AFTER THE BUBBLES

BOOK ONE of THE TOUCHERS

Also by Susan Berliner

THE SEA CRYSTAL AND OTHER WEIRD TALES

CORSONIA

THE DISAPPEARANCE

PEACHWOOD LAKE

DUST

Praise for Susan Berliner's books:

The Sea Crystal and Other Weird Tales

"Once you start reading anything written by Ms. Berliner, you had better clear your calendar. Her characters are haunting, memorable, and real. It takes a special talent to be able to create a scene in a few pages, from beginning to end, and this is where the author excels. As soon as the story begins, you are thrust into a little microcosm where things look ordinary...mundane even. But then...plants start talking, or someone disappears, or someone who is there turns out that they were never even there in the first place!" — K.W. Skultety, *Gimmethatbook*

"Her stories in this book vary in tone and content, but they're all rather solidly written and a ton of fun to read!...From chilling mirror images, to fairy tale lives, to a world of dark dreams that comes to life, there is so much to explore in Berliner's world...It was a lot of fun to try to figure out where the twist in each of these stories would be. Honestly, most of the time I was completely wrong about where I thought they were going. Which, of course, made it that much more fun!" — J. Nottingham, Hopelessly Devoted Bibliophile

"Around New Year's, my local cable station runs a marathon of Twilight Zone episodes...and that is sort of what this book put me in mind of - a little touch of the weird, but not too dangerous - something you could let kids read out loud during a sleepover. These stories are fun, and super-quick." — Rik Ty

Corsonia

"Well written and well paced." — *Julie's Book Review*

"Rich imagination. Vivid imagery. Superb characterizations. Snappy dialogue, capturing very believable conversations between two teenage girls/best friends. So many twists and turns, it kept me wanting to read more, and I resented having to put it down for silly things like making dinner and bathing!" — Linda Commodore

"I won't say *Corsonia* gave me nightmares, but my dreams were a bit more disturbing than usual! It was a great read, and gives the reader pause and makes you start thinking... could this actually happen? Not sure I ever want to find out!" — Judy Barnes

"Thoroughly enjoyable vacation read! The author has an innovative way of weaving factual incidents or occurrences into fast paced fiction." — Arlene Bender

The Disappearance

"*The Disappearance* is a terrific read...gratifying and suspenseful...for both young adults as well as adults. I highly recommend *The Disappearance*. Its message is thought-provoking and one young adults must keep in mind as they mature into adulthood."
— Night Owl Reviews (Top Pick)

"I enjoy reading books with time travel - and this book took you back and forth constantly! It was done in such a way that had me almost believing it was really possible."
— Michele Bodenheimer, *Miki's Hope*

"There are many modes of time travel, but this one takes the cake - so different from others I've read!...This group of characters working together to bring down one culprit is so different, so eclectic; it's a wonder they ever met each other! But that's what makes it work! I love 'The Sting' all over again."
— Lila L. Pinord

"I just loved this book! This is one of those books that will call you to pick it back up if you have the self-control to set it down for a moment. I was pulled in throughout the entire story because I could not wait to see what would happen next."
— Dawn Fitzpatrick

Peachwood Lake

"It is a marvelous coming of age horror story."
— *Night Owl Reviews* (Top Pick)

"Where else are you going to find a fish horror story that brings a young girl's life into focus?...I have no trouble recommending this book for the pre-teen/YA horror lover. Five out of five fairy kisses for this reader."
— Dottie Taylor, *Tink's Place*

"Great read. Fun and suspenseful. Best fish story since *Jaws*!"
— Peggy Derevlany

"I absolutely LOVED it! I can see this being a movie, a very awesome movie!"
— Heather Marts

Dust

"Susan Berliner gives us an amazing mysterious supernatural story in *Dust*. It intrigues and holds the readers' attention, while pulling them in and not letting them put it down."
— *Night Owl Reviews* (Top Pick)

"*Dust* picks you up and takes you on a whirlwind ride, pun intended, and doesn't let you go until the final climax. It's a great piece of escapist fiction and a book to easily get lost in."
— Patricia Lane

"I was able to read this book in its entirety within just a few hours, which added to its cinematic qualities; it was like watching a movie in the afternoon...The language in the book is relatively simple and casual, easy to read, and doesn't contain much in the way of profanity, so it can be enjoyed by a wide age-group spectrum."
— Andy S. Adams

AFTER THE BUBBLES

BOOK ONE of THE TOUCHERS

Susan Berliner

Published by SRB Books

ISBN: 978-0-9839401-7-3

Cover design by Cassy Roop of Pink Ink Designs
Layout by Rik of Wild Seas Formatting
Author's photo by Rachel Leib Photography

Published July, 2018

Printed in the United States of America

To Larry, my husband and fellow author

who always believes in me

and

In memory of Dawn Charles—

a terrific graphic artist

and a feisty friend

"This is the way the world ends

Not with a bang but a whimper."

– T.S. Eliot

CHAPTER 1 – The Bubbles

I first noticed the bubbles during seventh period geometry class. I always tuned out when Mr. Abruzzi explained theorems and it helped that I sat in the back row, right next to the window. I'd just finished drawing a unicorn and when I glanced outside, I saw them.

I call them bubbles, but they really weren't anything like little soap and water balls. These were big clear blobs with weird shapes, all different, and they were falling from the sky like some kind of new weather pattern: "Today's forecast is for bubbles."

I remember thinking that some person—or maybe even a super being—was sitting up in a cloud with a giant bubble wand, the kind little kids use, and blowing out these strange-looking shapes. They drifted slowly to the ground, hit the sidewalk, and then vanished. I didn't say anything because I was too fascinated by what was happening, just leaned closer to the window and watched as the bubbles kept falling, slowly but steadily.

A woman wearing a denim jacket rushed along the street, heading past the school. Maybe she was late for some appointment, maybe she didn't notice the bubbles, or maybe she saw them and didn't care. Anyway, she walked into one of the bubbles and it covered her completely. For a moment, it gave her an aura and she seemed to glow. Then the bubble disappeared just like the others did when they hit the sidewalk.

At first, the woman stood still. Then, instead of continuing up the street, she turned back and entered the school. I forgot about her and looked up at the sky again to watch the falling bubbles, thinking about what the shapes looked like. One long bubble looked like a shotgun, another resembled a giraffe...

"Excuse me. Are you looking for someone?"

I pulled myself away from the window when I heard the change in Mr. Abruzzi's voice. He was talking to the woman in the denim jacket. She stood inside the doorway of our classroom, which was on the first floor, near the main entrance.

"What do you want?" Mr. Abruzzi asked as the woman moved closer to him. Without answering the question, she touched his shoulder with her forefinger. He immediately crumpled and fell to the floor, lying there and not moving.

Then the woman walked to the first row and touched Steve Finnegan's leg. He fell down. She touched Cammie D'Amato and Cammie fell down too. All the kids started screaming and backing away from their chairs, trying to get away from the woman's outstretched finger. As I raced to the rear door, I saw the woman's finger brush Mandy Yu's arm and Mandy dropped to the ground.

"Don't touch any of the bubbles outside!" I yelled as I ran out of the classroom. I really hope all the other kids heard me, but I wasn't going to wait and make sure.

———

I reached the front entrance and the old cop who checked everyone coming into the building was lying face down on the ground. After flinging open the door, I raced outside.

I was lucky I lived just a couple of blocks from the high school. But I had to be out in the open during that time and those bubble things were still falling from the sky.

It was like a giant video game, only if I let one of those bubbles hit me, I was going to be worse than dead — turned into whatever that woman in the classroom had become.

To avoid the bubbles, I ran in a zigzag pattern. Out of the corner of my eye, I saw a bubble land on Mark Silverstein and made sure not to go anywhere in his direction.

I ducked into the porch of a house just before one of the bubbles splattered noiselessly on the ground only a foot away. Then I managed to stay clear of other falling bubbles until I reached my front door, thankful for the big porch so I didn't have to stand outside while fumbling for my key.

I was so nervous that a pen fell out of my bag as I searched. I finally found the damn key, jumped inside, locked the door, and stood with my back against it, panting heavily. Our dog, Muffles, waddled over and gave me a sloppy kiss.

"Erin, is that you?" Mom was off from work today, sick with the flu. I'd forgotten.

"Yes." I tried to say more, but the words wouldn't come out.

"You're home early. What's the matter?"

I ran up to her bedroom and immediately shut the open window and locked all three windows. I didn't know if those bubbles could drift inside, but I wasn't taking a chance. "I'll explain in a minute," I said.

Before Mom could question me, I raced through the house, shut a couple of open windows, and made sure all the others were locked. Muffles watched me, tilting his head trying to figure out what I was doing. When I finished, I returned to my parents' bedroom and sat on the bed, catching my breath.

My mother looked pale and sick with puffy bags around

her eyes. Knowing I wasn't going to make her feel any better, I told her what happened in school.

"Were the people unconscious?" she asked.

"I don't think so. I think they were all dead."

"Just from that woman's touch?" She stared at me for a long moment. "You have a vivid imagination, Erin."

I shook my head, too exhausted and scared to be insulted. "Mom, look at the bubbles outside. Do those things look normal to you?"

She tilted her head towards the windows. "They are different," she admitted.

"Turn on the TV," I suggested.

She grabbed the remote and hit "Power."

The channel showed two dopey cartoon animals running across the screen, chasing each other.

My mother smirked at me and shook her head.

"Try another," I said.

She switched channels and got two screens filled with static before finding a serious-looking newscaster giving a report: "...started falling early this afternoon and we don't know much about them yet," he said. "But they could be dangerous so, until we determine what they are, we urge you to stay inside and not touch the substances that are falling from the sky."

"The bubbles," I whispered.

"Shh."

"...have scientists trying to analyze the components of these clear falling objects," he continued. "According to reports, they are coming down over all parts of Earth. Please stay tuned to this station for further bulletins." The screen switched to a dumb pre-recorded talk show.

"Try a different channel," I said.

Mom turned to a major network station and the screen again showed a newsroom. But in this one, the anchorwoman was slumped over her desk and two men, dressed in jeans and wearing headphones, were sprawled on the floor in front of the news set. Nobody spoke or moved—either on the TV or in my house.

I jumped off my mother's bed. "What about Dad?" I asked.

Staring at me in horror, Mom reached for her cell phone on the night table, typed a quick text, and waited a moment. "I'm calling the office," she said, punching in a number and listening. "Busy signal." Then she looked at me and in a whispery voice, asked, "What about Danny?"

My twelve-year-old brother went to Grover Cleveland Middle School. "His bus doesn't come till after three," I said. "Call the school."

Mom pressed a key and again listened, this time for a while. "It's just ringing," she said, closing the phone. Pushing away the covers, she sat at the edge of the bed.

"What're you doing?" I asked.

"I'm going to drive to the school to get Danny."

"You can't do that!" I yelled. "The car's parked in the street. If you go outside and touch a bubble..."

"I can't just stay here and do nothing!"

"Let me go," I begged. "You're so sick, you can hardly sit up." It was true. She was holding her head in her hands and swaying. "There's no way you can do this. You'd never even make it to the car. I'll meet the school bus and get him home."

It would've been great if I could've used the car, but I hadn't taken driving lessons yet. Dad promised to teach me this summer.

"What if the bus doesn't make it here?"

That was a good question. But the middle school kids didn't have to stand outside except to get on the bus. It stopped at our corner—almost next to our house—and we were the second stop. "If no one got into his school, I think he'll be okay till the bus stops and he has to get off," I said out loud. "Then it'll be up to me and I already made it home once. I know I can do it."

Mom collapsed onto the bed and picked up her phone. "I'll try Dad again," she said, sending another text. She must have phoned him too because as I left the room, I heard the busy signal.

———

I flopped on top of my bed and grabbed my phone. First I texted my best friend, Marci. "R U OK?" I asked. Nothing.

I repeated the message to everyone on my phone list. Not one person answered.

Did anyone else make it out of John Adams—or did that woman in the denim jacket kill them all? I put my head under the pillow, wanting to disappear.

"Erin! What are you doing?"

"Resting! I'll be right in!"

I went back into Mom's bedroom, trying to be brave.

———

We checked the TV again. More channels had just static, the people in the newsroom were still lying there and hadn't moved, and one station had big words flashing across the entire screen that said, "DANGER! STAY INSIDE! DO NOT GO OUT! DO NOT TOUCH THE CLEAR OBJECTS FALLING FROM THE SKY!"

Mom asked me to get the laptop from the den and the radio from the kitchen. When she turned on the radio, we heard more warnings telling us to stay inside and not to touch anyone you didn't know.

"See," I said. "They must understand what happens when a bubble person touches you."

Mom frowned. "I don't like those words, 'bubble person.' It sounds creepy, like something from a bad horror movie."

"Well, that's what they are," I said, shrugging. "They touch you with just a finger and then you die."

"You don't know that for sure."

"I wasn't going to stick around Adams and check if those people that woman touched were still breathing." Grabbing the remote, I flipped stations until I found the screen with the three people in the newsroom. "Do any of these guys look alive?" I asked.

"Please turn the TV off," Mom said without answering my question. Instead, she powered up the computer and checked news sites. "There's not much here," she said. "It's mostly warnings to stay indoors. Also, it says those things have been falling everywhere in the world where it's daytime, except for places with rain."

"Do they say what they think it is?"

"No." Mom shook her head. "Just that they're studying the falling objects...I'll try Dad again." She texted him and then called his office. "Busy signal," she said. "I'm calling Grandma." Mom phoned her mother in Florida.

When I heard a busy signal again, I knew we couldn't reach anyone by phone.

"Let me check Facebook," I said, running into my room. Grabbing my iPad, I logged onto my page and checked the news updates from friends. "Look at this," I said, returning to my mother and pushing the screen close to her.

A Facebook friend, someone I didn't really know, had posted a picture of a busy street in New York City, taken from a window several floors above the ground. People were lying all over the street and the sidewalk. There must have been at least thirty bodies.

"Oh, my God!" Mom said, covering her mouth with her hand. She glanced at the clock. "Erin, it's almost time for Danny's bus."

———

I stood under the porch, ready to make my move the instant I heard the bus. Since the engine was so noisy, I'd know when it was almost at our stop. I thought about taking an umbrella, but decided against it because it would block my vision and more important, I didn't know if the umbrella would even protect me. Maybe the bubbles could go right through the fabric. I wasn't taking a chance.

When I heard the bus, I timed my zigzag run perfectly, getting to the stop just as the driver opened the door. Bobby Mitchell, Danny's friend who lived at the other end of the block, was the first one off.

"Bobby, don't let the bubble things touch you," I warned, dancing back and forth as one of those clear things splattered on the bus and another landed a couple of feet away from me. "Run!"

He looked at me, saw I was really scared, and dashed down the street towards his house.

Danny was next. "Follow my lead and don't touch the bubbles!" I shouted. "The rest of you, keep away from the falling bubbles!" I tried to let everyone on the bus know the danger, but I was concentrating on getting Danny safely home. My brother was a wiry kid—a great athlete, in fact—and he rushed behind me the short distance until we were both on the porch.

"C'mon," I said, pushing him inside and closing and locking the door. Muffles came over to greet us, but I nudged the dog aside.

"Erin! Danny!" Mom called.

"We're good!" I yelled back.

"What was that all about?" Danny asked. "What are those things?"

"I don't know, but they're dangerous." I ran into the dining room and looked out the side window that faced down the street. Danny followed me.

Two other middle-school kids lived on our block, Andrew O'Malley and Cyndy Louise Reade. As we watched, Andrew ran towards his house near the end of the street, with Cyndy Louise about ten feet behind him. She was a year older than my brother, a shy quiet girl who hardly ever spoke to anyone. Even now she walked quickly, but with her head down.

"Oh, no!" I moaned.

"What's wrong?" Danny asked.

"That bubble thing just landed on Cyndy Louise's head," I explained, pointing to the clear blob.

"So...?"

The bubble covered the girl's entire body, just like it had done to the woman at my school, and Cyndy Louise seemed to glow for a second or two. Then the bubble disappeared and she just stood there.

"What happened?" Danny asked.

"I don't know, but it's not good."

Cyndy Louise raised her head and dashed after Andrew, who was concentrating on dodging the bubbles and moving as quickly as he could to get home. He didn't notice Cyndy Louise as she ran past her house and caught up to him. Then, reaching out, she touched the back of Andrew's shirt with her left hand and he crumpled to the ground.

"What's wrong with Andrew?" Danny asked.

"I think he's dead," I whispered.

———

I forced myself to look away from Cyndy Louise, who remained outside after touching Andrew. Instead of going into her house, she continued to pace back and forth as if she was impatiently waiting for something. She paid no attention to

Andrew, who still lay on our sidewalk with his arms dangling in the street.

Danny hadn't said a word since asking about Andrew so I turned around and spoke to him. "Are you okay?"

He nodded, but there was a faraway expression on his face. "Let's go upstairs to Mom," I said.

Without saying anything, he followed me up the steps. Muffles, probably upset at being ignored, came too.

Mom was sitting up in bed, checking the laptop. She smiled when she saw Danny, opened her arms, and he walked into her hug. "Why were you two downstairs for so long?" she asked.

"We were watching outside," I explained. "A bubble fell on Cyndy Louise and..." I didn't want to talk about what had happened to Andrew because Danny still seemed out of it. His expression hadn't changed, even as Mom hugged him.

"Tell me," Mom ordered.

Since Danny was facing the other way, I mouthed, "she touched Andrew and he's dead."

Mom released Danny and stared at me. Then she picked up the phone and tried calling Dad again. This time, I didn't even hear a busy signal.

"No dial tone," she said, replacing the receiver. "Thank God, you two are safe." She patted the bed. "Now sit here and I'll tell you what I found out."

Danny and I sat on the bed and Muffles nuzzled closer and sniffed our legs. "I can't get any of the major news networks," Mom said.

"What about Google?" I asked.

Mom shook her head. "None of the search sites are working. But when I punched in today's date and 'falling from the sky,' I got some stuff."

"Like?" I prodded.

"Like a lot of people are blaming terrorists for what's

happening, but then you see messages from people who say that these clear bubble-like things fell in all the Arab countries too. And then I found this, which is supposed to be from Mexico, if it's true..." She turned the laptop so it faced us, but Danny looked away.

The screen showed a little baby in a busy city street. The baby was lying on top of a woman, maybe its mother, who had collapsed, and it seemed to be crying. Its mouth was open—but there was no sound with this picture so you couldn't hear anything. Around the baby, piled up on the floor, were about twenty people, all of them in crumpled positions, and all of them looked like they were dead.

"What do you think happened?" Mom asked me.

"I think a bubble landed on this baby and now lots of people want to help it, but whoever touches the baby just falls down and dies." I stared at my mother. "That's what I saw in school and outside with Cyndy Louise."

———

Without saying anything, Danny went into his room and closed his door. Mom remained on the bed with her eyes shut, but I knew she wasn't sleeping.

"Try the radio again," she finally said.

I checked the AM stations, but only got static. When I switched to FM, I heard a man, whose voice sounded very far away. After I raised the volume, we both listened.

"...the end of the world as we know it. This is God's will, a way to cut the population of the Earth, to weed out the unnecessary people, to..."

"Turn it off," my mother said. "We don't need to hear that garbage."

"Maybe it's true."

Mom opened her eyes and looked at me. "Whatever's

happening outside is not the end of the world or God's will."

"Then what is it?"

"I don't know." She closed her eyes again for a moment, but quickly opened them. "All right. We have to prepare ourselves. Erin, go to the downstairs hall closet and get flashlights and then gather up all the batteries you can find in the drawers."

I walked down the steps with Muffles following me. But before checking the hall closet, I looked outside. Cyndy Louise was still walking in the street. And the bubbles were still falling from the sky.

CHAPTER 2 – The First Day

None of us did much the rest of the afternoon. Danny stayed in his room and Mom stayed in bed. We were all shocked and scared by what was happening.

I spent most of the time staring out the dining room window into Walnut Lane, watching both the bubbles and Cyndy Louise. A couple of times, she went from house to house twisting doorknobs, ringing bells, and banging on front doors. But she couldn't break them and no one let her in. Mostly she walked back and forth along the block, still paying no attention to Andrew's body.

None of the phones worked. I didn't want to watch whatever was on TV—cartoons, movies, scary warnings, static, or dead people—and I was too wound up to check the iPad, read a book, or even draw.

The elementary school bus never stopped on Walnut Lane so the two little girls who lived down the street didn't come home. But a couple of cars did reach our block and I hope the people in them managed to make it into their houses without being touched by any bubbles or Cyndy Louise. I couldn't tell.

Late in the afternoon, Cyndy Louise's mother drove to her house across the street, in the middle of our block. When Mrs.

Reade saw her daughter, she opened the car window and yelled something to Cyndy Louise. Then she pulled the car into her driveway and waited.

I raced to the front door and opened it. "Close the window!" I shouted as loud as I could. "You can't let Cyndy Louise touch you!"

Mrs. Reade must've heard me because she shut the car window. But I guess her door wasn't locked because Cyndy Louise pulled it open and touched her mom's arm. Mrs. Reade tumbled out of the car, hitting her head on the driveway. And then she lay there, just like Andrew and all the others.

Cyndy Louise didn't even look at her mother. She turned away and marched up and down the street again.

I wiped the tears from my face. Mrs. Reade was a nice woman who gave out the best candy to kids on Halloween. I would miss her.

———

"Erin!...Danny!"

When Mom called my name, I moved away from my window post and slowly climbed upstairs with Muffles following.

"Go get your brother," she ordered.

I went to Danny's door and banged on it, but he didn't answer. "Mom wants you in her room—now!" I shouted.

A few seconds later, Danny stepped out and we entered Mom's bedroom together, both of us hopping onto the bed.

"I don't know how long this situation is going to last," she began. "But from what I've found out, we have to stay inside because of those things falling from the sky and people like..." Her voice faded and she didn't finish the sentence.

"Since we're stuck in the house," she continued, "and we don't know how long we'll have electricity, we have to be practical. To conserve our food, we'll eat the things that'll spoil first. For dinner tonight, we can have anything that's frozen—pizza, chicken, burgers. Either of you want to make a choice?"

Danny didn't say anything and I was quiet too. I wasn't hungry at all.

"We still have to eat," Mom said softly. "This will be over."

"You don't know that for sure," I whispered.

"That's true," she admitted. "But we have to believe it will."

Danny jumped off the bed and ran into his room, slamming the door hard.

———

I was about to put six hamburgers into the oven when Muffles pulled on my leg, dragging me towards the front door.

I'd forgotten about walking him like we always did before dinner. Kneeling, I patted the little dog's head. "Sorry, boy. You can't go outside today." I didn't know what the bubbles or Cyndy Louise could do to a dog, but I wasn't experimenting with Muffles.

I thought quickly about what we could use and remembered a plastic pie container. Happy that Muffles was a small dog, I grabbed the bowl from the kitchen cabinet and rushed upstairs to the hall bathroom with Muffles following closely behind.

"Okay, Muff," I said, placing the pie container on the floor and tapping it. "This is where you're going to do your stuff for now."

The dog tilted his furry gray head and looked at me.

"You're gonna go to the bathroom here like you do outside." I got down on my hands and feet and pretending to be a dog, lifted my leg as if I was going to poop in the plastic bowl. "See?"

Not just because he's my dog, but Muffles is really smart. Copying me, he lifted his leg and pooped and peed in the bowl, with just a little pee hitting the floor.

"Good boy!" I said as I poured everything down the toilet, cleaned the floor with toilet paper, rinsed the bowl with tub water, and poured that in the toilet too. Then, after scrubbing my hands, I went downstairs to work on dinner.

I left the pie container in the bathroom since I had no idea when Muffles would be able to use his outside toilet—and we weren't ever using it for pies again.

———

Following Mom's orders, I defrosted frozen broccoli and corn and when everything was done, dashed back upstairs. "Dinner's ready," I told her. "Are you okay to come down to eat?"

"I'm going to try," she said. "Tell Danny."

I knocked on my brother's door. "Dinnertime!" I called.

When Mom joined me in the hall, my brother still hadn't opened the door. "Danny," she said, leaning against the door and speaking softly. "You have to come out now. We're all going downstairs to eat dinner."

My brother opened the door, lowered his head, and walked silently down the steps.

We ate dinner without hardly any conversation except for table talk like, "Please pass the water" or "Thank you." None of us mentioned the bubbles or Dad or Andrew or Mrs. Reade or Cyndy Louise. At one point, I ran into the dining room to look out the window and see if Cyndy Louise was still there. She was.

Nobody ate very much. Three of the hamburgers and most of the vegetables were left over. After the meal, Danny went back to his room and Mom went upstairs to lie down again. She still didn't look good.

I put the uneaten food in the fridge, cleaned the table, and loaded the dirty dishes in the dishwasher. Danny was supposed to do the dishes, but I wasn't going to complain about him not doing his job. After I finished, it was almost dark outside so I rushed to the side window.

I saw one good thing and one bad thing. The good thing was the bubbles had stopped falling. The bad thing was Cyndy Louise was still out there.

I turned on the living room TV and ran through the channels, but got all static except for one station playing cartoons, another showing a movie, and a third flashing the "Danger! Don't go outside!" message. At least the newsroom with the dead people wasn't on any more. Switching off the TV, I went to my room, and started reading a romance novel. But I couldn't concentrate.

My dad never made it home that evening. He worked in the city, driving to the station every day and then taking a train to his office. My eyes got watery as I imagined what must have happened to him and the people in the cities.

If a bubble fell on someone and then that person went into a big building, got on an elevator, stopped on every floor, and walked into every office...It was like a deadly game of freeze tag. I didn't want to think about it any more, but I knew the cities must have been hit much harder than us in the suburbs.

I also knew that Dad was never coming home.

CHAPTER 3 – Day Two

It wasn't just a bad dream. When I woke up the next morning, the first thing I did was run to my window. The bubbles were falling again. My bedroom overlooked the street so I could see the bodies of Andrew and Mrs. Reade lying in the same crumpled positions, like thrown-away dolls. And Cyndy Louise was still there too, marching up and down Walnut Lane.

I stepped into the hallway and didn't hear anything. Both Danny's and Mom's doors were closed so, after taking a shower, I dressed and went downstairs.

Muffles ran over to kiss me, but more to remind me that he hadn't had breakfast or his morning walk. "We're trapped inside again," I told the dog as I poured his food and water and escorted him to the upstairs bathroom.

"Remember what you did yesterday and do it again," I whispered, setting up the plastic pie container. That dog is really smart! He did his stuff without needing a demonstration and we went back downstairs.

I turned on the TV. But now all I got was static on every station, not even any dumb cartoons. I didn't have the radio or laptop, which were both still in Mom's bedroom. I tried my iPad, but couldn't connect to the Internet.

With nothing to do, I just watched Cyndy Louise. I wondered if she'd been outside all night. Didn't she have to eat and sleep? *Maybe not.* Maybe she wasn't a person anymore. People didn't kill other people just by touching them—especially their own mothers. So what was she—some kind of freaky bubble person?

———

About a half hour later, I heard footsteps on the stairs and my mother entered the dining room. She had showered, put on a flowery tee shirt and jeans, and looked much better.

"How do you feel?" I asked.

"I'm okay, thanks. How about you?"

I shrugged. How could anyone feel good with what was going on outside.

Mom pulled out a chair and sat next to me. "The phones aren't working at all anymore," she said. "There's no dial tone. There's nothing on TV..."

"I know."

"...and the radio has a couple of stations that sound like people broadcasting from their homes."

"Did they say anything new?" I asked.

"Nothing more than we heard yesterday: Don't go outside, don't touch the bubbles, or let anyone from outside touch you."

"What about the computer?"

"There are no search engines, but for some reason, I can get feeds from England. It's the middle of the day and they don't have bubbles."

"Yesterday, people on the computer said rainy places didn't get the bubbles," I pointed out. "Did anyone say what the weather's like today in England?"

"Light rain."

I looked out the window again. "Well, we've got sun and

more bubbles so what're we going to do?"

Mom reached over and hugged me tightly. "We're going to get through this together—you, me, and Danny."

"What about Dad?" I whispered.

"I don't know," she said. "Let's hope he's somewhere safe inside."

If she wanted to believe that, I wasn't going to argue.

———

I had to bang on Danny's door again to get him out of his room for breakfast. He followed me downstairs, but still didn't say anything.

We ate waffles because Mom wanted to use up the frozen food. She did most of the table talk, trying to cheer us up. "So I thought we'd all play Monopoly this morning," she said, smiling. "Doesn't that sound like fun?"

It didn't, but I smiled at her anyway. She was just trying to take our minds off what was happening outside.

"After that, we can play some kind of card game—I haven't played cards in a long time. Maybe gin rummy. And tonight we can check our DVDs and find a movie we all like."

She had the whole day figured out—continuous family fun time.

"That'll be fine, Mom," I said, glancing out the window. The bubbles were still falling.

"Good...These waffles are really delicious, don't you think?"

This time, I just nodded. The happy act was getting more difficult for me. Danny didn't try to pretend; he sat with his head down, nibbling a waffle and not saying a word.

I gulped the rest of my orange juice and jumped up. "If it's okay, I'd like to go to my room now and draw."

"Monopoly in an hour?" Mom asked, still grinning.

"Sure." I bolted from the table.

———

After closing my door, I grabbed my pad and pencil and tried to draw a unicorn. But moments later, I heard a loud thump outside and rushed to the window.

Cyndy Louise must have picked up someone's flowerpot because she'd smashed it against a house across the street. Broken pot pieces and parts of flowers were scattered all over the Kaplan's front lawn.

As I continued to watch, Cyndy Louise walked down Walnut Lane, ignoring the falling bubbles and the bodies of Andrew and her mother. When she got back to where I could see her again, she was holding a lawn decoration—one of those ugly gnome things. Then she tossed it high into the air, way over someone's roof. I didn't remember Cyndy Louise being such a good thrower.

But when I saw her more closely, I realized she looked different. Although she still wore the same clothes as yesterday—a green tee shirt and black jeans—her hair was all messy. Stepping off the bus, it had been in a neat ponytail, but now her wavy brown hair was loose and uncombed.

She had carried a backpack on her shoulders, but that wasn't there anymore and I didn't see it on the ground. And what about her glasses? She had worn glasses yesterday afternoon, but they were gone now too. Could she still see clearly?

I never saw Cyndy Louise go inside or eat or drink anything. I never heard her say anything either, but the windows were all closed so if she was talking, I couldn't hear her.

During my watch, no cars drove into our street and none of the neighbors went outside. Like those rich people who have to stay in their homes with electronic cuffs on their ankles, we were all under house arrest.

———

"Erin?"

Hearing Mom's voice, I opened my door. She sat on my bed and in a whispery voice said, "I'm worried about Danny."

I shrugged. I knew what was bothering him—the same thing that was bothering all of us and probably everyone else who was still alive in this scary new world.

"You seem to be doing much better than he is."

Really? I didn't exactly feel wonderful.

"I think he needs to talk. Maybe you can go to his room and try..."

"No." I shook my head. "Give him some more time."

Mom leaned her head against the wall and let out a deep sigh. "He won't say anything to me. He just nods or grunts and goes back to playing video games on his iPad."

"That's not such a bad thing," I said. "It's probably a lot better than looking out the window and thinking about what's happened," *which is exactly what I'd been doing.*

"We should all be together right now, until things improve."

If they improve.

"Please, Erin. Talk to Danny and convince him to come out of his room and play Monopoly with us. It'll be better for everyone."

Obviously, it would be better for Mom. I stopped arguing and went to get my brother.

———

We played Monopoly, we played gin rummy, and we even played a couple of other old board games that Mom found. Danny still wasn't talking, but he didn't try to leave.

In between games, we ate lunch—yesterday's leftover hamburgers and frozen vegetables Mom insisted we finish in case we lost power.

Whenever I got up, I took a quick peek outside. The bubbles were still falling and Cyndy Louise was still patrolling. But at least she wasn't throwing things.

In the middle of the day, during one of the gin rummy games, Danny tapped me lightly on the shoulder and pointed to the window. When I looked outside, I realized the bubbles had stopped falling. But Cyndy Louise was still there.

"What do you think it means?" I asked Mom, who had followed me to the window.

"I don't know, but it's something positive."

My mom could put a good spin on anything. "How can you know that?" I asked. "Cyndy Louise is still in the street."

"Maybe she's back to her normal self now that the bubbles are gone."

I studied what I could see of Cyndy Louise. Her hair was a mess, her clothes were filthy, and she was marching back and forth along our block. "She doesn't seem to ever eat, sleep, or go inside. That's not normal."

"Maybe it'll take a little time for her to get back to normal...I'm going to check the TV." Mom flipped through the stations, but got just static. Then she dashed into the kitchen and returned with the portable radio. When she switched it on, we again heard only static.

"I guess we'll have to wait," Mom said. Then she smiled at Danny and me. "Okay. Let's get back to our game. Whose turn is it?"

CHAPTER 4 - Muffles

Mom finally ended Game Day and released Danny and me. Late in the afternoon, I sat at my desk trying to draw pictures of the bubbles. But I couldn't concentrate.

I kept glancing out the window every couple of minutes to see what Cyndy Louise was doing, not that she was doing anything much different: She walked back and forth along the street, only now she stopped for a longer time at our corner, looking in both directions like she was waiting for something. *What?* Was someone supposed to relieve her and take over patrol duties? I guess she could have used a break after spending the last day and a half outside.

When nothing happened, she turned and continued to the other side of Walnut Lane. Maybe she stopped and waited there too, even though we lived on a dead end. I couldn't see all the way down the block.

My door was partly open so Muffles came in and nuzzled my leg, the signal that it was time for his evening walk. "Okay, boy," I said as I entered Mom's bedroom, with Muffles following me. My mother was on her bed, using the laptop.

"Hi," she said. "Everything okay?"

No. It wasn't. But I knew she didn't mean that.

"Muffles wants to go out. Should I let him use the bathroom again or can he go in the backyard by himself?"

Mom considered the question. "I don't see why he can't go outside now that the bubbles are gone," she said. "He could probably use the exercise. Just be careful when you open the back door and close it quickly."

I nodded and skipped down the stairs. After peeking through the dining room window to check on Cyndy Louise—she was halfway down the street, heading away from our house—I continued to the sliding glass door.

Before opening it, I knelt to give Muffles instructions. "Listen," I said. "You can pee and poop in our yard today." I pointed to the back and lifted my leg to demonstrate. "But stay in the yard and scratch on the door when you're ready to come in." Again I showed Muffles what I wanted him to do.

"Okay, smart dog, do your stuff." After making sure Cyndy Louise was nowhere near our backyard, I slid open the door and let Muffles out.

———

While I waited for Muffles, I took my pencil and sketchbook downstairs and again tried to draw the bubbles. I sat in the dining room, facing the window, telling myself the lighting was better there. But that wasn't the real reason.

Every few minutes, I looked outside to see if Cyndy Louise was doing anything different. She wasn't.

"Woof!"

I rushed to the back door to let Muffles into the house. But I didn't see the dog. "Muffles?" Opening the sliding glass door, I quickly checked the yard. No dog.

"Muffles!" I yelled as loud as I could. "Come here now!"

No answer.

Racing to the dining room, I looked out the window. Cyndy

Louise was heading towards our house and Muffles was sprinting towards her.

I opened the window and shouted, "No, Muffles! Get away from her!"

"What's wrong?" Mom asked from the steps.

"It's Muffles. He's running up to Cyndy Louise and she's going to kill..." I started crying before I could finish explaining.

"Oh, honey." Mom put her arm around my shoulders and together we watched the scene in front of our house. Muffles stood next to Cyndy Louise, barking at her. Then she reached down and touched the dog—and nothing happened.

Muffles didn't fall down dead, he didn't stop barking, and Cyndy Louise didn't try to hurt him. Instead, she walked away with Muffles following her, barking as he ran. When she ignored him, the dog grabbed her jeans and bit the denim, but Cyndy Louise kept moving. Finally he turned and waddled slowly towards our house.

"Do you think Muffles is okay?" I whispered, drying my eyes with my hands.

"I don't know. You're the one who's seen what happens when people are touched."

"Yeah. They all die."

"But Muffles is very much alive."

"He's a dog, not a person. Maybe only people die, not animals."

"And maybe Cyndy Louise is normal again, now that the bubbles have stopped falling," Mom suggested again.

"Does she look normal?" I asked. "She looks worse to me." Her hair and clothes were totally disgusting. Before yesterday, she'd always been neat and clean.

At the back door, we heard a scratching noise. "Is it okay to let Muffles in?" I asked.

"Let me check the computer to see what people wrote about

touching animals."

While Mom did the research, I talked to Muffles. "Bad idea," I said through the glass door as the dog stared at me. "Naughty." I waved my forefinger at him. "You should have stayed in the yard like I told you. Why'd you go up to Cyndy Louise like that? Now you'll have to wait till we make sure you're safe."

Muffles tilted his head and looked like he was truly sorry and wanted to apologize.

I heard footsteps on the stairs as Mom returned. "From all the comments, animals aren't affected by the bubbles or by those people touching them so let Muffles back in."

I opened the sliding door and the dog dashed inside, jumped up on my legs, and tried to lick me. I guess Mom was right; I didn't feel any different.

―――――

I was in my room trying to read a magazine when I heard a loud crash of breaking glass. Running to the window, I looked outside just as Cyndy Louise stepped into the smashed living room window of the Kaplan's house across the street.

"What's going on?" Mom yelled.

"It's Cyndy Louise!" I called back. "She must've thrown a rock or something through the Kaplan's window and now she's gone inside."

Mom rushed into my room and together we watched from my window, but didn't hear another sound. A few minutes later, Cyndy Louise walked out of the house, closed the door, and continued pacing up and down the street.

"We've got to board up the downstairs windows," Mom said. "I think there's some plywood in the garage."

"I'll help you carry the stuff in," I said. Luckily we could enter our garage without leaving the house.

"We'll need the saw and hammer and nails. Go get Danny. He can help too."

We spent the next few hours nailing our first floor windows shut with the pieces of wood Mom found in the garage. When we ran out of wood, we broke a bookcase apart and used that. Then we took off the door to our laundry room and taped it over the glass part of the back door.

Now the house was mostly dark downstairs, but at least Cyndy Louise would have trouble breaking in. The boards didn't cover all the windows completely so we could still peek through the spaces of the dining room window to see what was going on down the street. But it was creepy, like we were living in a condemned house. And in a way, that was true.

———

"We have to talk," Mom said to us that evening as we ate our chicken dinner in the boarded-up kitchen. "I can't get any official information from the state or even anything national. Only a few places, like England, seem to have governments that are still working."

Considering the mess our country's been in, I didn't think that was such a bad thing.

"The problem is," Mom continued, "we can't all sit around the house every day waiting for the world to return to normal." She lowered her voice. "If it ever will." Then she turned to my brother, who stared at his plate and ate very slowly. "Danny, we have to move forward."

He ignored her words and kept on eating.

"So we're starting a new schedule. You're both going to school."

This time Danny did look up and we both stared at Mom.

"That's right," she said, nodding. "I'm going to be your new teacher. I've been checking the computer, working on lessons for the two of you and beginning tomorrow, we'll have classes every day from nine to one."

Wow! Not even a day off. "Every day?" I asked.

"It'll keep your minds busy." She smiled at us. "I've always wondered if I could do a better job than some of your teachers— and now we'll have a chance to find out."

Neither Danny nor I said anything. I don't know about my brother, but I wasn't exactly looking forward to being home-schooled.

CHAPTER 5 – School Days

Mom woke Danny and me at eight o'clock the next morning. After a breakfast of frozen pancakes, she told us to get notebooks and pens and come to the dining room for our first day of school. "And bring any textbooks you have here," she added.

"I don't have anything except an English book with poems and short stories," I said. "The rest of my books are still in my locker at Adams."

"Just bring that one then. Class starts in five minutes."

I shrugged and headed upstairs. Mom sounded real excited, like she was looking forward to her new "career." Who would've figured she'd always wanted to be a teacher?

As I got my stuff, I peeked out the window, although I knew what I'd see—a filthy-looking Cyndy Louise walking along an empty street. It had already been three days. *Was she going to stay out there forever?*

———

Mom was serious about her school. She had set up "classes" for both of us, starting with English. My first assignment was to read a story in the textbook I showed her. She had printed out a couple of poems for Danny and told him to read them carefully.

"Okay," she said when we both finished. "Erin, I want you to find five similes or metaphors in the story, write them down and explain them and Danny, you and I are going to discuss the poems."

Danny shook his head.

"Yes, hon, we are," Mom continued. "You have to talk. I know you're very upset about what's happened. Erin and I are upset too, but we all have to go on with our lives. Dad would want us to. You know that, Danny."

My brother was real close to my dad. Danny was an all-star pitcher and Dad coached his team. They went to games together and watched lots of sports on TV.

"He's dead, isn't he?" my brother whispered.

"We don't know for sure, but probably." Mom spoke very quietly.

"I need him," Danny said, tears flowing from his eyes.

"I need him too," Mom said softly. "We all do." She gave Danny a big hug. "But we can't change what happened and the three of us are stuck in the house for now so we have to do the best we can, together as a family."

———

After English, Mom gave us assignments in history, science, and geography with worksheets she'd found online. She told us the only subject she wasn't going to tackle was math because she didn't understand it. That was fine with me; I hated geometry.

Between classes, she gave us short breaks. During one break, I peeked out the opening in the side window to see if anything was different on Walnut Lane. Some of our neighbors' first-floor windows were now boarded up like ours, but otherwise nothing had changed. The street was empty except for the two dead bodies and Cyndy Louise, who continued her one-girl patrol.

I was still standing at the dining room window when Danny came over. "She's changing," he said.

"Huh?"

"Cyndy Louise—she's different."

"Of course she's different since the bubbles," I said. "She kills people by touching them and she doesn't eat or sleep or do anything except walk along our street, throw things, or try to break into houses."

"No. I mean she looks different."

"Of course she does. Her hair and clothes are filthy from being outside all the time."

Danny shook his head. "That's not what I'm talking about. Check her face when she comes closer."

"Erin and Danny!" Mom called. "Back to school!"

"Give us a second," I said. "Danny says we need to look at Cyndy Louise's face."

Mom joined us at the window. "What is it?" she asked.

"There!" Danny pointed to the girl's face as she neared our house. "Do you see it?"

"Her mouth," I said. "It looks like her lips are stuck together."

"Yeah," my brother agreed. "I think they're one piece now so they can't open."

My mother shook her head. "That would mean she can't eat or drink, or even talk. What is she?"

"Not a person anymore, that's for sure," I whispered.

We finished the first day of Mom School and it was better than I'd thought. My mother had spent a lot of time making up lessons, more time, I think, than my regular teachers did. Of course I missed going to John Adams and seeing my friends. I wondered how many kids had made it home okay during the bubbles, especially the ones in my geometry class. But I couldn't text anyone to find out.

After lunch we had free time, not that there was much we could do. Mom went to her room, probably preparing for the next day of school and Danny went to his room to play video games. I sat by the window, working on my unicorn drawings until I heard loud noises on the street.

Looking up, I saw Cyndy Louise bashing her mom's car with a lawn chair. But she was only able to dent the car before the plastic chair broke and she stepped around her mother's body and left.

"Mom! Danny!" I called. "Come see what Cyndy Louise just did!"

When my mother and brother joined me, I pointed to Mrs. Reade's car.

"Our car's parked in the street," Mom whispered.

I shrugged. We couldn't do anything about that.

"She's back!" Danny shouted. "With a rake!"

This time, Cyndy Louise attacked her car with a metal rake—a better weapon—so she quickly busted the windows and ripped through the tires. When she finally finished, her mother's car was totally destroyed.

"We've got to get our car into the garage," Mom said.

"How?" I asked. "We can't go out."

"We have to be ready for when we can go out," Mom said, turning to Danny and me. "This afternoon we're cleaning out the garage."

I groaned. Our garage was full of junk. My dad used it for his building projects and we'd just messed it up more cutting wood to board up the windows. Except for winter, we never put our cars in the garage, which is why Mom's Subaru was in the street.

"Let's go," my mother said.

We spent the next three hours cleaning the garage.

———

When I looked outside later, Cyndy Louise was back patrolling the block. I wondered how long she'd stay out there, keeping all of us trapped inside. *Would we spend the rest of our lives like this?*

I didn't like the way my thoughts were going so I went downstairs. Mom was in the kitchen reading a magazine with Muffles curled under her legs. As I sat, he licked me and I patted his soft head.

"My iPad doesn't work and I don't want to read or draw," I said.

"You can always do your homework."

"I have plenty of time to do it tonight. Can I watch a movie now?"

Mom hesitated before answering. "I don't want you getting into the habit of spending your spare time watching movies," she finally said.

"You said we'd lose our electricity."

She nodded. "I'm surprised we still have it. The computer's not working anymore so I'm glad I spent all those hours getting materials for our school. But even though we have power, I don't want you wasting your afternoons with movies."

"Danny just plays video games."

"Your brother needs time right now."

"And I don't?"

"Not as much. You're older and stronger."

I guess that was a compliment so I stopped arguing. "Just one movie. I promise."

For the next ninety minutes, I watched *Wild Child*, a dumb

comedy about a bratty girl shipped off to boarding school. It wasn't great, but during that time I didn't think about Cyndy Louise.

CHAPTER 6 – The Rain

The following morning, the sound of pouring rain woke me before Mom did. I opened the curtains and looked out the window. Cyndy Louise wasn't in the street.

Thinking maybe she was at the other end of the block—somewhere out of my sight—I went to the bathroom. When I returned to my room, she still hadn't shown up.

I ran into my mother's room, but she was sleeping. "Mom," I said, trying my best to whisper. "Cyndy Louise is gone!"

She opened her eyes and stared at me. "Are you sure?"

I nodded. "I don't see her anywhere outside. It's raining hard right now so do you think maybe the rain could've killed her?"

Mom sat up and shrugged. "I don't know. But considering what's already happened, I guess anything's possible."

———

After we finished breakfast—frozen pancakes again—I snuck a quick look through the space in the boarded-up side window. It was still raining and I still didn't see Cyndy Louise. Then we moved to the dining room for our second day of Mom School.

My mother went over our homework real carefully. "You

were supposed to explain the metaphors and similes, not just write them," she told me. "Also, it's very sloppy." She waved the paper in my face. "Is this the way you hand in your homework?"

"Mrs. Terkofsky's okay with it."

"I'm your teacher now and I'm not okay with it. I want you to do homework that you're proud of."

Proud? This wasn't a test or anything important, just homework for my mother.

"Don't think like that," Mom said, as if she could read my thoughts. "This is your school now and if I don't like your work, you're going to do it over." She gave the paper back to me. "Redo this for tomorrow."

Or what happens: Stay after school? Fail the class? But I nodded and didn't say anything.

My mother the teacher didn't like Danny's homework either. "How much time did you spend on this assignment?" she asked him. "Five minutes tops?"

He lowered his head and shrugged.

"This is not acceptable," she said, pointing to the paper. "You'll do it over along with today's assignment."

Mom was totally serious about this school stuff. But maybe her teaching career would be real short. We hadn't seen Cyndy Louise since last night.

———

We were almost finished with school—Mom was assigning homework and reminding us about how she wanted it done—when we heard a sharp series of knocks on the front door. We all stopped what we were doing and turned towards the sound.

"Cyndy Louise?" I mumbled.

"She hasn't banged on our door since the first day," Mom said.

Danny rushed to the entrance and peeked through the narrow glass partition. "It's Mrs. Perez," he said. "Can I open it?"

"Not yet," Mom said. Moving Danny aside, she smiled at our next-door neighbor through the closed door. Mrs. Perez was divorced and lived by herself. Her younger daughter, Christina, used to be our babysitter. "Are you alone?" Mom asked.

"Yes," Mrs. Perez said.

"Do you see Cyndy Louise anywhere?"

She shook her head. "I haven't seen her since yesterday."

My mother opened the door to let our neighbor inside and quickly shut it. "I'm sorry for the questions, Norma, but I had to be sure you were all right."

Muffles came over to Mrs. Perez and nuzzled her leg.

"I understand," she said, petting the dog. "You don't know who is who anymore. Look at what's happened to Cyndy Louise..." Her voice faded away.

"Please come in and sit down," Mom said, ushering Mrs. Perez towards the living room. "We were just finishing school."

"Oh." She glanced at our notebooks on the dining room table and tried to smile. "I guess you're managing pretty well then."

Mom shrugged. "We're trying our best. How are you doing?"

"I'm okay for now. But I don't know how long I can do this. In a few days, I'll need to go out and get food and..." Again her voice trailed off and her eyes got watery.

"Maybe Cyndy Louise is really gone," I said. "We haven't seen her since it's been raining."

"I know," Mrs. Perez agreed. "But there must be others."

"Maybe the rain killed all of them," I suggested.

No one said anything for a long time. Then Mom spoke.

"We have plenty of food," she said. "You can always stay here with us."

"No," Mrs. Perez said. "I'll be all right...Did Bill make it home?"

My mother shook her head.

"I'm so sorry," our neighbor said as she rose. "Well, it was good talking to all of you and knowing that you're here. It's been so lonely not having anyone to talk to. I can't even phone my daughters to find out if they're okay."

"Maybe Cyndy Louise and the others are gone," I repeated. I really wanted to believe this nightmare was over.

"How about some coffee?" Mom asked, remembering she had a guest.

"No. If she's still out there, I want to go back before she shows up again."

We all knew who "she" was.

———

Danny, Mom, and I ate lunch together—peanut butter and jelly sandwiches—and then split to do our own things.

I was able to concentrate for a couple of hours—reading and drawing—as I listened to the soothing patter of falling raindrops. If rain meant no more Cyndy Louise, then I loved this wet weather.

In midafternoon the rain stopped and the sky brightened, becoming almost sunny. When I looked outside, there was Cyndy Louise again, marching along the street like nothing had happened.

Damn! I was so mad that I kicked the wall and punched it hard with my left hand.

After I finished feeling sorry for myself, I turned back to the window and studied her. She didn't look at all wet so she must have stayed somewhere inside during the rain. But she was still a filthy mess so she hadn't used the time away from the street to clean up.

I tried to get a closer view of her mouth. If anything, her lips looked a little more attached. But something else about Cyndy Louise's face was different. Staring at her as she approached our house, I tried to figure out what it was. Then I saw it—her nose. It had gotten smaller and flatter, like it was melting into her face. And I didn't see any nostrils.

I raced out of my room and down the steps, into the kitchen. "Mom!" I yelled. "Cyndy Louise is back and her nose is all smooshed up."

My mother followed me into the dining room with Muffles trailing behind.

"You're right," Mom agreed. "Her nose is closing, just like her mouth."

"Then how can she breathe?" I asked.

Mom shrugged. "I don't know."

"She's not a person anymore," I whispered. "So maybe she doesn't have to breathe."

CHAPTER 7 – The Dark

The night after Cyndy Louise's return, things got worse. We'd just finished dinner when the lights went out.

"It had to happen," Mom said, sighing deeply. With our boarded windows, I could barely see her as she held onto the wall, feeling her way around the kitchen. I heard jingling noises in one of the drawers before she returned to the table, shining a flashlight and holding two others.

"Here," she said, giving me one of the flashlights before turning to Danny. "You can't use it to play your games all night because we don't have enough batteries. Do you understand?" She handed him the third flashlight.

Danny took the flashlight and nodded, but he didn't look happy.

Mom sat and switched off the light. "We're going to have to change almost everything we do," she began, "because we can't count on getting our power back till this is over. From now on, we're going to sleep early and waking up early so we can use all the daylight.

"After we clear the table, we'll rinse the dishes, leave them in the sink, and clean them tomorrow morning. Then we're going upstairs to bed. I know you're both not tired, but we have to get into this new routine. I'm setting the alarm for six o'clock because we'll start school early too."

I guess changing almost everything didn't mean no more Mom School.

———

The next day was tough. You don't think about electricity until you don't have it. With the refrigerator not working, we had to either eat the food that would spoil or throw it away. We'd already finished most of the frozen stuff, but without a stove we couldn't heat anything so the eggs were no good.

We still had bread, jelly, crackers, a few apples—not real exciting—and we were nearly out of milk and orange juice.

"What're we going to do when we run out of food?" I asked Mom as I nibbled American cheese on buttered crackers.

My mother smiled at me. "We have plenty to eat for now so don't worry." She tilted her head towards Danny.

What did she mean by "for now"? A week? A month? I didn't ask because of Mom's signal. I guess she figured I could deal with all this better than Danny, but I was getting really scared too.

It was bad enough that we were trapped inside our house, but now we didn't have lights and a lot of our food was no good. We still had water, but without power, that would soon turn cold so I'd be taking freezing showers. At least it was mid-May and warm.

———

Without lights and with boarded windows, it was too dark downstairs so we moved school to Mom's bedroom. Danny and I pushed the two small end tables from the sides of the bed to the outside wall and brought in our desk chairs. We were both reading silently in our new classroom when we heard two sharp, booming noises coming from down the block.

"What's that?" I asked.

"It sounds like gunshots," Danny said as he rushed to my window. Mom and I followed.

"Look!" Danny pointed to a man standing at the door of a home across the street from us, two houses down. "It's Mr. Muldare and he's shooting at Cyndy Louise!"

Carrying a rifle, Mr. Muldare left his porch and followed Cyndy Louise, who was walking quickly towards the other end of the block, nearly out of our sight.

"I can hardly see her," I said, opening the window.

"Just the top," Mom ordered.

As I pulled the window halfway down, we heard Mr. Muldare scream, "Don't run away from me! Turn around or I'm gonna shoot you in the back!"

"What's he doing?" I whispered.

"He thinks he can stop her," Mom said.

"But she's not a person anymore," I murmured.

Cyndy Louise turned and headed right at Mr. Muldare, who aimed his rifle and fired at her face. The bullet bounced off her skin—or whatever now covered her face—and didn't even slow her down. She was only a couple of feet away when he fired a second shot. Although that bullet hit her in the chest, it bounced off like the first one and she kept walking.

Mr. Muldare dropped his rifle and ran towards his house, making it to the front porch. But Cyndy Louise moved really fast and as he reached for the door, she touched his shoulder. He crumpled to the ground, just like the others.

Cyndy Louise opened the front door and went inside Mr. Muldare's house. After that, Mom made me close my window and Danny and I went back to doing our schoolwork. But as I was reading, I'm pretty sure I heard a woman screaming.

―――――

I couldn't concentrate on school the rest of the morning and I know Danny couldn't either. Every time I looked up, he was either staring into space or glancing at the window. But Mom kept right on with her lessons, not saying anything about what had happened outside as if that would keep us from thinking about Mr. Muldare and Cyndy Louise.

Finally I couldn't stand it any longer. "Do you think Cyndy Louise is some kind of zombie-person now?" I asked.

"The bullets didn't hurt her at all," Danny whispered. "She's like Superman."

"We don't know that," Mom said. "We only know that she's—well, different."

"Yeah, different in a way that she can kill us and we can't kill her," I muttered.

"We don't know that for sure either," Mom argued. "Just that the rifle bullets didn't penetrate her skin."

"They bounced right off," Danny added.

"You think we can kill her another way—maybe burn her, set her on fire?" I suggested.

Mom shrugged. "I don't know. But somebody would have to get very close to her—and that's too dangerous." She shook her head. "I can't believe we're talking like this about that nice little girl."

"Cyndy Louise's not a girl anymore, Mom," I said. "You have to stop thinking of her as a person. She's something bad now, something that only wants to kill us."

"If we stay inside the house, we're not in any danger," Mom said. "So that's what we're going to do." She smiled at us and then glanced at her lesson plans. "We're up to you, Erin. Please explain the causes of the Revolutionary War."

CHAPTER 8 – The Neighbors

When Mom woke us the next morning at dawn, I heard the rain pounding on the roof so I immediately ran to my window and checked the street. No Cyndy Louise.

I rushed into my mother's room. "Can we skip school this morning or switch it to the afternoon?" I asked. "It's pouring again and Cyndy Louise is gone so maybe it's safe to go outside."

Mom shook her head. "I don't know, Erin..."

"We can stand in front of the house so if we see her coming, we can run back inside." I sighed and played the guilt card. "It would really be good for me and Danny to be out." Parents always want their kids to get fresh air.

"Let me think about it. If it's still raining after breakfast and Cyndy Louise isn't on the street, we'll talk about it again."

I nodded and went to the bathroom to wash up. The water was barely warm, but at least the toilet still worked.

Danny and I had cold cereal for breakfast, using the last of the milk before it spoiled. When we finished, it was still pouring.

Mom opened the back door to let Muffles outside. "I want to see if Cyndy Louise shows up," she said. We all went to the dining room and looked out the opening in the side window. Cyndy Louise wasn't anywhere on the street.

"Please, Mom," I begged.

"All right," she said. "After I put the car into the garage, we'll all stand together in front of the house."

While Danny and I got into our raincoats and found umbrellas, Mom drove the car from the street into our now clean garage. Then my brother and I stepped outside, leaving the front door halfway open. As Mom joined us, Muffles rushed from the backyard, barking happily and jumping up and down our legs in excitement.

"This is almost normal," I said, patting the dog's wet head.

"Yeah," Danny said. "We always stand outside in the rain in front of our house doing nothing."

My brother could be a smartass. "Well, it's good just to be able to go out," I answered back.

"I can think of better..."

"Hi."

Danny stopped talking in mid-sentence as our next-door neighbor, Mrs. Perez, approached, holding a large black umbrella. "Can I join you?" she asked, smiling.

"Sure, Norma," Mom said, moving a few steps to make room. "We're getting a little wet fresh air since it seems safe to be outside during the rain."

"True," she agreed. "But the rest of the time..."

"Look," Danny interrupted. "Here comes Mr. and Mrs. Douglas."

Our neighbors from right across the street—seniors in their 70s, I think—headed towards us, wearing identical bright yellow raincoats and matching shiny rain hats.

"It's great to see all of you and know that you're okay," Mr. Douglas said, hugging each of us. "We need to get everyone on the block out here and come up with a plan."

"Do you think it'll be safe?" Mom asked. "If Cyndy Louise returns..."

"We have to do something, if only to figure out a way to communicate," Mr. Douglas said. "And we have to bury the dead." He nodded towards the bodies of Mrs. Reade and Andrew in the street.

We couldn't see Mr. Muldare's front porch, but I'm sure he was still lying there too. And we don't know what happened inside, but I remembered the woman's screams.

"Can we knock on everyone's door?" I asked.

Mom shook her head. "What if Cyndy Louise is in one of the houses? We can't take that chance."

"How about if we yell for people to go outside to the middle of the street?" Danny suggested.

"Then we're too far from our own house if Cyndy Louise comes back," my mother said.

"We're willing to go to the middle of the block," Mr. Douglas said, glancing at his wife who nodded. "It's our best shot so I think we should try it. Tell everyone who comes out to leave their doors open so if the girl returns, we can all run into the nearest house."

"If we're trapped together, what'll we do about food?" my mother argued.

"I agree with Harold," Mrs. Perez said. "We should get everybody out here now and come up with a plan. We can't go on living like this." She turned to my mother. "Let's give it a try, Maura."

"If we do that, we still need someone to stay here by the corner and watch for Cyndy Louise," Mom said. "Make sure, if she's somewhere else, we know if she comes back to the street."

"Let me do it," Danny offered.

My mother nodded. "Okay, but be careful."

I think she liked the idea of my brother staying near our

house. The rest of us walked down the block shouting that Cyndy Louise wasn't outside and asking everyone to join us and to leave their doors open.

———

I counted the people who stood in the middle of Walnut Lane. If this was everybody, then sixteen of us still lived here. Since we had fourteen houses on our block, that wasn't very many people.

Besides my family, Mrs. Perez, and Mr. and Mrs. Douglas, there was Danny's friend, Bobby Mitchell, and his mom; Connie Chou and her two-year-old daughter, Emily, who I had babysat; Mr. Ortega, who lived by himself; and two families at the other end of the block that I didn't know: a woman named Rhonda Weiss and her little boy; and the Santangelos—a man, woman, and baby.

Six of the houses either had no one alive inside or no one who was willing to come out, including the homes of Cyndy Louise, Mr. Muldare, Andrew O'Malley, and Mr. and Mrs. Kaplan.

After lots of hugs, kisses, and tears—especially by the two moms with the little kids in the strollers—Mr. Douglas spoke to everyone. "Thanks for coming out," he began, the rain bouncing off his yellow hat. "We think this is the only time it's safe to be outside, when it rains, because then that girl isn't on the street." He nodded towards the bodies lying nearby. "We have to bury the dead. That should be the first thing we do."

"What if we become like her if we touch them?" Mr. Santangelo asked. He was a muscular guy who looked strong enough to lift a car.

"Or what if after we touch them, we die too?" Bobby Mitchell's mom added.

Mr. Douglas shook his head. "We can't just leave the bodies

outside to rot," he argued.

"What about Mr. Muldare?" I asked. "And I heard a woman scream inside his house."

"It's too dangerous to go inside the Muldare's place," Mr. Douglas said. "Same with the Kaplan's house. But we have to get all the outside bodies buried. We'll wrap them in blankets first, wearing gloves so we don't touch them." He glanced at everyone and then turned to his wife. "If no one else is willing to help us, Lynne and I'll do it ourselves."

"I'll help you," Mr. Ortega said. He worked from his house, running some kind of computer business.

"So will I," Mrs. Perez said. "Let's get shovels and blankets."

———

The people on our block dug three graves in front of Mr. Muldare's house, with Mr. Santangelo and Mr. Ortega doing most of the work. No one said anything about using the Muldare's front lawn for the bodies, but everyone was afraid to go into a backyard. Since we still had no idea where Cyndy Louise was, it seemed safer to be in the street. At least then we could run inside an open house.

When the graves were ready, the Douglasses, Mr. Ortega, and Mrs. Perez—all wearing gloves—wrapped Mr. Muldare in the donated blankets. Then they lifted his body and lowered him into the first hole. After we gathered around the grave and Mr. Douglas said a short prayer, Mr. Santangelo took the shovel and covered the hole with wet dirt.

Connie Chou came forward with two sticks she and her friend, Mrs. Weiss, had tied together with pieces of thick grass and she wedged the handmade cross into the new grave.

Then the same four people wrapped the bodies of Andrew and Cyndy Louise's mother and carried them to the gravesite. Those two bodies smelled really bad, I guess because they had been outside all this time. After Mr. Douglas said a few quick prayers, Mr. Santangelo shoveled in dirt, and Connie and Mrs. Weiss added crosses made from the branches.

———

After all the bodies were buried, everyone helped clean up the broken glass and flowerpot pieces outside the Kaplan's house and the plastic, glass, and busted tires around Mrs. Reade's smashed car.

It was still pouring hard when we formed a circle in the middle of the street. "Now we have to figure out a way to communicate when it's not raining and we're stuck in our homes, assuming that girl comes back into the street," Mr. Douglas said.

"How about telephone?" I suggested.

Some neighbors looked confused, but Connie Chou and Mrs. Perez nodded their heads.

"Like the game where you pass messages along to each other?" Connie asked. "You think we can do it from house to house?"

"If we shout," I said.

"But what about the homes where nobody's there?" Mrs. Douglas asked.

"Maybe we have a few different talk lines," my mom suggested. "On our side of the block, we can do four houses before the empty one."

"We're the only homes on the end," Bobby's mother said to Mr. and Mrs. Santangelo. "We'll have to shout across to each other."

Mr. Santangelo nodded.

"It could work," Mr. Douglas said.

"And Walnut Lane's quiet enough that we should be able to hear each other," Mr. Ortega pointed out. "Cyndy Louise doesn't say anything."

"She can't even talk anymore," I said. "Did you see how her mouth is closing?"

Several people nodded. "Yeah," Mrs. Perez agreed. "And her nose is almost gone."

"So how can she eat and breathe?" Mrs. Weiss asked.

"She doesn't have to," I murmured.

No one spoke for a few seconds. "We all know that she's not a person anymore," Mr. Douglas said. "She's changing, but we don't know what she's turning into. Let's keep watching and monitoring her and talk to each other through the upstairs windows."

"But she'll hear what we're saying," Mrs. Santangelo said.

Mr. Douglas shrugged. "If she's not human anymore, maybe she won't understand or care about what we say."

"Or maybe her ears will disappear too," I offered. "Then she won't be able to hear us."

My mom shook her head. "I don't think that'll happen, Erin. Living creatures need to hear."

"But they also need to eat and breathe," I argued. "And Cyndy Louise doesn't so that means she's not a living creature."

"Then what is she?" Mrs. Santangelo asked.

Again everyone was quiet until Connie spoke. "We don't know," she said.

———

It was still raining, but not as heavily, and we were all getting antsy about being in the middle of the street.

"Let's go home and try our new form of communication," Mr. Douglas said.

As the meeting broke up, Bobby Mitchell came up to Mom and me. "Can I see Danny now?" he asked. He'd wanted to join my brother watching for Cyndy Louise, but his mother wouldn't let him.

"We have to go back to our house," Mrs. Mitchell said, looking nervously in the direction of her home at the other end of the block.

"Please," Bobby begged. "Just for a minute."

Bobby's mother nodded and he dashed towards Danny, who'd left his post to join us. The boys met near our house, and after a quick hug, began talking and gesturing to each other, huge smiles covering both their faces.

"It's good for them," Mom said, staring at the pair.

"I know," Mrs. Mitchell agreed. "But it's dangerous out here. We have to go back...He's all I have left."

Like my dad, her husband hadn't come home. Neither did Bobby's older brother, Rick, who'd been a freshman at Adams.

"Give the boys a couple more minutes," my mother said. "They've been through a lot."

As my mother continued talking to Mrs. Mitchell, I stood nearby watching Danny and Bobby and tried not to be jealous. None of my friends lived on our block—if I still had any friends who were alive. But I didn't want to think about that.

———

We were upstairs, doing schoolwork in Mom's bedroom, when we heard a whistle. Without saying a word, Danny and I dropped our books on the bed and raced into my room. The whistle blew again and we saw Mr. Douglas standing in front of an open upstairs window across the street, waving a whistle at us. His wife was in front of a window in the next room and she smiled and waved too.

Mom opened my window halfway. It was drizzling and Cyndy Louise wasn't in sight.

"You heard the whistle?" Mr. Douglas shouted.

"Yes!" Mom yelled back.

"Good!" Mr. Douglas shouted. "That can be our signal!"

"I'm here too." Another woman, whom we couldn't see, spoke the words, which we could barely hear.

"That's Norma Perez," Mom said to us.

"If I go to my room, I can see her and also hear her better," Danny said, stepping away.

"Maybe later," Mom said as she grabbed his arm. "Right now, stay here."

"Ramón's with us too!" Mr. Douglas shouted. "He just waved to me! Can you hear him?"

Danny, Mom, and I looked at each other. I shrugged and Danny shook his head. We couldn't see or hear Mr. Ortega, who lived next door to Mrs. Perez.

"No!" Mom yelled out the window.

"I'll have Ramón shout our messages down the block!" Mr. Douglas hollered. "Let's set times for these meetings—maybe twice a day!"

"How about ten and four?" Mrs. Perez called.

"Did you hear that?" Mr. Douglas shouted. "We'll talk to each other every day at ten and four!"

"That's fine!" Mom yelled back.

"Ramón says those times are good too!" Mr. Douglas called to us. "We're going to pass this message along to the rest of the people on the street!" After a wave, he closed his window.

Mom shut my window and we went back to her bedroom for school. I felt a little better. At least we had a way of keeping in touch with our neighbors.

CHAPTER 9 – The Fight

It continued raining lightly through the rest of the afternoon and early night so we didn't see Cyndy Louise that entire day. When I woke up the next morning, I immediately ran to my window. The sun was shining again—and there was Cyndy Louise, marching up and down the street like nothing had happened.

As she got closer to our house, I stared at her to see if anything else had changed. She still wore the same filthy clothes, torn in lots of places, and she swung her arms and legs as she walked. But now her hair looked different. It was still just as messy, but I think there was less hair on her head. *Was it falling out?*

Then Mom yelled that it was time to get up and begin our day. At breakfast—dry cereal and water—I mentioned Cyndy Louise's hair.

"Maybe she doesn't need it anymore," Danny suggested. "Like her nose and mouth."

"I guess," I said. "She's still got arms and legs though."

"She needs them to move around and touch people." Danny frowned and extended his arm towards my face.

I swatted his arm away.

"Finish up," Mom said, pointing to the kitchen clock. "It's almost time for school." Our new school hours were seven to eleven-thirty to take advantage of the daylight. I had argued that it was more time than before, but Mom wouldn't listen.

"You have the rest of the day for yourself," she had said. "After you eat lunch and finish your homework, you've still got plenty of spare time."

I had complained because extra school didn't seem fair. But Mom was right about the time—and there wasn't much else to do anyway.

———

We were upstairs in Mom's bedroom, reading in school, when I heard noises outside. "What's that?" I asked.

"Sounds like banging," Danny said as he closed his book and ran into my room.

When Mom and I joined him, Danny pointed to our street corner. "Cyndy Louise's got company."

I looked out my window and saw two other toucher things—a man and a woman—standing next to Cyndy Louise. There was a garbage can nearby, laying on its side.

"Can we open the window so we can hear what they're saying?" I asked Mom.

She nodded.

I opened the window, but we just heard grunts, not words.

"Their mouths don't work no more," Danny said.

"Any more," Mom corrected.

"They don't like each other," I said. "See their body language." The man toucher thumped his fist against his chest, reminding me of a gorilla bragging about how strong it was. Then the man-thing moved next to Cyndy Louise and punched her hard in the stomach.

"Ow!" Mom cried.

But Cyndy Louise didn't fall down or back off. Instead, she threw herself against the guy toucher, knocked him to the ground, and pounded him with her hands.

The woman toucher jumped on Cyndy Louise and hit her in the face so Cyndy Louise stopped punching the man and began using her fists on the woman.

"Wow!" Danny muttered. "A girl fight!"

"They're not girls," I reminded him. "They're some kind of toucher things."

"Yeah, but whatever they are, Cyndy Louise is winning," Danny said.

And he was right. She was beating up both the man and woman things. When she stopped hitting them, she took the garbage can cover and swatted them with that. We heard several loud grunts from the pair as they both turned and ran out of Walnut Lane. After Cyndy Louise stared at them for a moment, she began walking to the other end of the block again.

Reaching over, Mom closed my window.

"So what was that all about?" Danny asked.

"It reminded me of a wild animal defending her territory," Mom explained. "Like a lion or tiger."

"And we're her territory," I whispered.

———

I was answering questions about the climate in India when I heard the whistle.

Mom checked her watch. "It's ten o'clock," she said. "So that must be Harold Douglas. We'll take a quick break to hear what he's got to say."

Danny, Mom, and I raced to my bedroom again and Mom opened the top part of the window.

Mr. Douglas waved at us. "Hello!" he shouted. His wife stood at another second floor window and waved too.

"Hi, Harold!" Mom yelled back. "Did you see the fight?"

"Yes! Our girl won!"

"We don't know if that's such a good thing!" Mom hollered.

Mr. Douglas shrugged.

"At least we know what she's like," I heard a woman say. It must have been Mrs. Perez next door. "We don't know those others."

"I'm sure they're all the same!" Mrs. Douglas shouted. "They're all just as dangerous!"

I heard the faint sound of a man's voice, but couldn't make out what he said.

"Okay, Ramón!" Mr. Douglas hollered. "I'll ask!" He turned towards us. "Did you hear that?" he asked.

"No!" Mom shouted.

"Ramón said we have to find some way to attack the girl, figure out her vulnerability!"

"What's that?" Danny asked.

"Find a weak spot so we can kill her," I explained.

CHAPTER 10 – The Store

We were having our usual breakfast of cold cereal when Mom shook her head and pointed to the wall calendar with her spoon. She'd been marking off the days since the bubbles fell and there were nearly two weeks worth of "X"s.

"Since there's no easy way to say this, I'm going to do it quickly," she said. "We're running out of food so I have to go to the supermarket."

"You can't!" I shouted. "Not with Cyndy Louise outside!"

"I'll take the car the next time it rains."

"I'm going with you," Danny said.

"Me too," I echoed.

Mom frowned at us. "I don't want either of you to go. It's much too dangerous."

"But it's just as dangerous for you," I argued. "And what happens to Danny and me if you don't come back? If we all go, we can protect each other—watch out for them."

"What if we see the toucher-things?" Mom asked. "We still don't know how to stop them." We'd had telephone talks with our neighbors for nearly a week, but no one had come up with a plan for killing Cyndy Louise.

"I have an idea," Danny whispered.

Mom and I turned and looked at him.

"Cyndy Louise is never outside when it rains so that's gotta mean they don't like water. Maybe we could shoot water at them with a water gun."

Mom shrugged. "What do you think?" she asked me.

"It could work," I said. "It might keep them away."

"Do you have any water pistols?" Mom asked Danny.

"I looked for them all day yesterday and found a couple. I thought I had more, but I don't know where they are."

My brother isn't the neatest kid in the world. But I'm not the one to criticize him since I'm just as big a slob.

"Bring the water guns downstairs and let's try them out," Mom said.

———

I'd forgotten how much fun a water fight could be—and it was a lot better way to spend the morning than having classes at Mom School. Danny gave me one of his loaded guns and I squirted his chest, getting his shirt real wet. Then he sprayed me in the leg and ran into the other room, hiding behind the couch.

"Not in the living room!" Mom shouted. I guess she was still trying to protect the furniture.

Muffles, who had been watching Danny and me, started barking so I squirted him too. He shook himself dry, getting the kitchen floor full of water.

"That's enough," Mom said as she used a rag to wipe the tiles. "We can see that the water pistols still work."

Danny came back into the kitchen, pointing at his weapon. "But shouldn't we test them out more to check our aim?" he asked.

"No," Mom said. "I'm not spending the rest of the day mopping up the house. Your aim is fine."

"Does that mean we can go to the store with you?" I asked.

Mom glanced up from the floor. "I don't like the idea," she said. "But I'm afraid of leaving you two by yourselves so..."

"...we can go?" Danny interrupted.

My mother nodded her head.

———

Mom didn't want to mention her plan of going to the supermarket during the telephone talks with our neighbors. "I don't know how much Cyndy Louise hears and understands," she explained. "We can't take a chance."

"But it'd be better if a bunch of us go together," I said. "We could all watch out for each other."

"I'll mention it the next time we meet on the street," Mom said. "In the meantime, I'm going to write down everything we need and make a map of the store, with as many aisles as I can remember, so we can get everything as fast as possible. Without any lights, it'll be dark in the back."

I had forgotten that. This adventure was starting to sound creepy.

"Help me," Mom said. "Let's put our heads together and see what we remember about Stop & Shop."

I didn't go to the supermarket very often so I couldn't think of much. I just remembered where the cookies were and told Mom I didn't think that would be tops on her list.

"Actually it is important, Erin," Mom said. "Crackers will be in the cookie aisle and since we can't get fresh bread, we need lots of crackers."

Danny knew the location of a few aisles and Mom remembered most of the rest so she was able to design a pretty good store map. Then she took her list and put it in order, according to the aisles. When she finished, she read it to us and asked for suggestions.

"What about more fruit?" I asked. We'd eaten the last of our apples and I missed having bananas at breakfast.

"After no power for more than a week, that section's going to smell bad—almost like the meat department—with lots of spoiled food, but we can try for apples and melons," she said. "And maybe we can find some raisins and other dried fruits." She grabbed her pen and added those things to the list.

"Can we get Three Musketeers bars?" Danny asked.

Mom smiled. "It's not a priority, but we'll see if we can grab a couple bags of candy." She made a note on the paper and then glanced at us. "Okay, I think we're pretty much set. Now all we need is a heavy rainstorm."

———

"Erin! Danny! Time to get up!"

After hearing the now-familiar early morning wakeup call, otherwise known as the Mom Alarm, I stretched and sat up in bed. But as I did, I heard the unmistakable sounds of raindrops pounding on the roof.

I rushed into Mom's bedroom even before heading to the bathroom. "It's pouring out," I said. "Does this mean we're going to the store?" It had been two days since my mother told us about her shopping plans.

"I hope so." She was already dressed in jeans and a tee shirt and brushing her dark blonde hair.

"No school today?"

"Not this morning if the weather stays like this."

"Great—I'll tell Danny." I ran to my brother's room and banged on his door. "Get up!" I yelled. "It's raining and we're going to the supermarket!"

"Really?" Danny opened the door and stood there in his pajamas, rubbing his eyes. "I'll get the water guns ready."

"Fill up an extra bottle with water just in case we need

more."

"Good idea," he said. "Meet you downstairs." He closed the door in my face.

"Right." I stood outside my brother's door for a moment taking in his comment. Danny said I had a good idea. Things were really different—both outside and inside our house.

———

We ate breakfast quickly as Mom reviewed her plans for the supermarket trip. "It's still pouring so we're on for this morning," she said, looking through the narrow opening in the boarded-up kitchen window. "But first I'm going to check with Norma, and also with Harold and Lynne, to see if they want to come with us."

"What about Connie and the others?" I asked.

Mom shook her head. "Too many. We can fit three more in our car, but that's it."

"Are we gonna take Muffles?" Danny asked. Hearing his name, the dog walked over to my brother to be petted.

"No," Mom said. "I don't want him barking in the store. We need to be quiet."

"We have to make some noise," I pointed out. "We'll use shopping carts and the wheels on them are noisy. And even if we whisper..."

"It's not the same as loud barking," Mom argued. "Muffles isn't coming."

"But he could warn us if the toucher things are around," Danny said.

"He could also let them know that we're around," Mom replied. "We're shopping without the dog." She carried her cereal bowl and glass to the sink. "Finish up and get ready. After we make sure Cyndy Louise isn't on the street, I'm knocking on Norma and Harold's doors. Then we're heading to

Stop & Shop."

———

Mr. and Mrs. Douglas didn't want to come with us, but Mrs. Perez did. At nine o'clock, Mom drove our Legacy out of the garage and into the rain.

"I'm glad the car started," Mom said as Mrs. Perez got into the front seat while Danny and I slid into the back. "I only drove it into the garage since all this happened."

There were now fifteen "X"s on our calendar.

Turning left, Mom headed for the supermarket, which was near our house, just about two miles away. But my mother drove real slow. "We don't know what's going on anywhere else," she explained.

I looked out my window and checked the houses and streets as we passed them. It was spookily quiet everywhere. There were a couple of moving cars on the road, although there were lots of wrecked ones that had crashed into other cars or jumped the sidewalk and then rammed into buildings. My mother swerved around all the messed-up autos like she was playing an arcade game—the kind with an obstacle course where you sit inside a booth and turn the steering wheel. Only she was moving in slow motion.

And she didn't have to stop for any traffic lights. None of them worked. I didn't see any live people and I stopped counting the dead bodies in the street and on the sidewalk after I got to twenty. That's without the ones in the crashed cars because I couldn't tell how many people were inside.

"At least no touchers are out here," I said, trying to be positive.

"Where do they go when it rains?" Mrs. Perez asked.

"Hopefully someplace far away from here," my mother said as she pulled into Stop & Shop's parking lot, which had about ten empty normal-looking cars, plus two that had crashed head-on and a bunch of dead people on the ground that I tried not to look at.

"Everybody out and stay together," Mom said.

As we walked towards the entrance of the store, avoiding the body on the sidewalk, Danny and I each carried a loaded water pistol and Mrs. Perez held an extra bottle of water. Mom clutched her shopping list, although it probably wasn't necessary since she had memorized everything on it.

―――――

The automatic entrance door didn't work. But someone— or something—had smashed in part of the front window and made a huge hole. "Be careful not to touch the glass," Mom whispered as, one by one, we entered the store through the broken window.

"Yucch!" Danny said as he stepped inside.

"Shh," Mom whispered.

But I understood my brother's comment. It smelled really, really bad—like some animal had crawled into the supermarket and died surrounded by a bunch of rotten, spoiled food. It was gross. Also it was hot and dark. Mom had brought a flashlight and so had Mrs. Perez. They both shined their lights on the floor in front of us.

After Mom and Mrs. Perez each grabbed a cart, my mother nodded towards the first aisle on the right where we had decided to start and we all moved as quietly as we could in that direction. It was even creepier than I'd figured—the smells, the dark, and lots of strange little scurrying sounds that didn't belong in any supermarket.

"What's that noise?" I whispered to Danny.

"Probably rats."

Oh, God! I held my water pistol in front of me and moved

closer to my brother as we reached the bread aisle and stopped. There was hardly anything on the shelves, especially the bottom ones. Most of the food was all over the floor and many of the packages were open. Chewed slices of bread and animal poop were everywhere.

As soon as Mom and Mrs. Perez shined their flashlights, the creatures on the floor all scattered. And Danny had been right. They were rats—lots and lots of them.

Mom motioned towards the next aisle, which had laundry and cleaning stuff. The shelves looked okay and I didn't see any rats on the ground. We entered the aisle and Mom and Mrs. Perez picked up a couple of bottles and packages of detergents. Then they turned the carts around and we quickly moved into the next aisle.

This was the paper section—toilet paper, tissues, and paper towels—and it was also in good shape. My mother and Mrs. Perez put paper stuff in their carts and then turned the wagons around to the front. I knew we were staying away from the back part of the store because that was where the most disgusting smell was coming from—the meat department.

So far we hadn't seen anything gross except rats and poop. But when we walked into the fourth aisle, we immediately stopped. A dead body blocked the way. It was a woman, lying on her stomach, her arms stretched out like she was reaching for the can of tomato sauce that lay on its side near her head.

This was the canned vegetable aisle and someone needed to go in there and get food. Mom turned to us, signaling she and Mrs. Perez would give Danny and me their flashlights, leave the carts, and they would go to the shelves and get the cans.

While Danny and I waited, each aiming a flashlight and water pistol in front of us, Mom and our neighbor walked around the body and into the aisle to get cans of vegetables, bringing back a few at a time. These shelves were only half full so other people must have been here and gotten out okay—just not the dead lady on the floor.

The next aisle had cookies, crackers, and cheese spreads, but also more dead bodies. I counted one man and three women sprawled near the center, surrounded by a bunch of cookie boxes, most of them unopened. I heard that creepy shuffling sound as some rats must have seen us and run away.

Again Mom motioned that she and our neighbor would get the food while Danny and I kept watch. That was fine with me. I didn't want to step around a group of dead people. And these bodies must have been in the store longer than the other lady because they smelled real bad.

We turned into the canned fruit and juice aisle next. Some dented cans covered the floor, but none were open, and even better, there were no dead people. Mom and Mrs. Perez again gave us their flashlights and Danny and I shined light on them as they picked up juices, canned fruits, and jars of applesauce. I liked fresh fruit a lot better, but from the smell coming from that end of the store, I knew I wasn't going to like the fresh fruit selection.

The next aisle had canned fish and canned and dry milk. But it also had lots of bodies all over the floor. Luckily the dead people were towards the back and the food we wanted was in the front. We pushed both carts in a little bit and emptied tuna and sardine cans into our cart while Mrs. Perez got a bunch of milks.

We reached the candy aisle next. Two more dead people blocked the back and the floor was full of squashed chocolate pieces, mostly M & Ms, and lots more rat poop. Mom ran in quickly and picked up a few bags of Three Musketeers and Skittles, which I liked.

The next two aisles had frozen food so they were

completely worthless to us. The aisles smelled bad, but at least they didn't have any dead bodies and I didn't see or hear any rats.

After we passed the soups, we pulled up to the soda and iced tea aisle. Danny and I had argued for soda because it was boring to just drink water. Although Mom had refused, saying we were eating enough junk these days, she had agreed to get iced tea and fruit drink packets. And this aisle was in good shape. In this store, "good shape" meant no messed up cans or bottles on the ground, no rats, and of course, no dead bodies.

We reached an important aisle next because it had pet food and we needed stuff for Muffles. Unfortunately, the aisle was a disaster. Bags were ripped up all over the floor and the rats here didn't even run away when we showed up. Even worse, the one body in the front was lying face up—if you could still call it that. The woman's face was all bitten and chunks of her flesh had been ripped out. I looked away before I threw up.

I don't know who went into the aisle for dog food, probably Mom. I just couldn't look at that dead body. My mother tapped me on the back when we were ready to move and we headed towards the large produce section that took up the whole left side of the store. The smell of rotten fruits and vegetables was really gross. *So much for "fresh" fruit.*

Mom motioned that we should stay together with the carts and she would get dried fruit and other stuff that wasn't spoiled. I nodded and held my nose with my left hand and the water pistol with my right. Danny walked closer, aiming the flashlight and his water gun ahead of him. Mrs. Perez aimed her flashlight too.

Mom made a couple of trips through the section, picking up apples and then packages of dried fruits. As she emptied the stuff into the cart, I felt something small and furry climb onto my foot.

"No!" I shouted, shaking my leg. That one little word sounded very loud in the quiet store.

Mom frowned at me and pointed to the front door. That's when we heard their footsteps.

The toucher things must have been sleeping, resting, or doing whatever they did, someplace in the back of the store. And my scream had awakened them. There were three—a boy-thing about Danny's age and two women—and they raced down the main grocery aisle towards us.

"Move fast!" Mom shouted, taking the cart and pushing it in front of her while Mrs. Perez did the same.

Danny and I walked right behind them, holding the flashlights and water pistols. As the touchers continued running in our direction, my brother turned and squirted the boy, hitting the thing's foot. The toucher stopped and shook off the water.

"He doesn't like it," I said, using my gun to squirt the older woman-thing whose mouth looked like it was pasted onto her face. I hit her in the arm and she also stopped to wipe away the water.

But the other woman toucher kept coming. "Now!" I shouted and Danny and I both fired all the water left in our guns at her.

She stopped and fell to the floor, not making any sound, but she sure didn't seem happy.

Now our guns were empty. "We need water!" I yelled and Danny grabbed the extra bottle that Mrs. Perez handed him.

The boy and older woman were moving again and were just a couple of feet from us when Danny opened the bottle and flung the water at both their faces. My brother, the all-star Little League pitcher, threw strikes! The toucher things immediately dropped to the floor.

Danny and I caught up to Mom and Mrs. Perez and we

pushed the carts through the exit door, which we were able to pull open. Then we all stepped into the safety of the pouring rain.

———

We wheeled both wagons to the car and quickly dumped the stuff into the trunk, nervously checking the front of the store every few seconds to see if any of the touchers were coming after us. But none of them did.

Mom drove back to Walnut Lane as fast as she could, avoiding the crashed autos and dead people, while all four of us sat quietly, nobody talking. Again I looked out the window, but this time I didn't bother counting the bodies we passed; there were too many.

Mom turned into Mrs. Perez's driveway and everyone got out of the car. Walnut Lane was quiet—no Cyndy Louise on the street and none of our neighbors either. After we helped carry food and supplies into Mrs. Perez's house, Mom drove into our garage and the three of us unloaded our groceries.

When we were finished, we sat in the kitchen. Muffles wandered up to me to be petted and I stroked his soft, furry neck.

"You two did a great job of saving us in the store," Mom said.

"We wouldn't've needed to do anything if she didn't scream," Danny said, scowling at me.

"I'm sorry, but I couldn't help it." I shrugged and turned to my mother. "A creepy rat crawled up my leg."

"You must've woke those things up," Danny continued. "We could've all been killed."

"Well, we weren't. The water guns worked." I smiled at my brother. "That was a real good idea."

"Yeah," he agreed, nodding at me. But he kept on scowling.

CHAPTER 11 – The Water

We were preparing lunch—tuna on crackers—when we heard a knock on the front door. Danny jumped up to check it out. "It's Mr. and Mrs. Douglas!" he yelled to us.

"Don't touch the door!" Mom warned as she rushed to intercept Danny. After peeking through the narrow opening in the wood, she unlocked the door and greeted our neighbors, saying, "Please come in."

"No," Mr. Douglas said. "We're dripping wet so we'll stand here. We just wanted to find out how your shopping trip turned out."

"We saw you drive the car into the garage," Mrs. Douglas added. "And now you're all back safely." She smiled at us. "Were you able to get inside the store and bring back food?"

"Yes," Mom said. "But it wasn't easy." After convincing the neighbors to take off their yellow raincoats and hats and come into the house, she invited them to join us for lunch.

"No, thanks," Mr. Douglas said. "We just ate."

The Douglasses sat on the couch in our dark living room and Danny and I lay on the floor while Mom told them what happened in the supermarket.

When she finished, Mr. Douglas shook his head. "You were

very lucky not to have been killed," he said. "It's too bad those bubble things formed a group to work together, unlike Cyndy Louise. But what you discovered could help us."

"They really hate water," Mrs. Douglas murmured.

"Not enough to kill them," Danny said.

"But enough to slow them down," I added. "Every time the touchers got wet, they immediately stopped to wipe off the water."

"I wonder if we could use hoses on them," Mr. Douglas said. "Stop Cyndy Louise and the others with a steady stream of water."

"It's worth a try," my mother said. "Whenever we're outside, we should have water guns and hoses ready in case the rain stops and she, or one of the others, comes after us."

"I'll mention the water hose idea later this afternoon at our next block talk," Mr. Douglas said, standing. "But now, Lynne and I will get out of here so you can enjoy your lunch. You must be starving after your ordeal this morning."

"Can we give you some food to take home?" Mom asked. "We were able to get quite a few things."

Mrs. Douglas waved her hand at my mother. "No, thank you. We really are well stocked," she said. "Harold and I hoard food like crazy. We always buy too much."

———

We were exhausted from our morning at the store so after lunch, we went into our separate rooms to relax. Picking up my sketchpad, I sat by the window and thumbed through my drawings, stopping when I reached a colored-pencil picture of a unicorn.

I closed the pad and stared at the falling rain. Just two weeks ago, I had finished drawing that unicorn in geometry class when I looked out the window and saw the bubbles.

It seemed so long ago, like another lifetime. Sighing, I leaned my elbows on the sill, holding my head on my hands. *Why did this happen—and when would it end?* As I sat quietly, feeling sorry for myself, I heard the soft sounds of crying through my open door.

The noise was very faint, but it was definitely crying—and it was coming from Mom's room. As carefully as I could, I tiptoed into the hall and rested my ear against my mother's closed bedroom door. She was crying softly, maybe into a towel or something, trying not to be heard.

Danny's door wasn't open so maybe he didn't hear it. I lifted my hand to knock on Mom's door, but then quickly pulled it back. I hadn't realized how bad she felt. I should have figured—I mean, she could have lost her mother and she did lose Dad. He was my father and I loved him, but he was her husband. *What could I say to her?* I went back into my room and this time, closed the door.

———

Just before four o'clock, Mom and Danny knocked on my door. "Time for our telephone talk," my mother said, pointing to her watch. Opening the window wide, she waved to the Douglasses across the street. "Hi!" she shouted through the soft drizzle. "It's still raining! Should we meet outside?"

"No!" Mr. Douglas yelled. "This light rain could stop at any time! Let's just get the word out about the water!" He blew his whistle and waited for nearly a minute before turning towards Mrs. Perez's house.

"Hi, Norma!" he shouted. "Tell Ramón about what happened with the touchers in the supermarket! That they don't like to get wet! Water guns slowed them down so we want to try using hoses!"

We heard a faint, "Okay," before Mr. Douglas called to us

again. "Next time we meet outside in the rain, let's connect hoses to the fire hydrant!" he yelled. Our hydrant was in the middle of the block, across the street between Mr. Muldare's and Cyndy Louise's property.

"Pass that message along!" he shouted to Mrs. Perez. "Everybody should bring water hoses and we will connect them to the hydrant!"

"And they should take water pistols!" Danny yelled.

"Good idea!" Mr. Douglas called, smiling at my brother. "Norma! Tell people if they have water guns to bring them outside too!"

―――――

The drizzle turned into a heavier rain overnight and when Mom woke us the next morning, it was still pouring.

"We should go outside and set up the hoses like Mr. Douglas said," I suggested during breakfast.

Mom shook her head. "We didn't have school yesterday because we went to the store. We'll go outside in the afternoon if it's still raining."

"But shouldn't we get some fresh air?" I asked, using the line that had worked before.

"You were out in the fresh air yesterday."

"We were mostly in the store," Danny muttered. "And that was real bad air."

Ignoring his comment, Mom gazed at the kitchen clock. "Finish eating and get your books and notebooks. Be in my room in ten minutes for class."

―――――

After we finished Mom School and ate a quick lunch, the three of us put on our raincoats, grabbed umbrellas, and headed to the middle of the block where a bunch of our neighbors were standing.

"Welcome!" Mr. Douglas said, smiling as we approached. "We've been getting the hydrant ready. Fortunately Ramón had a hose adapter that fit." He nodded towards Mr. Ortega, who held a large wrench. "Take a look." We walked with Mr. Douglas and Mr. Ortega to the fire hydrant.

"Are you sure Cyndy Louise isn't somewhere inside?" my mother asked, tipping her umbrella in the direction of the Reade house.

Mr. Douglas shrugged. "We can't be sure she's not in there," he said. "But if they don't like having water on them, then even if she's in the house, she probably won't come outside into the rain. Besides, we've been out here all this time talking and she hasn't shown up."

When we reached the fire hydrant, a long hose, maybe eighty feet, was attached to it, looking like a huge green snake.

"How do we turn the water on?" I asked quietly. "Someone has to be out here to do it when it's not raining and Cyndy Louise is around."

"You're right," Mr. Douglas agreed. "Ramón has already loosened the valves so it's all set, but we'll have to think of a way to start the water."

———

When I woke up the next morning, the sun was shining. Jumping out of bed, I rushed to the window to check out Cyndy Louise.

She looked different than a few days ago. Her nose was much flatter, like it was being absorbed into her cheeks and I couldn't see any nostrils. Her mouth was disappearing too. It was just a dark pink outline on the bottom of her face. I didn't notice any space between her lips so I'm not sure she could open them any more.

What was happening to Cyndy Louise? What was she? She was

alive, but not like anything we knew.

As she walked, I stared at her face again. Her eyes and ears hadn't changed at all. Little Red Riding Hood and the big bad wolf popped into my head: "The better to see you with, my dear!" Like the wolf, she needed to see and hear in order to touch us. She needed her legs and arms and hands and feet too. But she didn't need to eat, drink, breathe, or smell.

I guess she didn't need to be clean either. She stayed away from water and hadn't washed herself with anything else either. Also, she hadn't changed clothes since the bubble landed on her so her shirt and jeans were now filthy rags. What was left of her hair was all tangled and knotted and she was covered with dirt. I bet she smelled real bad too, but I didn't want to get close enough to find out.

———

We always had a school break at ten o'clock for the telephone talk. When we heard Mr. Douglas' whistle, Mom and I dashed into my room and now Danny went into his room to talk to Mrs. Perez.

Mr. Douglas and his wife waved at Mom and me. "We're ready to test the hose this morning!" he shouted.

"How?" my mother called back.

"When Cyndy Louise is on the other end of the block, Ramón will run across the street and turn the water on!" Mr. Douglas explained.

"But if it doesn't work and she touches him..." Mom didn't finish her sentence.

"Maura, we have to try something!" Mrs. Douglas shouted. "We're all trapped in our homes like animals in cages!"

"But we can't be sure the water will keep her away!" Mom yelled.

"We have to try this!" her husband called. "Ramón

volunteered and he's the closest to the hydrant! Everyone agrees it's the best plan!"

"Yes, it is." I recognized Mrs. Perez's voice. "What time will he do it?"

"Eleven o'clock!" Mr. Douglas shouted. "Pass the information to the others!"

———

The alarm in Mom's bedroom went off at 10:55. I dropped my pen and notebook on the bed and we all ran into my room.

As we watched, Cyndy Louise walked to our corner, swung around, and headed down the block. When she was all the way at the other end, Mr. Ortega rushed out to the hydrant and used his wrench to turn on the water. Then he tossed the wrench and held the hose, water gushing into the street as he waited for Cyndy Louise to return. When she got close, he lifted the hose and squirted the water at her head.

She flinched and stepped back, wiping her face continuously. Then, still trying to rub off the water, she ran into her front yard.

Mr. Ortega followed her movements, trying to keep the hose pointed at her. But Cyndy Louise was so fast that he couldn't do it. She kept running until she was in the back of her yard and we couldn't see her anymore.

"Get out of there!" Mr. Douglas shouted. "Ramón, go home!"

Mr. Ortega dropped the hose in the gutter and raced to his door as Cyndy Louise crossed the street, rushing after him.

I held my breath and none of us spoke. We heard a door slam followed by heavy pounding noises, but we couldn't see anything. Finally we heard Mr. Douglas. "He made it back inside!" he shouted. "Ramón's safe!"

———

We stayed next to my window for a few minutes after Mr. Ortega's adventure with the hose, listening to Cyndy Louise bang on his door. Then the sounds stopped, but we still didn't see Cyndy Louise. She must have been walking on the sidewalk on our side of Walnut Lane because water from the hose was still pouring into the middle of the street from the sidewalk where Mr. Ortega had been standing.

"We've got to turn off the water!" Mr. Douglas shouted. "We don't know how much of a supply we have!"

"Very dangerous!" my mother yelled.

"She won't come near the water!" he called back. "I'm going out!"

Danny tapped my mother's shoulder. "Let me take the water guns," he said. "I can cover him like I did at the store."

Mom shook her head.

"I've got to—I don't think Mr. Douglas even has a water pistol."

"I can go too," I offered.

"No," Danny said. "I shoot much better than you."

I didn't argue with him because he was right.

Danny ran out of the room and seconds later we heard the water running in the bathroom. Then he walked back into my bedroom carrying two filled water pistols. "I'm going," he said.

"Danny..." my mother pleaded.

"I'll stand behind Mr. Douglas and if she comes after me, I'll shoot her and run," he said. "You know I can run fast."

I looked out the window and saw Mr. Douglas heading towards the middle of the street. "He's on his way," I said.

Danny rushed out of the room and we heard the front door slam shut. I raced downstairs, locked the door, ran to the dining room window, and peeked through the small opening. Mom pulled out a chair and sat next to me.

"I don't like this at all," she whispered. "My little boy..."

"I haven't liked anything that's happened since the bubbles started falling," I said. "But Danny's the right person to do this and he'll be fine." I hoped what I said was true.

———

Mom and I watched in silence as Mr. Douglas picked up the wrench Mr. Ortega had left near the hydrant and used it to twist the valves. Much less water flowed into the street from the hose, but it didn't stop completely.

My brother stood behind our neighbor as he struggled to turn all the water off. Then we saw Cyndy Louise heading towards them, moving crazy fast.

"They've got to get out of there now," Mom murmured. Leaning out the window, she yelled, "Danny! That's enough! Come home!"

Mr. Douglas gave a valve one final twist with the wrench, said something to Danny that we couldn't hear, and then ran as fast as he could—which wasn't very fast—towards his house.

Danny ran behind him and when Cyndy Louise was about ten feet away, he stopped and fired his water gun. That kid had some aim! He hit her right in the middle of her face—on what was left of her nose. She stood still, rubbing the water as if it was poison.

By the time she started moving again, Mr. Douglas had reached his front door and Danny was safely inside our house.

CHAPTER 12 – Block Party

It's weird how you change the way you think about things. Before the bubbles, I loved to go outside on sunny days. I hated when it rained because then I was stuck in the house or if I went out, I had to wear a raincoat or use an umbrella and of course my hair didn't look good.

Now it was just the opposite. It sucked when the sun was shining because that meant we were trapped inside. But when it rained, we could leave the house—not that we could go far—but at least we could see our neighbors. And I stopped caring about my hair because none of my friends were around to see how bad it looked.

Three days after the fire hydrant incident, we were near the end of our school morning when raindrops began pounding the roof. Danny and I grinned at each other and Mom checked the bedroom clock.

"I hear the rain too," she said, smiling at us. "Let's stop a little early today, have a quick lunch, and go..."

Before she finished talking, my brother and I darted down the stairs, ready to eat.

"Wash your hands first!" my mother shouted.

———

By the time we went out, nearly everyone was on the street. Mr. and Mrs. Douglas were in front of Mr. Ortega's house, having a conversation with him and Mrs. Perez. Further down the block, Connie Chou and Rhonda Weiss had positioned their covered strollers foot to foot so the two little kids could look at each other while the moms stood nearby, holding umbrellas and talking.

As we walked towards our neighbors, Bobby Mitchell raced to meet us. "Hi, Danny," he said, grinning at my brother. "Wanna come over my house?"

"Can I, Mom?" Danny asked.

My mother nodded her head. "Just for a little while. But if the rain lets up..."

"I know," my brother interrupted. "Then I'll come right back home."

I watched as Danny and Bobby dashed happily to the Mitchell's house at the other end of the block. There was no one my age here—girls or boys. *Boys*...I'd never had a real boyfriend and now I never would.

Mom must have sensed how I felt because she put her arm around my shoulder. "You miss your friends," she said.

"I don't even know who's alive," I whispered. "That first toucher lady in my geometry class could've gone into every room in the school." I shrugged. "Nobody knew to be scared of her."

Mom squeezed my shoulder and gave me a quick hug. "Oh, Erin honey, I wish I could tell you everything will be okay. But I hope the worst of this is over and we'll soon find a way to get rid of them." She smiled. "We already know they don't like water. That's a start."

Leave it to my mother to find something positive. I tried to return her smile, but it's hard to fake being happy when you feel lousy. Seeing my neighbors talking and laughing together didn't make me feel good. It made me feel lonely.

———

We joined the Douglasses and Mr. Ortega, who had gone across the street to examine the fire hydrant. They must have turned off the water all the way because the hose, although still attached to the hydrant, was no longer leaking.

Mr. Douglas greeted us and pointed to the hydrant. "Ramón, Lynne, and I were just trying to decide if we should unhook the hose or leave it on."

"Why take it off?" Mom asked. "If we leave it on, we can squirt her with it again."

"But what if she damages the hose so we can't use it?" Mr. Ortega said.

"There's lots more hoses, right?" I asked. I figured every house had at least one.

"True," Mr. Douglas agreed. "But this one is nearly a hundred feet long. We'd have to combine three or four to get this length."

"I say leave it on," Mrs. Douglas said. "Erin's right. If Cyndy Louise destroys it, we have others. But we need to find a better way to attack her with it." She nodded towards Mr. Ortega. "She almost killed Ramón."

Shaking his head, Mr. Ortega waved at the Reade's property. "She ran around the back so fast, I couldn't believe it," he said. "That's not normal speed."

Duh! "Cyndy Louise's not normal," I whispered, stating the obvious.

"She doesn't need her mouth or nose because whatever she's turning into doesn't eat or breathe," Mrs. Douglas said, ignoring my comment. "But she seems to need everything else—and her legs must be changing so that she can run much faster."

"I haven't seen anything different," Mom said.

"That's probably because she's still wearing jeans," Mr. Douglas pointed out. "They're torn, but not enough that we can see her skin or muscles underneath. When the clothes fall off, we may see changes."

Yucch! The thought of a naked Cyndy Louise thing was gross.

"So we'll leave the hose..." My mother didn't finish her sentence because she noticed what we'd all just realized. The rain had stopped.

———

"Run home, everybody!" Mr. Douglas shouted. He grabbed his wife's hand and the two of them raced towards their house.

I reached for Mom's hand, but she was staring down the block. "Danny..." she murmured.

"We can't get him now," I said, pulling her forward. "He'll be safe with Bobby." I hoped I was right. *Did Danny have his water gun?* I wasn't sure. As we ran, I turned and took a quick look and didn't see the boys outside.

"She's back!" another woman yelled.

I heard a crashing noise in the street and then someone shouted, "Leave it! Just run!" Doors slammed around us as Mom and I made it inside our house and quickly locked the door.

After catching my breath, I climbed the steps and ran to my window. Cyndy Louise was heading our way. She must have come from the dead-end part of the street, maybe through the woods.

Danny... That's where Bobby's house was. I prayed silently that the two boys had been inside when the rain stopped. *But what if that's where Cyndy Louise had been staying?*

"You look very pale, Erin. Are you all right?"

"I'm fine." I turned and smiled at my mother.

She walked to the window and peeked outside. "Did you see something that scared you?" she asked, grabbing my hands and looking into my eyes. "Danny?"

I shook my head. "No," I said truthfully. "I didn't see anything."

———

The crashing sound I'd heard must have come from a falling stroller because one lay upside-down in the middle of the block, half on the sidewalk and half in the street. Thankfully, it was empty. I guess Cyndy Louise didn't want the stroller there because she picked it up with one hand and heaved it into her own front yard. It landed a few feet from the house.

"How'd she get so strong?" my mother whispered.

"Maybe that's something else about her that's changing," I replied. Neither of us said another word on that subject, but we both knew the change wasn't good.

Mom opened my window and leaned out as far as she could. "I can't see all the way down the street," she said.

To the Mitchell's house she meant.

"I have to make sure he's okay."

"We have the afternoon telephone," I pointed out. "What time is it now?"

Mom looked at her watch. "Ten after two."

I gave her my widest smile. "I'm sure Danny's fine," I said. "He and Bobby are both real fast runners—and they could've even been inside the house." *Without Cyndy Louise,* I hoped.

———

Danny and Bobby were okay. The message came from Mrs. Perez who heard it from Mr. Ortega, who relayed it from Connie Chou, who got it from Mrs. Weiss, who spoke to

Bobby's mother.

Everyone else on the street was all right too, although Mrs. Weiss' stroller didn't make it. She'd been holding her little boy when the rain stopped and tried to run home while pushing the stroller at the same time. *If she hadn't left it in the street...*I shook my head, not wanting to think about what could've happened to the two of them.

We also found out that nobody else but Bobby had water guns—and Bobby had only one. Since we couldn't exactly go shopping for them, we'd have to be real careful not to get trapped outside if it suddenly stopped raining.

I spent the rest of the afternoon upstairs in my room, feeling very sorry for myself and very lonely. I hadn't been spending a lot of time with Danny, except for school. But even when I'd been in my room by myself, I knew he was next door. Now he wasn't. He was with Bobby Mitchell at the end of Walnut Lane. It was just six houses away, but it felt like a thousand miles. Looking out my window, I hoped for rain.

CHAPTER 13 – Food Hunt

Since it was just me and Mom in the house, I thought we'd forget school till Danny came back home. But that's not what happened.

"Of course we're having classes tomorrow morning," Mom said, giving me a puzzled look when I suggested a break. "Why wouldn't we?"

"Because Danny's not here?"

"But you're here."

"It's not fair," I argued. "Why do I have to go to school when Danny doesn't?"

My mother shook her head. "You're wrong about that. I gave Jennifer Mitchell seventh grade lessons for Bobby when we were outside last week and she was very grateful. She told me she'd start classes for him immediately." Mom smiled at me. "Now Bobby's got a classmate, at least until the next rainstorm."

I marched out of her bedroom and into my room, slamming the door.

―――

I was bored and unhappy. After lunch, Mom challenged me to a game of Texas Hold 'Em poker, but I turned her down. Even Muffles noticed my bad mood. He followed me around, nuzzling and licking my arms like a concerned parent until I barricaded myself in my room.

I stayed there all afternoon, drawing in my sketchpad and watching Cyndy Louise patrol the block. She usually just walked from one end to the other, but a couple of times she got creative. Once I heard a strange thumping noise and when I looked outside, she'd yanked the hose out of the hydrant and was stomping on it.

After nothing happened, she ran into her backyard and came back with a long stick, which she used to beat and stab the hose. When she finished, about ten raggedy pieces of hose were lying all over the sidewalk and then she tossed the branch into the side of her yard like it was a little twig.

Danny and my dad were big Red Sox fans. If they'd seen Cyndy Louise's throw, I'm sure they would've wanted her to pitch for their team. But Danny was in the Mitchell's house, my dad was dead, and there was no more baseball.

———

Four days later, at about eleven o'clock in the morning, it finally rained. When I heard those wonderful pattering sounds on the roof over Mom's bedroom, I rushed to the window and opened it.

"Can we end school a little early and go out?" I asked with my head still outside the window as drops of water pelted my hair and face.

"All right, Erin."

Shutting the window, I turned towards my mother. "Really?" I hadn't expected her to agree. Maybe she felt sorry for me; I'd been pretty miserable and made sure she knew it.

Mom closed her lesson book and bounced off the bed. "We deserve a little break," she said, smiling at me. "We'll wait a few minutes to make sure the rain is for real and Cyndy Louise is gone and then head outside." She smiled again, this time much wider. "I want to see Danny too."

———

After a quick lunch of cheese spread on crackers, Mom and I put on our raincoats, grabbed umbrellas, and I shoved a loaded water pistol in my pocket. It was raining steadily, but I remembered what happened last time.

No one was outside yet as we hurried down the block, staying on our sidewalk since the messed up water hose was all over the road and the opposite sidewalk. We passed Connie Chou's house just as she opened her door, with Emily in the stroller. "Hey!" I called, waving to both of them.

"Rin," Emily said. That was how she pronounced my name.

I ran to their front door and gave the little girl a quick hug. "Hi, Emmy. How are you?"

"Rin!" she repeated, louder and with a big smile. "Rin! Rin! Rin!"

"She really misses you, Erin," Connie said as we hugged each other. "I do too."

I turned to my mother who had just reached us. "Can I stay here with them for a little while?"

"I think we can work something out," Mom said, nodding her head. "Maybe even later today if it's still raining. But right now, I want you to come with me to get Danny."

I don't know if my mother figured it was safer for both of us to be together or if she was just too scared to walk down Walnut Lane by herself. Either way, she had agreed I could see the Chous so I didn't argue. After waving bye-bye to Emily, we continued along the block past the two empty houses— including Andrew O'Malley's—and crossed the street to the Mitchell's home.

———

Mom knocked and Mrs. Mitchell looked through the peephole and then let us in. "We were coming outside too," she said.

The two of us stood in the hallway, rain dripping from our umbrellas. "How's Danny?" my mother asked, skipping the small talk.

"The boys are fine," Mrs. Mitchell said. "It's good for them to be together." Turning around, she called, "Danny, come down! Your mom and sister are here!"

"Okay!" my brother replied.

"I hope he wasn't any trouble," Mom continued.

"Not at all and I've been using the lesson plans you gave me." She chuckled. "Danny complained that he'd done some of the work before, but we managed."

"Great," my mother said. "Next time, Bobby can stay with us for..."

"Hi, Mom," Danny said, jumping from the bottom step into the hallway with Bobby right behind him. Both of them looked real happy.

My mother hugged Danny like she hadn't seen him for weeks, not just a few days. "We missed you so much," she said, kissing his cheek.

My brother pulled away from her grasp. "Please stop," he whispered, his face turning red.

Mom didn't say anything, but she kept holding his hand and looking at him. I was getting uncomfortable too so I decided to end our little visit. "Goodbye," I waved. "Thanks for everything."

Danny quickly put on his raincoat and together we managed to guide our mother out the door.

———

"Why'd you do that?" Danny asked as the three of us crossed the street and walked to the middle of the block where a bunch of our neighbors had gathered.

"I'm sorry if I embarrassed you," Mom said. "I guess I was more frightened than I realized."

"Yeah, okay."

My brother didn't say anything else. I think he just wanted to drop the subject.

All the other people from our block, except the Santangelos, stood in a circle in front of Connie's house: Rhonda Weiss, Mr. and Mrs. Douglas, Mrs. Perez, and Mr. Ortega. The two little kids were both in strollers so Mrs. Weiss must have found an extra one, although this stroller had a makeshift plastic-bag covering to protect her son's head.

"Come and join us," Mr. Douglas said. He and his wife moved closer together so we could fit in. "We were just talking about food."

"Oh?" my mother questioned.

"We're running out of supplies," Mrs. Weiss explained.

"Well, I wouldn't recommend going to the supermarket," Mom said. "We almost got killed there."

"I heard what happened from Norma," Mrs. Weiss said, motioning to Mrs. Perez. "But soon Jake and I won't have enough to eat. We also need flashlights and toilet paper."

"We can give you a couple of rolls and a flashlight," Mom said.

"Thanks." Mrs. Weiss smiled at my mother.

"On the food problem, what about checking all the empty houses here?" Mr. Ortega suggested. "We've got..." He used his fingers to point and count. "There're six of them with no one inside."

"That's not really true," I whispered. "Someone's probably dead inside Mr. Muldare's house—and there could be more dead people in those other houses too."

"And what about Cyndy Louise?" Danny asked. "She's gotta be staying someplace inside when it rains, like those other touchers in the store."

Connie Chou shook her head. "It doesn't sound like fun, but we've got to get food. I only have about another week's worth myself and checking the pantries in the vacant houses here seems like a better idea than going to the supermarket."

"Maybe we should set up a hose again," Mr. Douglas suggested.

"For outside," Mr. Ortega said. "It's much too clumsy for indoors."

"Use the water guns," Danny said, twirling his pistol. "Or just take some water balloons or bottles filled with water to throw at them."

"When do you want to do this?" Mrs. Douglas asked.

"Right now," Rhonda Weiss said. "I need food—and what if it doesn't rain for another week?"

"You shouldn't go," Mr. Douglas said, pointing to the little boy in the stroller. "You've got Jake to take care of and the same goes for Connie." He looked at the rest of us. "Any volunteers to search the empty houses?"

Danny and I looked at each other and both raised our hands.

"No," my mother whispered, shaking her head.

"Mom, I'm a pitcher and my reflexes are great," Danny argued. "I got away from the touchers twice already—and I run real fast."

"Me too," I said. Although I wasn't a pitcher like my brother, I was a good runner.

"I'm going too," Mr. Ortega said. "I'll fill a plant sprayer and carry a couple bottles of water."

"We've got to do this," I said, looking at my mother and

then at Danny, who nodded. "You know we've got the best chance to find the food and get out okay."

"She's right," Mr. Douglas agreed. "They're both young and agile. Let them do it, Maura."

"I'll be with them and if we hear or see anything, I'll make sure we leave immediately," Mr. Ortega said before turning to Danny and me. "I'll get some big garbage bags, a flashlight, and the water and meet you back here in five minutes."

———

While we waited for Mr. Ortega, Connie went home and returned with a key, which she handed to me. "This'll get you into the Fisher's house," she explained, pointing to the home next to hers.

When Mr. Ortega came back, I gave him the key and he put it in his pocket. "I still want to search the empty houses in order," he told us.

That meant starting with the Kaplan's, the second house on the block across the street, next to the Douglass'. Mr. and Mrs. Kaplan both worked in the city so I didn't really know either of them. When the bubbles fell, I figured—like my dad—they'd never made it home. But we weren't sure.

Since Cyndy Louise had already broken the living room window of the house, we climbed inside, one at a time, careful not to touch the glass, and holding our water weapons in front of us. It smelled musty, not bad like in the supermarket, just damp and unpleasant.

"Yucch," I whispered.

"Shh," Mr. Ortega said, putting his finger next to his lip and motioning towards the kitchen. Danny and I still held our water guns, just in case.

It was pretty dark in the kitchen so Mr. Ortega turned on his flashlight. I heard scurrying sounds as a bunch of bugs scattered from the countertop. Not as bad as the supermarket, but still gross.

Mr. Ortega waved his other hand at the top cabinets and carefully opened the first one. It just held dishes. The next two had more dishes and cups and glasses. Then he moved to the bottom cabinets. One had pots and pans, another had cleaning stuff, but the third was packed with snack food.

I held the flashlight as he dropped bags of popcorn, pretzels, crackers, and chips into the big garbage bag. Then he opened a large top cabinet and that had more food—cans of tuna, sardines, and vegetables, a jar of peanut butter, ketchup, mayonnaise, and a bunch of things that weren't so good because they had to be cooked, like soups and rice. But Mr. Ortega dumped them in the bag too.

I felt something touch my arm and jumped before I realized Danny had tapped me. When I looked at him, he pretended to be drinking and then pointed down. *The basement?* Check downstairs for drinks?

I shook my head. It would be totally dark and creepy—more bugs, or maybe rats—and what if Cyndy Louise was resting there? She could have crawled through the living room window just like us. "No," I mouthed.

———

We left the Kaplan house by the front door so we wouldn't have to climb through the broken window again. The garbage bag must have been heavy because Mr. Ortega dragged it behind him on the sidewalk.

"Want me to help you with that?" I asked.

"No, thanks," Mr. Ortega replied. "I'm fine."

"We didn't get any drinks," Danny said, turning and making a face at me.

Mr. Ortega didn't see the nasty look. "That's not important," he said. "The water's still working so there's plenty to drink."

"I bet they had lots of soda in that house," my brother grumbled.

"You heard Mr. Ortega," I said. "Soda's not important." I stuck my tongue out at him.

When we reached Connie's house, Mom and Mrs. Perez were still standing outside, talking to Connie and Rhonda Weiss.

"We got food!" Danny announced, sounding like the leader of our little search party.

"Thank you so much!" Rhonda Weiss exclaimed. She grabbed Danny by the shoulders and gave him a big hug.

My brother moved away quickly, his face reddening.

"Here," Mr. Ortega said, dropping the heavy bag in front of Mrs. Weiss. "This first batch is all yours." Then he spoke to Connie. "We're going into the Muldare's house next and we'll find food for you."

I wasn't looking forward to that visit at all. I still remembered the woman's screams.

————

The Muldare's front door was unlocked so the three of us were able to walk right in. The house didn't smell musty, but it didn't smell good. I wondered which room the woman who screamed had been in because I figured that's where the bad smell was coming from.

Holding the water gun in front of me, I tried to concentrate on protecting us from Cyndy Louise. Although it was quiet, she could have been somewhere in the house. The front door had been open and she'd already been inside after killing Mr. Muldare.

When we entered the kitchen, I realized I'd been wrong about the source of the bad smell. There was gross food on the counter—a half-eaten apple and some other rotting things that I couldn't even recognize. Flies buzzed around the food and I swatted them away, trying to close my nostrils and not think about the smell.

Mr. Ortega quietly opened each cabinet and when he found food, tossed the bags, boxes, and cans into his garbage bag. This house had a lot of cheese stuff—macaroni and cheese mixes, cans of cheese spreads, and cheesy crackers. I was wondering if Connie and Emily liked cheese when I heard footsteps coming down the stairs.

"Run!" I yelled.

Danny and I rushed out the kitchen into the hallway, just as Cyndy Louise reached the bottom step of the stairs. Danny turned and squirted her, hitting what was left of her face. I squeezed my water pistol too, but my aim wasn't so good and I just nicked her arm.

She stopped moving and rubbed the water off her face like it was painful as Danny and I raced out the front door into the rain.

"Where's Mr. Ortega?" I asked.

"He's still in there," Danny said. "I'm going back."

I grabbed my brother's arm. "You can't!"

Pushing my hand away, he ran inside.

———

I stood there for a moment—scared out of my mind—and quickly reviewed my options: I could stay in the rain and wait, I could go back inside, or I could try to get help. There wasn't time to round up the neighbors and if I did nothing, Cyndy Louise could kill Danny.

Without giving myself a chance to chicken out, I walked though the open door, holding my water pistol as I crept into the hallway. I saw Danny right away. He was a few feet in front of me, peeking into the kitchen with his gun aimed.

"Danny," I whispered.

"Shh," he said, motioning me next to him.

When I glanced inside the kitchen, I understood why my brother was so fascinated. Danny couldn't save Mr. Ortega; he was already dead, lying on the floor, face up, still clutching the garbage bag. But Cyndy Louise was there too, kneeling next to him and continuing to touch his dead body, her hand on his arm.

Something was happening that we hadn't seen before. It looked like sparks or electricity was shooting from Mr. Ortega's arm into Cyndy—like she was using his body as a battery to charge herself.

And her face had changed again. It wasn't even a face anymore—just a round ball. She didn't have any nose or mouth, not even the outlines of where they had been. But she still had eyes and ears so she could see and hear us. We'd been lucky she was so engrossed in whatever she was doing with Mr. Ortega's body.

I gave my brother's arm a tug and this time he followed me outside.

———

"What the hell was all that?" Danny whispered as we rushed down the block to my mother, who was still talking to Mrs. Perez in front of Connie's house.

"It was like she was getting some kind of power from Mr. Ortega. It reminded me of a fill-up at the gas station."

"Did you ever see her do that with any of the other dead people?"

I shook my head. "She just walked away from them before. But she's changed..."

We didn't say anything else until we reached Mom. I

surprised myself by rushing into her arms and bursting into tears.

"Erin, honey, what's wrong?" My mother held my shoulders and looked into my eyes. "Where's Mr. Ortega?"

"He's dead," Danny whispered. "Cyndy Louise got him."

"She was in there with you?" Mrs. Perez asked.

I nodded, wiping my tears. I wasn't shaping up as much of an action hero. Danny was doing a much better job.

"We...left...the...food," I stammered.

Mom kissed me and hugged me tightly. "You both could have been killed," she whispered before reaching for Danny, who moved inside her open arms.

CHAPTER 14 – The Strangers

The days after Cyndy Louise touched Mr. Ortega in the Muldare's kitchen were normal for us: school in the mornings, afternoons off, homework, and sleep. The only contact we had with our neighbors was through the street telephone.

Mr. Douglas was especially sad about Mr. Ortega. They had been good friends. "We have to come up with a better way to get inside the houses for food!" he called to us.

"Next time, I won't let Erin and Danny go!" Mom shouted back.

I didn't argue with my mother. I'd dreamt about Cyndy Louise killing Mr. Ortega and when I woke up I'd been real scared, so I wasn't planning to volunteer to raid the other empty houses on the block.

But Danny felt differently. "I'm gonna go," he told Mom after the neighborhood telephone talk.

"No! You're not!"

"Mom, they need me. Mr. Douglas is old, he can't move fast, and he's the only guy. Then there's his wife, the mothers with little kids, you and Mrs. Perez, and Bobby's mom—and I can shoot a water gun better than all of them."

"They'll have to find someone else—maybe that man we

met, the one who lives at the other end of the block with his wife and baby."

"Mr. Santangelo?" I asked. I remembered his name, but we hadn't seen him or his family in a while. "We don't even know if he's okay anymore," I whispered.

Mom didn't say anything and Danny stopped arguing.

———

It was almost a week until the next heavy rain. Mom shortened school and we ate a quick early lunch, got into our raingear, and rushed outside. Mr. and Mrs. Douglas were in front of their house, talking to Mrs. Perez.

"We're trying to decide how to get more food," Mrs. Perez said. "After last week..." She didn't finish her sentence.

"And I want to give Ramón a decent burial," Mr. Douglas whispered. "It's the least I can do for him."

"You can't go back in there after what happened," Mrs. Douglas said, grabbing her husband's arm. "Erin and Danny said she was doing something to his body—and maybe that's where she's been staying every time it rains, in the Muldare's house."

"I'll connect the Kaplan's hose, turn it on, and then take it with me next door into the Muldare's." Mr. Douglas shrugged. "I just need enough time to get inside the kitchen and drag his body out."

"You can't do all that by yourself," his wife argued. "If you insist on going in there, I'm going with you."

"Mom, please let me help them," Danny begged. "I know I can stop Cyndy Louise. I've already done it twice."

My mother shook her head emphatically. "No more rescue missions for you."

They were still arguing when we heard the now uncommon sound of a car's engine. As we watched, a banged-up blue auto turned into Walnut Lane and parked in front of our house. I could see at least two people inside.

"Run!" Mr. Douglas shouted as he grabbed his wife and rushed to his front door.

Mrs. Perez made a diagonal dash for her house.

As Mom, Danny, and I stood together on the sidewalk, I realized if we ran home, whoever was in the car would be able to reach us before we got inside. Danny took out his water pistol.

"It can't be touchers," I whispered. "They don't go out in the rain and I've never seen them drive cars."

"But it could be robbers or worse," my mother said. "Nobody comes into this street anymore."

"Maybe they'll think these are real guns," Danny said.

"What if they have real guns—and shoot us?" I replied.

Then the front doors of the car opened and Mom pushed us forward. "This way!" she ordered and we raced to the Douglas' house.

———

Mr. Douglas opened his door just before we reached the entrance and locked it immediately after the three of us stepped inside. We all looked through the openings of his living room window—pieces of a wooden chair were taped over it—to see what the people from the car were doing.

There were two of them, both men, dressed in jeans, not rags, and they weren't touchers. They had regular faces and as they headed towards the Douglas' house, I saw they weren't really men—they were teens, my age or a little older.

One of them rang the doorbell and they both stood there, smiling. "Who are you and what do you want?" Mr. Douglas asked.

"We're not gonna hurt anyone," the shorter guy said. He

had long curly brown hair, blue eyes, and a cute grin. "We just want to talk to y'all." He didn't sound like he was from any place around here.

"Yeah," the other guy said. He was very tall with shorter dark hair, not so cute, and wasn't smiling anymore. "No weapons—See?" He held out his hands to show that nothing was in them. "We've got a business proposal."

"Are you going to let them in?" my mother asked Mr. Douglas.

He turned to his wife. "Lynne," he whispered. "While I question them, get four steak knives for you and the Fredericks. Then I'll see about opening the door."

"Well...?" the taller guy said. "We're waiting."

"What kind of proposal are you offering?" Mr. Douglas asked as his wife returned and handed each of us a sharp knife. I put mine in my jeans pocket, hoping I wouldn't stab myself.

"It's not about makin' money, that's for sure," the shorter guy replied, smiling again. "No one cares about money anymore. We're talkin' about somethin' everybody wants—food."

He said the magic word!

Mr. Douglas looked at each of us. His wife, Danny, and I nodded and Mom shrugged. Then Mr. Douglas unlocked the door and opened it.

"Thanks," the cute guy said, continuing to smile at us. "We thought we could work somethin' out." He nodded towards the living room. "Mind if we sit down?"

"Go ahead," Mr. Douglas said, waving them inside.

The two of them sat on the couch and the Douglasses settled into the cushiony chairs opposite. As Mom, Danny, and I leaned against the wall, I tried to hide behind Danny. My hair looked gross from not being washed and standing in the rain. I hadn't figured on visitors.

"I'm Blaine Erstad and this is Zach Williams," the cute guy said, nodding towards his friend. "We used to go to UMass, but now we're kind of..."

When he paused, Zach finished the sentence. "...wanderers, doing jobs for food along the way."

"Yeah," Blaine said. "We're tryin' to make it back home."

"Where are you from?" Mom asked.

"Delaware," Zach said.

"Atlanta for me," Blaine said.

"That's a long way," Mr. Douglas whispered.

Blaine nodded. "And we can only drive when it rains so we have to find different places to stay."

"What do you know about those bubble people?" Mr. Douglas asked. "We call them touchers."

"That's a good name," Blaine said, glancing at his friend. "We just call them 'things.'"

"How many of them have you seen?" Mr. Douglas continued.

Blaine didn't answer right away. "Hundreds," he finally said.

"Do they travel in groups or alone?"

Blaine looked at Zach, who shrugged. "We've seen both kinds," he said.

"Are they everywhere you've been?" Mr. Douglas asked.

"Yeah," Blaine said. "Men, ladies, kids—at least that's what they used to be before the bubbles. I don't know what they are now."

Curiosity forced me to speak. "The toucher here—a girl—killed a man on our block last week," I said, still scrunched behind Danny. "And then after he was dead, she did something with his arm, like she was using him as a battery for power. Did you see anything like that?"

Blaine thought for a moment. Then he shook his head and

turned to his friend.

"No," Zach agreed. "But we haven't seen many of them real close. That's why we're still alive."

No one said anything for about a minute until Mrs. Douglas spoke. "You mentioned a business proposal that involves getting food," she said. "What's your plan?"

Blaine smiled that cute grin again. "You got houses here that are empty, right?" he asked in his soft drawl.

We all nodded.

"Me and Zach'll go inside all the empty houses and take out the food," Blaine said. "In return, we get to stay in one of the homes and eat as much food as we need. Then we'll leave at the next heavy rain."

Mr. Douglas looked at his wife and then at my mother. "What do you think?" he asked.

"Do it," Mom said. "These boys need a place to stay and we can't just throw them out—and we don't have an alternate plan for getting food."

Mrs. Douglas nodded.

"All right," her husband said. "It's a deal—but with one condition." Quickly, he told Blaine and Zach what he needed them to do.

———

With help from her husband and Mom, Mrs. Douglas drew a rough map of Walnut Lane, labeling who lived in all the houses and circling the empty ones. "Here," she said, handing it to Blaine.

Then Mr. Douglas gave Blaine and Zach a rundown of Cyndy Louise's movements and what we'd done so far. "...and during the last rain, we got food from the Kaplan's house and collected food in the Muldare's kitchen, but Cyndy Louise was somewhere upstairs in that house." He turned to Danny and me. "When you left, Ramón's body was in the kitchen with the bag of food. Right?"

My brother and I nodded.

"Like we promised, we'll get the dead guy and that food out for you first," Zach said.

"But be careful," Mom warned. "That's where she was staying—in the Muldare's—so maybe she goes there every time it rains."

Blaine smiled at her. "Thanks for the concern. You remind me of my mother." Then his smile disappeared and he didn't say anything else.

"I think we're good," Zach said, moving towards the door.

"Do you have water guns?" Danny asked.

"Yeah." Zach smiled at my brother. "We've been collecting them."

Mr. Douglas put his hand on Mom's shoulder. "Maura, we should go back outside and tell Norma and everyone that these boys will be staying on our street, going in and out of houses collecting food. Otherwise they'll be very frightened when they see them."

"You're right. Erin and Danny will go with me too."

So as Blaine and Zach got started, the Douglasses and us knocked on our neighbors' doors and told them what was going on. It was kind of like Paul Revere, but instead of, "The British are coming!" our message was, "The two guys are coming!"

I actually felt pretty good that afternoon—until we knocked on the Santangelo's door.

CHAPTER 15 – The Santangelos

We divided the street into two sides. Mom, Danny, and I told Mrs. Perez and Connie about Blaine and Zach and what they'd be doing and the Douglasses told the neighbors on their side— Mrs. Weiss and the Mitchells. Our last stop was the Santangelo's house at the end of the street. We knocked on the front door and waited. When no one answered, we knocked again—harder. Again nothing happened.

Danny tried twisting the knob, but the door was locked.

"They could all be sleeping," Mom suggested.

"Maybe the baby and the mother, but not the father too," I said.

"You think Cyndy Louise got them?" Danny asked.

"I don't know," I said, remembering we hadn't seen the Santangelo family outside the last couple of times it rained. "Danny, you can scream real loud so yell something."

"Hey!" my brother shouted. "We're your neighbors from down the block! Open the door so we can tell you about food!"

"Good job," I said. His message would have gotten my attention. But nothing happened.

We peeked into the garage and two cars were parked there.

"What do we do now?" I asked Mom.

"We go home and tell the Douglasses about this."

"Should we check the windows in the back first?" Danny asked. "Maybe we can see something inside."

Like our house, the front windows were covered with pieces of wood and all the curtains were closed. The rear windows faced the woods.

"We're not walking to the back," Mom said. "Cyndy Louise or the others could be hiding somewhere in the trees and bushes."

That didn't make much sense to me since the touchers didn't stay outside in the rain. But I didn't argue because I didn't want to go behind the house either.

———

The Douglasses and Blaine and Zach were standing in a circle on the sidewalk in front of Mr. Muldare's house. When we reached them, I saw two things: Blaine was holding a partly filled black garbage bag and a man's legs were lying on the ground.

I took a step backwards. My hair still looked gross and I didn't want to get close to Mr. Ortega's body. But I was curious about what Cyndy Louise had done to him so, after taking a deep breath, I moved next to the others.

"...and we should bury him before we do anything else," Mr. Douglas was saying.

"Shouldn't we at least wait for the rest of the neighbors?" Mom asked.

Mr. Douglas held out his hand, palm up. "I'm afraid the rain might be stopping so we should do it now." He shook his head. "I don't want to take the chance of leaving him out here until the next rain."

While Mom briefed everyone on the missing Santangelos, I glanced at Mr. Ortega. He looked pale, but otherwise sort of peaceful. He wasn't chewed up like that woman in the supermarket. Cyndy Louise had done something to him, but whatever it was didn't show.

Then I remembered the key. "Mr. Ortega's got the key to the Fisher's house," I mumbled.

Blaine rummaged through the dead man's pockets until he found the key.

"Is it safe to touch him?" I blurted out.

"Yeah," Blaine said, smiling at me. "See? I'm still alive."

I lowered my face, which felt warm.

Mr. Douglas lifted the garbage bag. "Blaine and Zach also retrieved this—and collected the rest of the Muldare's food," he said. "After the boys take their share, we'll deliver the remainder to Connie." He faced the guys. "Thank you."

"No problem," Blaine said. "The girl toucher-thing wasn't in the house."

"But she could've been," Mrs. Douglas said. "You risked your lives getting this."

Zach shrugged and Blaine stared at the ground.

"The boys have offered to dig the grave for us too," Mr. Douglas said. "I appreciate it since I seem to be the only remaining man on the block. After the funeral, we'll figure out what to do about the Santangelos."

———

While Blaine and Zach dug up the wet grass in Mr. Ortega's front yard, Mom, Danny, and I went back to the houses of the neighbors we had visited—minus the Santangelos—and to the Mitchells and Rhonda Weiss and told them about the funeral.

When we returned to Mr. Ortega's yard, his body had been wrapped in a gray blanket and was lying next to the hole Blaine and Zach had dug. After about five minutes, everyone showed up except Mrs. Weiss, who'd told us her little boy was napping.

Mr. Douglas said a few words about what a good man Ramón Ortega had been—a wonderful friend and neighbor—and how much he would miss him. I felt bad I hadn't known him better and now would never have that chance. Then Blaine and Zach lowered the body into the hole, covered it with the loose wet soil, and patted it down.

Just as the short ceremony ended, Mrs. Weiss arrived with her son in the stroller with the plastic-bag cover on top. When she joined us, Mr. Douglas spoke again. "We have a new problem," he began and told everyone about the missing Santangelos. "Has anyone seen them lately?"

"No," Bobby's mother said. "I didn't see them outside the last time it rained. But since I've never had much to do with the family, I thought they weren't interested in getting together with us. Now I'm sorry I never checked."

"Maybe they went somewhere," Connie suggested.

"Without a car?" I asked. The block was so quiet now that someone would have heard an engine—and we'd seen two cars in their garage.

Connie shrugged.

"Could they've walked through the woods?" Mrs. Perez asked. "To the homes on the other side?"

"Why would they have taken a chance doing that—and with a little baby?" Mrs. Douglas said.

Bobby Mitchell shook his head and made a face. "You guys all know what happened to them, but you don't wanna say it."

"Bobby..." his mother said, grabbing her son's arm.

He wrenched free of her grasp. "Cyndy Louise!" he shouted. "She got into their house. That's why nobody's seen 'em, 'cause they're all dead!"

———

None of us said anything for what seemed like a very long time. Blaine and Zach had been standing outside our little circle during the funeral, but now Blaine took a step forward. "We'll go into that house and check it out for y'all," he said in his cute drawl.

"No." Mr. Douglas shook his head, rain bouncing off his shiny yellow hat. "That's not something you boys have to do."

"We're goin' into all the empty houses," Blaine continued. "And now this one's empty." He turned to Zach. "You okay with this?"

"Sure." Zach sounded excited—like he really wanted to check the house.

"I wanna go in there too," Danny said, turning to Mom. "I'm the best shot."

She shook her head.

"I'll go with Danny," Bobby said. "I've got a water gun too."

Mrs. Mitchell grabbed Bobby's arm and held him tightly.

"Nobody should go into that house," Mr. Douglas said. "Zach and Blaine have already agreed to check the other vacant homes for food so there's no need for anyone to enter the Santangelo's house. Let's drop that idea for now."

"What if they're hurt and need our help?" Connie asked.

"Do you really think that's the case?" Mrs. Douglas said softy.

"Probably not."

"Did any of you hear a baby crying inside—or any other sounds?" Mr. Douglas asked us.

"No," I whispered. Mom and Danny shook their heads.

Since it was still raining and everyone was already outside, people separated into small groups. I saw Mom talking to Mrs. Perez and Bobby's mother. I thought about going over to Blaine and Zach. But my hair was such a mess—and what was I going to say? I'd already said something dumb. While I was composing my great opening line, Danny and Bobby ran up to the guys and the four of them walked quickly towards the other end of the street.

So much for that idea. If I ran over to them now, I'd look like a real jerk. Changing direction, I joined Connie and Emily in front of their house. As I knelt to talk to Emmy, Mrs. Weiss walked up to us with her little boy, Jake, parking his stroller next to me. Jake was a little older than Emily, about two-and-a-half, and he talked much better.

"I want Bethie," he said as his mother turned to say something to Connie. "Where Bethie?"

She must have been his older sister, the little girl who went to James Madison, our elementary school. I remembered she was about seven, with dark brown hair and a big smile.

"What do you like to play?" I asked, changing the subject.

"Where Daddy?" he said.

I didn't want to ask Mrs. Weiss about Jake's questions so I backed away from him and thought about my own dad, who I knew I'd never see again. Then I walked home feeling worse than I'd felt in a long time.

CHAPTER 16 - Missing

I lay on my bed, suffering from a severe case of self-pity. Finally there was someone close to my age on the block—Blaine was cute and seemed like a nice guy—but he'd probably be gone before I even had a chance to talk to him.

Picking up the pillow, I hit my face with it. *Dumb! Dumb! Dumb!*

I heard a knock on my door. "Go away!" I yelled.

"It's important," Danny said.

"Leave me alone!"

"Really, Erin. I've gotta talk to you."

I tossed the pillow aside and walked to the door, wondering what could be so damn important.

Danny came into my room with Muffles trailing. The dog nuzzled my leg and I patted his soft head. "So?" I asked.

"They're not in the house."

"Who?"

"The Santangelos—they're not in their house."

"How do you know that?"

"Me and Bobby walked over there with those two guys, Blaine and Zach, and Zach tried the back door and it was open. Then Bobby gave Zach his water gun and him and Blaine went in the house and Bobby and me stood right outside 'cause I still had my gun." He shook his head. "But nobody was in there, Erin. Those people just disappeared."

I studied his face. "Mom told you not to go into that house."

"I didn't go inside."

"You're playing with words," I said. "You know what Mom meant. What if that's where Cyndy Louise was hiding?"

"But she wasn't...Erin, where'd that family go?"

I shook my head. "I don't know."

———

After Danny and Muffles left, I returned to my bed, trying to figure out what could have happened. Cyndy Louise was very powerful—she killed people she touched and she'd done something to Mr. Ortega's body after he was already dead. But she hadn't made anyone vanish.

So why did the Santangelos leave their house and where did they go?

I played the question over and over in my head until a new thought hit me. Jumping out of bed, I checked my window and saw it was still raining pretty hard so I raced out of my room and banged on Danny's door.

"Did they check the basement?" I asked when he opened the door.

"I dunno. I didn't go inside the house with them, remember?"

"What if that's where they're hiding or that's where Cyndy Louise...?" I didn't want to finish the question.

"But you just told me we're not allowed in there." He stuck his tongue out at me.

I sat on Danny's bed, next to Muffles who lapped my arm. "What if we get Blaine and Zach to go back inside?"

"I guess that'd be okay," my brother said, smiling.

———

It was still raining hard when Danny and I went out again.

"Where are you two going?" Mom called. She was sitting on a lawn chair with Mrs. Perez on our next-door neighbor's front porch.

I gave my brother a quick look. "To Bobby's house," I said.

"Don't go inside." Mom stood quickly and headed towards us. "I don't want you to get stuck there like last time so I'm going with you."

"No need." I held out my arm to stop her. "We've both got water guns and we'll stay outside. I promise." Then I nudged Danny and we ran down the middle of the street. When we reached the end of the block, I was relieved Mom hadn't followed us.

"Where...are...Blaine...and...Zach?" I panted.

"They're going through the empty houses in order, remember?" Danny didn't sound at all out of breath. "They'd have gone into Mr. Ortega's, but he couldn't have much food, so by now they'd probably be in the Fisher's or the O'Malley's."

"Can you call them?" I'd promised Mom we wouldn't go inside and I didn't want to lie to her.

"Sure." He stood between the two houses. "Blaine! Zach! Could you guys come out here?"

We heard footsteps and the front door of the O'Malley's house opened. Zach held a pretty full garbage bag and Blaine stood next to him, a flashlight in his hand. "What's goin' on?" Blaine asked.

Danny and I dashed to Andrew's house and met the guys on the porch. I had put my hair in a ponytail and added some lip-gloss so I'd look a little better. "Did you ever check the basement?" I asked, nodding towards the Santangelo's house.

"No," Blaine said. "You think those missin' people could be down there?"

I looked into his big blue eyes and nodded.

"What about that toucher girl?" Blaine asked. "Couldn't she be hidin' in the basement?"

Danny shrugged and no one said anything.

"I'm checking it out," Zach said, dropping his bag and walking quickly towards the Santangelo's. After a few steps, he stopped and turned, staring at Blaine, who still stood on the O'Malley's porch. "Are you coming?"

"Sure," Blaine said, winking at me. Then with his water gun aimed in front of him, he followed his friend.

———

Danny and I stood outside the Santangelo's house, waiting for Blaine and Zach to return.

"They've been gone a while," I said. I wasn't wearing a watch so I didn't know exactly how long it had been.

Danny checked his watch. "It's only been five minutes, Erin. It would take them that long just to go up and down the stairs—and they gotta be real slow and careful, make sure Cyndy Louise's not there."

"I guess." I looked at the boarded windows in the front of the house. "Too bad we can't see what's going on inside."

"Yeah."

We were quiet again. I was sorry I'd promised Mom we wouldn't go in there. But I had already kind of lied about what we were doing and I didn't want to make things worse. And what if Danny and I went inside and Cyndy Louise was there and she touched us and...

The Santangelo's front door swung open, jolting me out of my scary thoughts, and Blaine rushed over to us, smiling. "You were right," he said to me, his blue eyes twinkling. "That whole family was downstairs, hidin'. Zach's leadin' them back up now."

———

After that, I didn't think about my promise to Mom. Danny and I followed Blaine into the Santangelo's house and we stood in the kitchen, waiting for the others.

"Are they okay?" I asked Blaine.

"I think so," he said, shrugging his shoulders. "I didn't really ask them anythin'. Just ran right up to tell you."

We heard footsteps and Zach entered the room. Mr. Santangelo, carrying the sleeping baby, came next, and then his wife. They all looked kind of pale and Mrs. Santangelo must have been crying because her eyes were wet and puffy.

"I never thought we'd ever get back upstairs," she whispered as she sunk into one of her kitchen chairs.

"I told you it'd be all right, Nikki," Mr. Santangelo said, smiling at Zach and Blaine, who leaned against the sink and the surrounding cabinets. "You boys was real brave to come downstairs to look for us."

"Don't thank us," Blaine said, nodding in my direction. "It was her idea."

"Thank you," Mr. Santangelo said to me.

"How long have you been in the basement?" I asked, speaking very softly.

Mrs. Santangelo stared at me. "Nearly two weeks, I think." She sighed. "It felt like forever."

"It wasn't so bad, Nik," her husband said. "We had food and a bathroom—even the old couch to sleep on."

"But that monster was upstairs. And then when that thing banged on the door and you leaned against it, I thought it would break through and come downstairs to get us." Mrs. Santangelo started crying again. "I was so scared."

Her husband put his arms around her. "But the monster thing didn't get in. I got the basement door bolted and it couldn't touch us."

"Was it Cyndy Louise?" I asked. "The girl from our block?"

"I don't know which of them it was," Mr. Santangelo said. "We didn't see it and all we heard was grunts. Didn't say no words."

"Whatever it was, it wasn't human," his wife added.

"But now it's all over, Nikki." Mr. Santangelo squeezed his wife's shoulders. "And we're back upstairs in our house again."

Mrs. Santangelo looked at Zach, Blaine, Danny, and me. "It's raining now, right?" she asked.

We all nodded.

"But when the rain stops, they come out again, don't they?"

We nodded again.

Mrs. Santangelo glanced up at her husband and shook her head. "Then it's not over, Frank. It's not over at all."

———

No one said anything because we knew Mrs. Santangelo was right. It wasn't over. Cyndy Louise and the others like her were still out there, changing into whatever they were becoming, killing those of us they could find and touch along the way. And although they didn't like getting wet and water slowed them, it didn't hurt or stop them.

We stayed in the Santangelo's house for a few more minutes listening to the rest of the story of how they had ended up trapped in their basement.

"That thing which used to be a human," Mr. Santangelo began. "It came in through the back door, made lots of noise, but didn't break no glass, so maybe the door wasn't locked." He looked at his wife.

"The lock was broken," Blaine said. "The toucher must've busted it."

"I told you I didn't leave the sliding-glass door open," Mrs. Santangelo said, turning to her husband. "That morning we were all sitting in the kitchen, eating breakfast, and it got real loud..."

"...so I grabbed the baby and we ran downstairs to the basement," Mr. Santangelo continued. "We made it just in time." He patted his sleeping son's soft brown hair. "And we was real lucky. What if Frankie'd been upstairs in his crib?"

"Don't even talk about that." His wife shook her head and her eyes started tearing again.

After a moment, Zach spoke. "You people shouldn't stay in this house anymore," he said. "You've got the woods behind you, those toucher-things are always looking for places to stay inside when it rains, and they've already been in here. And now your back lock is broken..."

"Where'll we go?" Mrs. Santangelo asked.

I shrugged. "There's lots of empty houses on the street."

"How about Mr. Ortega's?" Danny suggested. "It's boarded up good and we know Cyndy Louise hasn't gotten in."

"What happened to Ramón?" Mr. Santangelo asked.

"Cyndy Louise touched him," I whispered.

It was quiet again until Blaine spoke. "Let's do this," he said. "We'll help you move there right now. Me and Zach have been goin' through all the empty houses, pullin' out all the food we can find and sharin' it with the people on the block, but we'll stop doin' that and get your family into that house safely."

———

Mom wasn't happy when I told her about finding the Santangelos. "You lied to me, Erin."

"Not really."

"Yes, really. You said you were going to see Bobby, but you never had any intention of going there."

I squirmed and tried to think of a good comeback. When I couldn't think of anything smart to say, I lowered my head and studied my feet.

"I trusted you," Mom continued. "Then you made it worse by going inside that house. What if Cyndy Louise or one of those other touchers had still been in there?"

"But she wasn't," I whispered. "And we didn't go inside until Blaine and Zach said it was clear. We freed the whole family."

"That part is wonderful—but it could have been done without you and Danny going inside the house—and without all the lies."

"I'm sorry," I whispered.

"Everything now is very dangerous," Mom said, her eyes filling with tears. "I've got to at least know that you're both being honest." She looked at me and then at Danny. "Our lives depend on this—and I can't lose you. Do you understand?"

We both nodded.

CHAPTER 17 – The Changes

Mom, Danny, and I settled back into our boring routine. But at least we had our twice-a-day telephone so we could communicate with our neighbors and talk directly to the Douglasses and Mrs. Perez.

I knew Blaine and Zach were down the block, staying in the Fisher's house. But I couldn't talk to Blaine or even hear his drawly voice on the street telephone. A couple of times, Mr. Douglas relayed messages from them—nothing important. Like the rest of us, they were trapped inside until the next rain.

Cyndy Louise was the only thing interesting because she'd changed much more. She was nearly bald now, except for a few tangled brown hairs. And her raggedy clothes were nearly gone: She was topless—no shirt and bra anymore—so her boobs were exposed.

I would have been embarrassed checking out a half-naked girl with my twelve-year-old brother, but Cyndy Louise's boobs didn't look like breasts because she had no nipples. In fact, she looked less like a person and more like a partly-finished dirty doll with no face except eyes and ears.

As for the rest of her body, her arms were straighter—like they didn't have any fat on them—and her lower half was still covered with filthy pieces of torn jeans. And from what I could see, she continued to walk on two human-looking legs with shoes.

But the biggest new change was her skin, only it didn't look like skin anymore because it was no longer the color of any person's flesh. Her skin had turned a pale yellow and it glowed, kind of like what happened when the bubble first covered her.

Everyone on the block noticed the changes in Cyndy Louise. But nobody knew what any of the changes meant.

––––––

Mom and Danny watched Cyndy Louise from my window while I lay on my bed petting Muffles as we waited for the start of our afternoon telephone talk.

"Maybe the bubbles will fall again and just float Cyndy Louise and all the others up into the sky," my optimistic mother suggested.

"Yeah, right," Danny muttered, rolling his eyes.

"I wonder if the glow's got something to do with what she did to Mr. Ortega after she killed him," I said. "She held his hand like she was trying to transfer something from his body into hers. Maybe whatever she got from him gave her the yellow color and the glow."

Danny shrugged. "I dunno about that, but at least we can see her coming real easily."

"But it's got to mean some..."

We heard Mr. Douglas' whistle so I stopped talking and joined my mother at my window while Danny went into his room to speak to Mrs. Perez.

"Good afternoon!" Mr. Douglas yelled. "Anything to share?"

"We're trying to figure out why Cyndy Louise is yellow and glowing!" Mom called.

"The boys say they haven't seen that before either!" Mr. Douglas shouted. "It must be something new!"

"Erin thinks it's connected to what she did to Ramón!" my mother yelled.

"She's probably right!" Mrs. Douglas called.

"Some kind of energy, I bet," I heard Mrs. Perez say through Danny's open window. She must have been shouting, but I could barely make out her words. Too bad you couldn't turn up the volume on this phone.

Then we heard the faraway sounds of another woman's voice, which must have been Mrs. Santangelo and we waited for Mrs. Perez to pass the message to Danny and the Douglasses.

"Nicole says maybe Cyndy Louise is like a battery, charging herself in the sun and then turning herself off when it rains!" Mr. Douglas relayed.

"But if she gets power from the sun, why does she have to touch us and kill us?" I shouted.

Mr. Douglas just shrugged.

———

After the telephone session ended, I lay on my bed again and thought about Blaine, wondering if he was thinking of me.

Why should he? I'd hardly talked to him and besides, he was leaving with Zach the next time it rained. At most, I'd say goodbye and he still wouldn't know anything about me. He'd totally forget me by his next stop and I'd never see him again.

I covered my face with the pillow and tried not to think about how I had messed up my one—and probably only— chance to hang out with a cute guy. *Dummy! Not even any competition since you're the only girl here.*

What if I never got off the block—never got to go anywhere else—just lived and died here in this house, with only Mom and

Danny and seeing our neighbors when it rained? *What a life!*

I took the pillow away from my face and placed it under my head. Then, closing my eyes, I cried quietly until I felt my face being licked. Without opening my eyes, I hugged the dog. "At least you love me," I whispered, caressing Muffles' soft fur.

———

Early next morning, the thunder woke me. It boomed so loud and strong that the house seemed to shake. When the flashes of lightning followed, I gave up on sleeping, crept to my window, and peeked through the curtains.

The wet street was empty, of course. Cyndy Louise had gone into some house or building to escape from the rain and sleep, rest, recharge, or do whatever the touchers did. I rested my elbows on the windowsill and hoped the storm would last long enough for me to see Blaine again.

What's he doing? Sleeping? Or maybe the thunder woke him too. I closed my eyes and tried to picture him in the Fisher's house, sitting in front of a bedroom window and thinking about me. Maybe if I concentrated real hard, I'd be able to connect our brains. *Erin to Blaine: Are you there?*

Yeah, sure. Like a sci-fi movie on mind control.

Dad loved the original "Star Trek" TV series and Mom got him the DVD. I watched some of the shows and I remember the serious guy with the pointy ears—Spock—doing a mind meld.

That's what I wanted to do, link my mind with Blaine's. Actually, I would have rather linked my lips with his. But it didn't matter because none of that was going to happen. If the rain stopped, I wouldn't see him and if it kept raining, I'd only see him long enough to say goodbye.

I walked back to bed feeling sorry for myself.

———

I must have fallen asleep because the next thing I heard was Mom's wake-up call. Opening my curtains, I glanced outside and when I saw Cyndy Louise, I knew it was no longer raining.

We were half finished with school when I again heard the wonderful sound of raindrops falling. Danny must have heard them too because he looked up from the book he was reading and smiled at me.

"Can we stop school a little early today and go outside?" I asked Mom. "It's been like weeks since the last time it rained."

She gave me a funny look. "I mark each rainfall on the calendar and it's only been five days, Erin. But it's tough for all of us being cooped up in the house so let's finish English and then, if it's still raining heavily, we'll head into the street."

By the time the four of us went outside—I held Muffles' leash—it was pouring and the wind was really strong. We heard thunder in the distance followed by a couple of zigzagging lightning bolts.

"We're not staying outside if the lightning comes much closer," Mom said.

Great. Just my luck.

"Good morning," Mrs. Perez called, waving to us from her front porch. "I'm sitting here enjoying the fireworks show in the sky."

Danny nodded. "It's pretty cool."

"Come and join me," Mrs. Perez said. "You're getting soaked standing out there."

The heavy wind was pulling our umbrellas in all directions. I was having trouble keeping mine over my head and holding the leash at the same time.

We stepped onto our neighbor's porch, dripping puddles of water.

"Sorry, I don't have enough chairs for all of you," Mrs. Perez said, petting Muffles' wet head. "But I can get more from the shed."

"That's okay," Mom said. "We sit all the time. It's just good to be here and see you. Has anyone else been out?"

"I saw the Douglasses about a half hour ago, but they didn't stay outside very long and then I saw the two boys who've been living at the Fisher's house."

My heart did a quick flip. "Oh," I said, trying to sound casual. "What were they doing?"

Mrs. Perez looked at me, her lips forming a slight grin. "They said they were going to finish checking the O'Malley's house and then go to the other empty one across the street."

"That's right," my mother said. "They stopped looking for food last week to help the Santangelos move into Mr. Ortega's house." She turned towards Mrs. Perez. "Have you seen the husband or wife today?"

"No, but I've been talking to them on our telephone."

"How are they?"

"Fine, considering what they went through." Mrs. Perez shuddered. "I can't imagine being trapped in the basement for that long."

"We've been trapped in our houses for much longer—more than a month," I whispered. "It's not so different."

"Cyndy Louise wasn't inside our house, Erin," my mother said.

I shrugged and didn't argue. But I didn't agree with Mom. I didn't think it was much different at all.

———

We stayed on Mrs. Perez's porch until I noticed that, although it was still pouring, the wind wasn't blowing as hard. "Can we go back on the street?" I asked. "It's not so stormy right now."

"Yeah," Danny added. "No thunder or lightning either and

I wanna see Bobby."

Mom nodded and we said goodbye to Mrs. Perez. "Can we stop at Connie's and say 'hi'?" I asked my mother as we walked. "Emily loves Muffles." And Connie was right next door to the Fisher's, which just happened to be the current home of Blaine and Zach.

"Sure."

I ran onto Connie's porch with Muffles and rapped on her front door. Connie peered at me through a tiny slit and smiled when she opened the door.

"Visitors!" she exclaimed as Mom and Danny caught up to me. "What a nice surprise. Do you guys want to come inside?"

"No," Mom said. "We're too wet. Now that the thunderstorm is over, we're taking a walk, and were passing your house so..."

"Rin!" Emily shouted, her arms raised as she rushed to the door. But Muffles stepped in front of me, blocking her path. "Wow wow!" she said happily, touching the dog's wet fur. Then the little girl glanced at her wet fingers in amazement. "Wawa?"

We all laughed and it felt real good. It seemed like I hadn't laughed for a very long time.

———

Mom, Danny, Muffles, and I left Connie's house and again stood in the rain, holding umbrellas over our heads. "I wonder if Blaine and Zach finished checking everywhere for food," I said casually.

Mom smiled at me. "We can knock on the Fisher's door and see if they're inside," she said.

"We're stoppin' at every house for Erin," Danny whined. "I don't wanna go there. I just wanna see Bobby. Can't I run across the street and you and Erin stay here?"

"No. Remember what happened the last time we did that?"

"It's pouring too hard now," Danny argued. "This rain's not gonna stop."

"You can't be sure of that so we're all staying together."

Danny puckered his lips and scowled.

"That doesn't mean you can't see Bobby," Mom continued. "But it's his turn to visit us so if his mother agrees, Bobby can stay in our house—with you in your room—till the next rain."

If I didn't know better, I'd have thought she was planning an ordinary sleepover—just two boys getting together—and I didn't like the idea at all. They'd make lots of noise, which I'd hear through the connecting wall—more reminders of friends I no longer had. But I forced myself not to complain. Danny was my brother and he deserved some fun in this awful new world.

As Mom knocked on the Fisher's door, I held Muffles' leash and tried not to be jealous.

———

No one answered the door at the Fisher's house.

"You think they're okay?" I whispered.

"Yes." Mom nodded her head. "I bet those boys are across the street at the house next door to Bobby, gathering the rest of the food." We didn't know the name of the people who lived there—or at this point, used to live there. They'd moved in just a few months ago and kept to themselves.

"Can we check...?" I started to ask.

"You said I could see Bobby," Danny interrupted. "Erin's knocked on every door on the block."

"We'll do both," Mom said. "Erin can check the empty house while you go to Bobby's. I'll stand in the street between the two houses and watch both of you."

Smart solution. Sometimes my mother surprised me.

I dashed to the house next to Bobby's and rapped on the door. I heard footsteps and when the door opened, I was staring at the twinkling eyes of Blaine.

"Hi," he said, smiling first at me and then at Muffles. "What's up?"

I felt my face turning red as I realized I didn't have a good reason for being there. "Hi," I began. "We were walking down the block 'cause my brother wanted to see his friend and I thought I'd check on how you were doing." *Check? Why'd I use that word? Was I his boss?*

But Blaine didn't seem upset at my choice of language. "Who's this little guy?" he asked, squatting to study the dog.

"His name's Muffles."

"Hi, Muffles," Blaine said, reaching down to pat the wet fur on the dog's head. "How you doin', boy?"

I loved that soft drawl. "He's doing better than us, that's for sure. Cyndy Louise can't hurt him."

"Yeah, those toucher things don't kill animals, just people." Blaine opened the door wider and pointed towards the hallway. "You and Muffles want to come inside while Zach and me finish raidin' the kitchen?"

I did, but Mom was standing behind me, watching. "Is it okay if I go inside?" I called.

"I'm sorry. No."

Great. My mother won't let me out of her sight like I'm two-years-old.

As I tried to think of a clever way to explain why I couldn't go into the house, Blaine spoke. "I understand," he said. "They can be hidin' anywhere."

"And my brother got stuck in his friend's house one time when the rain suddenly stopped and Cyndy Louise came back on the street. My mom's afraid that'll happen again."

He nodded.

"Well, I guess this is goodbye," I said, forcing a smile. "You and Zach said you're leaving during this rain."

Blaine grinned at me. "Oh, I don't know about that. We found a lot of food on this block and it's been real comfy livin' in that house so we might be stayin' here a little while longer."

"Great!" I knew I sounded overly excited, but I couldn't help it.

———

"Food's here!" Blaine shouted as he and Zach each dragged two big bags through the rain to Connie's porch. "Come and get it!"

Carrying their own garbage bags, our neighbors hurried to Connie's and nearly everybody took something, although Connie, the Santangelos, and Bobby's mother split most of the food. Mom just grabbed some toilet paper for us since we still had enough stuff to eat from our trip to the supermarket.

During the food distribution, I noticed Danny and Bobby in deep conversation with Blaine and Zach. Although I was curious about what they were saying, I didn't interrupt them because I had something else on my mind.

"This is the end of the food on the block," I said to Mom as we headed home together, Danny and Bobby trailing behind because Mrs. Mitchell had agreed to let Bobby stay with us until it rained again. "What'll happen in a week or two when all our food's gone?"

Mom didn't answer right away. "Don't worry about that, Erin," she finally said. "We'll deal with it when the time comes, just like we did before."

Before? I thought of the dead bodies, the rats, the smell — and, of course, the touchers — and stood still, feeling like I had to throw up. "You mean we'd go back to the supermarket?"

"Not necessarily." She put her arm around my shoulders and pulled me next to her as she started walking again. "Really, hon, we won't starve. We'll find more food when we need to. I promise."

    I don't know if she had a plan or just said what she did to make me feel better. Either way, it helped a little and I forced myself to stop thinking about food.

CHAPTER 18 – Bobby's Visit

As soon as we got back to our house, Danny and Bobby ran to my brother's room and slammed the door shut. Even though I closed my door, I could still hear them and there was no way to drown out the sound—no music, TV, phone, computer.

My mother's door was open so I jumped on her bed. "What's wrong?" she asked, glancing at me from her desk with Muffles curled up on the floor nearby.

"They're too loud. I can't stay in my room."

Mom rolled her eyes and chuckled. "They're twelve-year-old boys, Erin. Cut them a little slack."

Flipping onto my stomach, I leaned my elbows on the bed. "I understand that. But I can't read or draw or concentrate on anything with all that noise."

"It's just temporary." Mom sat on the bed and hugged me. "I know you're lonely, hon. How about you and I do something together—play a board game or cards?"

"No, thanks." I rolled away from her and stood. "I'll be okay." I didn't want to start the games again. They were boring and Mom was only offering to play because she felt sorry for me.

"I'm always here if you want to do something together."

"I know and I appreciate it." *A play date with my mother. My life really sucked.*

"Can I go outside again for a little while? It's still raining."

My mother shook her head. "It's barely drizzling now."

I rushed back to my room and slammed the door.

———

Dragging my desk chair to the window, I sat, trying not to cry. I figured I'd watch the street—see if anyone was still out and if it stopped raining, check on changes in Cyndy Louise. There wasn't much else I could do before dinner.

"Shut up!" Danny's yell was followed by a loud laugh. Then Bobby said something I couldn't make out and both of them burst into giggles. After that they must have shoved each other around the room because I heard a loud thump as bodies crashed against the wall by my bed.

I leaned closer to the window and looked outside. It wasn't raining anymore because Cyndy Louise was back and even though she was walking away from me, I could see that she was different. The color of her skin—or whatever now covered her body—wasn't pale yellow anymore. It was much brighter and glowed more than before. *Like a light bulb.* It would be even harder for her to sneak up on us, especially in the dark.

Her face—if you could call it that—still had the eyes and ears of a person with no mouth or nose. Like before, she was topless, but her little nippleless breasts were now flat so she didn't look at all female. Torn bits of her jeans still covered her lower body so I couldn't tell what was going on down there, but I bet her vagina had disappeared too.

Whatever she was turning into, it wasn't going to be a girl, woman, or anything feminine. But I don't think she was turning into a man either. Whatever she was becoming didn't have a sex.

With Bobby joining us, we had three students in Mom School the next morning. He'd brought his notebook and shared Danny's textbooks.

Mom assigned us stories to read and questions to answer. As I opened my English anthology, I let out a huge yawn.

"Didn't you sleep well?" my mother asked.

"I guess not," I said, shrugging. I really did feel tired. The boys hadn't made too much noise during the night, but I kept waking up, conscious of every little sound.

"You're not sick, are you?"

"I don't think so."

"Let me know if something hurts."

"Sure." I smiled, trying to reassure her I was fine. It was hard because I didn't feel fine, but I don't think anything was physically wrong. I was just depressed and seeing Danny with Bobby made me feel worse. I was glad Danny had a friend, but I had no one. I didn't even know if Marci or any of my friends were still alive.

Having Bobby in the house meant a lot of groans for me. He was a good kid, but he loved to tell jokes and had a weird sense of humor.

"Did you hear the one about the duck and the grapes?" Bobby asked the next morning at breakfast.

"Spare us," I whispered.

"This duck walks into a grocery store," he said, ignoring my plea. "And it asks the guy at the counter, 'Got any grapes?'

"The guy says, 'No' and the duck leaves.

"The next day, the duck walks back into the store and asks the same guy, 'Got any grapes?'

"The guy gets mad and yells at the duck. 'I told you

yesterday, I don't have no grapes! If you ever come back and ask me that question again, I'm gonna nail your duck feet to the floor!'

"The duck walks out of the store, but then the next day, it comes back. 'You again,' the guy at the counter says. 'Whaddyu want?'

"'Got any nails?' the duck asks.

"'No,' the guy says.

"'Good,' the duck says. 'Got any grapes?'"

Danny fell out of his chair, laughing like it was the funniest joke he ever heard. Mom smiled to be polite. I shook my head and prayed for rain.

———

Of course it didn't rain. Instead, the weather was warm and sunny, allowing Cyndy Louise to patrol our street all day and all night.

One early evening after dinner—three days into Bobby's visit, I think—I was sitting by the window trying to draw, but mostly watching Cyndy Louise, when I heard footsteps behind me. I'd left my door open and Danny and Bobby had walked right in.

"Go away," I said, silently cursing myself for not closing the door. "I'm busy."

"No, you're not," Danny said as he shut my door. "We gotta talk to you about something important."

I smiled at my brother. "What's so important? Are you two on some secret spy mission?"

Danny bounced onto my bed. "Really, Erin, we're serious. This isn't a joke."

"Yeah," Bobby said, sitting next to Danny. "We've been talking a lot, figuring out stuff, and we came up with a plan."

"What kind of a plan?"

"A plan to kill Cyndy Louise," Bobby said.

I looked at both boys and neither was smiling. "What are you two talking about? We don't know how to kill her, but we sure know how she can kill us."

"It's the water," Danny said. "We know they don't like water, right? So we're gonna drown her."

"And just where are you drowning her?"

Bobby smiled at me. "In the Fisher's pool."

———

For a few moments, no one said anything. Then, finally, I spoke. "It's not a bad idea, but it's something you need to discuss with everybody on the block."

Bobby shook his head. "They're all too scared."

"Of course they're scared," I agreed, staring at him. "Haven't you seen what the touchers can do?"

"Yeah, but I don't think their brains work so good anymore so we can fool her."

Their brains... Maybe Bobby had a point. If their bodies were becoming less and less human, it's possible their brains were changing too, making them dumber. I hoped he was right. "At least, let's tell Mom," I argued.

"No," Bobby said. "I tried to tell my mother, but she wouldn't listen. You can't tell your mom 'cause then she's not going to let us do it."

"So it's just you two?"

"Blaine and Zach are gonna do this with us," Danny said.

Aha! I looked at both of them. "So whose idea was this really—yours or Blaine's and Zach's?"

Bobby stared at his knees. "I was talking about how water bothers them and then Zach said there was a pool in the back of the house they're staying in..."

"It was Blaine who said we gotta figure out a way to get her into the water," Danny added.

"Is the pool filled?" I asked.

"They said there's a cover on it with lots of water underneath," Danny explained. "They were gonna take the cover off before the last rain stopped."

I nodded. "Okay, so the water's there. But you can't touch Cyndy Louise and push her in. Since we know she hates water, how do you intend to get her to go swimming?"

"We knock her in." Bobby pretended he was a baseball player swinging a bat.

"With what?"

"They got a big long metal pole," Bobby continued. "It's something for the pool."

"Blaine and Zach are going to hit her with this pole?"

"Yeah," Danny said.

"Then what are you two doing?" I was afraid of the answer.

"We gotta get her to chase us to the back of the house," Bobby said.

I stared at them. "You're the bait."

Danny shrugged.

"You boys can't do this," I whispered. "She's so strong and super fast and..."

"She's not smart," Bobby repeated, interrupting me. "Cyndy Louise used to be real smart, but..."

"She's still smart enough to kill you, especially since all she has to do is touch you."

The boys didn't say anything.

"So when is all this supposed to happen?" I finally said.

"Tomorrow afternoon," Danny said. "Tomorrow at three o'clock."

———

Again no one spoke for a long time. "This is really crazy," I finally said, shaking my head. "How are you even going to make it down the street to the Fisher's house?" I counted quickly. "That's four houses away—and there's absolutely nothing wrong with Cyndy Louise's hearing. Her ears still work perfectly fine."

"We found an old CD player with batteries in it," Danny said. "We tested it out today and when we're ready, we're gonna put in a song, turn the sound up real loud, and leave it blasting on our porch."

"And when Cyndy Louise comes here to check out the noise, we'll run through the back to Blaine and Zach," Bobby added.

I remembered something. "What about the fence around Connie's backyard?"

"They already cut big holes through it during the last rain," Danny explained.

"Does Connie know?"

Bobby nodded. "They told her it was in case of Cyndy Louise and we had to get through the back fast."

I looked at my brother and then at his friend. "Are you both sure you want to do this?"

The two boys nodded seriously.

"Danny, this isn't an adventure like in the movies. Remember what happened with Mr. Ortega?"

"We're not gonna get trapped like that and let her get close enough to touch us, Erin."

"It's our best chance to kill her," Bobby said.

I shook my head again. "But we don't know for sure that being in the water'll kill her."

"We still have to try it," Danny said as he stood. "We're doing this tomorrow and we wanted you to know so when we leave, you can explain it to Mom."

"I'm coming with you." The words were out of my mouth before I realized I'd spoken.

"You don't have to," Danny said. "We've got everything all figured out."

"If you're doing this, then I'm going too," I repeated.

CHAPTER 19 – The Pool

I slept badly that night and was real nervous the following morning—so much that Mom noticed. "What's wrong, Erin?" she asked during school. "Are you sick?"

"No." I forced myself to smile, hoping I looked convincing. "I'm fine."

"You're not concentrating on your work. Whenever I ask you a question, I have to repeat it."

"Sorry." I shrugged, still smiling my phony grin. "I guess I'm just daydreaming." Then I glanced at my paper, hoping to end the conversation.

Danny and Bobby were doing a much better job of pretending it was a normal morning in our not-so-normal lives. I snuck a few peeks at the boys and both were reading the textbook and answering the questions Mom had assigned them.

I checked my watch again and it wasn't even eleven o'clock. Four long hours till the boys' plan. I sighed, quietly I hoped, and tried to focus on the world history pages I was supposed to be reading.

———

I got through the rest of the morning and lunchtime without having to answer more questions about my health. Then, finally, we were dismissed and I escaped to my room. Since I was already totally exhausted, I fell into bed and closed my eyes, hoping I'd feel better after a short nap.

Almost immediately, I heard a soft tap on the door. "Go away," I mumbled. "I'm trying to get some rest."

But my protest didn't do any good. The doorknob turned and someone entered my room. "Erin," Danny whispered. "Are you okay?"

Grudgingly, I opened my eyes and faced my brother, who leaned over the bed, looking worried. "Physically, I'm fine," I said. "But mentally, I'm a complete wreck about this afternoon."

"It'll work. She won't touch us."

"How can you be so sure?"

"I'm too fast for her—and so's Bobby."

"Danny, she's much faster now than a regular girl. You know that."

He shrugged. "You won't tell Mom?"

"No."

"Are you still coming with us?"

I nodded.

———

I don't think I napped for more than a half hour, but I woke up feeling a thousand percent better. When the boys knocked on my door a little before three o'clock, I was ready to go.

"You're good?" Danny asked nervously when I opened the door.

"Yeah."

"Okay," Bobby whispered. "Here's your water gun." He handed me a loaded pistol. "Let's go."

"What about Mom?" I asked, suddenly realizing how

138

scared she'd be when we all disappeared.

Danny waved a slip of paper. "I wrote her a note," he said.

That wouldn't make her less scared, but at least she'd know what was going on. Glancing at my mother's door, I saw it was closed.

The three of us tiptoed down the stairs. At the bottom, we were met by Muffles.

"Shh," Danny whispered to the dog, crouching and putting his finger to his lips.

Muffles turned his head sideways as if to ask, "Huh? What're you doing?"

"Good boy," Danny whispered, petting the dog's head. "Stay."

Bobby led the way to the dining room and looked through the opening. "She's heading to us," he said softly. "After she starts going back, we'll set up the CD player on the porch and turn it on when she's all the way down the other end of the street."

We waited and watched. When Cyndy Louise was out of our sight, Bobby opened the door as quietly as possible and he and Danny stepped onto the porch. "Now," he whispered.

Danny turned on the music and booming rock sounds exploded into the quiet afternoon. They'd chosen the loudest CD they could find—"Old Time Rock 'n Roll"—a song my mother used to blast when she cleaned the house.

After the boys shut and locked the front door, we all hurried around to the back and into the yard. I imagined by now Mom would have already called Danny and me and— getting no answers—run downstairs to find out where all the noise was coming from.

Danny had left his note on the dining room table. *She'd better find it.* I shook my head, trying to sweep away my fears and concentrate on what we needed to do.

The three of us raced past Mrs. Perez's backyard and Mr. Ortega's property, where the Santangelo family was now living, and wriggled through the openings Blaine and Zach had cut in the fence behind Connie's house. Then we were standing in the Fisher's backyard, next to an in-ground rectangular pool filled with water. And Blaine and Zach were there too, smiling at us.

"Welcome," Blaine said in his cute drawl. "Glad y'all could make it." He smiled at me. "Didn't know you'd be joinin' us."

I returned his smile. "Thought I might help."

Zach held the net part of a long pole the Fishers must have used to clean their pool. "Okay, boys," he said, waving the pole. "Get her to come back here."

"What do you want me to do?" I asked Blaine.

"Stand off to the side under cover and yell when you see the kids runnin' this way," he said smiling. "But don't get anywhere near her."

"Of course I won't." *Did he think I was that dumb?*

I backed away, crouching behind a wide bush that separated the Fisher's house from Connie's, held my water gun, and waited. A few minutes later, I saw the boys, followed by the sounds of running footsteps. "They're coming!" I yelled and ducked into my hiding place again.

"She's here!" Danny shouted as he and Bobby jumped into the pool—with clothes and sneakers—swam to the center, and treaded water. I hadn't figured they'd do that, but it made perfect sense. The pool was the safest place; Cyndy Louise certainly wouldn't jump in.

But what if Blaine and Zach didn't kill her? She'd probably be fine with staying right here and waiting for them to come out of the water. And they'd have to come out sometime.

While I was considering the terrible possibilities, Cyndy Louise entered the Fisher's backyard. Close up, she looked even more like an unfinished rag doll—a face with no mouth or nose, just eyes and ears—practically no hair, except for a few long dirty strands. Her arms and legs were all muscle. Except for shoes, the rest of her body was nearly all uncovered and pretty much flat. Nothing looked female anymore—no breasts or vagina. And she was a brighter shade of yellow.

She hesitated when she saw the boys in the water and then took a big step backwards.

Blaine and Zach had positioned themselves behind a row of bushes that surrounded the pool. "Here I am!" Blaine now shouted, coming forward and waving his arms.

Moving quickly, Cyndy Louise ran along the side of the pool towards Blaine while Zach stood nearby, holding the pole upright. When Cyndy Louise was about ten feet away from him, Blaine jumped into the pool and swam to the center, joining Danny and Bobby, who continued to tread water.

That left Zach holding the pole. He smashed it hard at Cyndy Louise, hitting her squarely in the middle of the back.

She dropped to the ground by the edge of the pool and didn't fall into the water. She didn't make a sound either. But of course she couldn't because she no longer had a mouth.

Bobby swam closer, splashing at Cyndy Louise, trying to get her wet. Blaine and Danny did the same until she crawled away from them. As she lay there, Zach hit her again several times with the long pole and used it to try to push her into the pool.

But none of it did any good. The pounding didn't hurt her and she continued to crawl further away from the water. And then she rose to her feet.

"Jump into the pool!" Blaine yelled.

"Not yet!" Zach shouted. "I gotta try this first!" He heaved the long pole at her, smashing Cyndy Louise in what was left of her face. With one powerful motion, she flicked the pole away and Zach fell to the ground, his water gun tumbling from his pocket and out of his reach.

I squirted Cyndy Louise from the bush, but the water didn't reach her. Blaine, Bobby, and Danny tried splashing her, but she was too far away. "Into the pool—now!" Blaine yelled, swimming towards his friend.

Then it was over. Cyndy Louise reached down and touched Zach.

————

She did that strange stuff with the dead body again, like with Mr. Ortega. We were lucky she was so focused on Zach because it gave us time to escape.

One by one, the boys climbed out of the pool and crept into the house. She ignored them. Instead, she continued to hold Zach's hand and concentrate on whatever she was doing with him. When I ran from my hiding place, still aiming my gun at her, she didn't even look up.

The three dripping wet boys and I stood in front of the sliding glass door watching Cyndy Louise. Like with Mr. Ortega, flashes of sparks seemed to go from Zach's hand into Cyndy Louise's yellow arm. "What do you think is happening?" I whispered.

"She's drainin' his energy," Blaine said as he wiped his eyes. "Some kind of weird power transfer." He shook his head and then lowered it, covering his face with his hands.

"I'm so sorry," I said. "I know you two were friends."

"Yeah." He didn't look up.

Danny walked over to us, his eyes full of tears. "I shouldn't have got you into this," he said to me. "Now Zach's dead and Mom's all alone."

I shrugged. It was too late for second thoughts. We were stuck together in this house until the next rain.

CHAPTER 20 – Housemates

Blaine, Danny, and Bobby got towels to dry themselves and then Blaine gave the boys clothes to change into.

When Danny and Bobby returned to the kitchen, I couldn't help giggling because the two of them looked so funny. The shorts and shirts they wore were much too big. Danny was taller than Bobby, but even he looked like he was dressing up in his father's clothes. The black tee nearly reached his ankles and the blue shorts dangled way past his knees.

"At least roll them up," I said, pointing to the shorts.

"I gave them Zach's stuff," Blaine whispered. "He won't be needin' any more clothes."

"Sorry." I felt guilty for my momentary lapse into happiness.

"It's okay," Blaine said. "They both do look kinda funny." He smiled, but his smile looked sad.

"I have another idea about Cyndy Louise," Danny said, taking a seat at the kitchen table.

The three of us turned towards my brother.

"She didn't chase us when we came out of the water, right?" he asked.

"Yeah," Bobby agreed. "She was too busy doing that stuff

with Zach's body."

"But what if that's not the whole reason she didn't try to get us?" Danny continued. "What if she didn't want to touch us?"

"Why not?" Blaine asked.

"Maybe 'cause we were all soaking wet from being in the pool."

"That's a good theory," I said. "But you're forgetting about me. I was completely dry behind the bush."

Danny nodded. "She could've gone after you, but I think she just didn't see you."

"Even if you're right, how would that help us?" I asked. "We can't stay in the pool all the time or just go outside when we're soaked."

Danny shrugged.

"It could help," Blaine said. "If we're outside and she's chasin' us, we know we can jump in the pool, get wet, and then come out..."

"Only if Danny's right that she won't touch us if we're real wet—and we still don't know that for sure," I pointed out.

———

We were ready for the four o'clock telephone talk, which I didn't want to miss. At least we could tell Mom—and Bobby's mother—we were okay.

I knew my mother would be mad at me and Danny for running out like we did, but I hoped she'd feel so relieved that she'd forgive us. She'd have time to get over her anger. Today was a beautiful sunny day so we weren't going home anytime soon.

We stood in a large upstairs bedroom that faced the street, Danny and me in front of one window and Blaine and Bobby in front of the other. I heard a faint whistle and across the street, Mrs. Weiss waved at us, looking puzzled.

"Danny and I are okay!" I shouted. "Please tell my mother!"

I couldn't see Connie, but I heard her voice from next door. "I'll pass it along!" she yelled. A minute later, I heard Connie holler something about us from another window that I hope the Santangelos understood and relayed to Mrs. Perez.

"This is Bobby!" Danny's friend shouted. "I'm okay too!"

I heard a faint reply from Bobby's mom at the end of the street, who we could barely see. It sounded like she said, "Thank God, but what are you doing over there?"

"I'm with Danny, Erin, and Blaine!" Bobby yelled back, waving at her. "We're all fine!"

That was true, but it didn't answer his mother's question. Also, he didn't say anything about Zach, who most certainly wasn't fine.

"What happened?" Rhonda Weiss called to us. "Why are all of you in that house?"

The four of us looked at each other before saying anything. "Let me talk," Blaine said. Sticking his head out the window, he yelled, "We thought we could kill the toucher girl by drownin' her in the pool! But it didn't work!"

That was obvious since we could see the back of Cyndy Louise's yellow body as she headed up the block.

"She didn't drown?" Mrs. Weiss asked.

"No!" Blaine hollered. "We couldn't get her into the water!"

"What about your friend?" Connie called.

"She touched him!" Blaine answered, his voice cracking.

"I'm so sorry!" Mrs. Weiss called.

"Me too!" Connie shouted.

———

After the telephone talk, I asked Blaine a question. "Just how are we going to do this?"

"Do what?"

"You know..." I didn't want to say 'sleep' because I knew my face would turn red.

"She means where're we all gonna stay?" Danny, my interpreter, explained.

"Oh," Blaine said. "Well, there're two more bedrooms besides this big one. I was in here and Zach used another..." His voice trailed off as he mentioned his friend's name. "You kids can share that one." Then he turned to me. "And you can have the third bedroom. Follow me."

Blaine pushed open a door to what must have been a guest room. It had a large bed—though not as big as the one in the other room—a dresser, and two end tables. "For you guys," he said to Danny and Bobby. "Think you can share that bed? If not, I'll switch with you." Although he made the offer, Blaine didn't sound anxious to move into his dead friend's room.

Danny must have sensed Blaine's feelings. "We'll be okay here," my brother said quickly. "Right?"

"Sure," Bobby agreed.

Continuing down the hall, Blaine entered another bedroom. "This one looks perfect for you," he said, smiling a little. It was painted pale pink, obviously a girl's room. But it was for a little girl because it was filled with dolls, mostly Disney characters. I recognized some—Cinderella, Belle, Ariel, and Tinkerbell—and there were many more on shelves and on top of the dresser. Even the bedspread featured an Indian princess—Pocahontas maybe?

I touched the bed cover lightly, forcing myself not to think about what happened to the little girl who slept here—one of the kids on the elementary school bus that never reached our street.

"Is this all right?" Blaine asked softly.

"Yes." I tried to smile. "I'll be fine. Thank you."

———

We all ate dinner together. Hopefully, Blaine had enough food for the four of us until the next rain. But nobody said anything about that. We ate plain tuna without mayonnaise, cheese spread on crackers, and drank water mixed with strawberry Kool-Aid. I'd hoped for something different, but this was pretty much what we'd been eating at our house the past month.

"You guys have enough?" our host asked.

Everyone nodded.

"Now for dessert." Reaching into an upper shelf, Blaine pulled out four individually wrapped pieces of chocolate pound cake.

Each of us grabbed a cake, opened the wrapper, and gobbled the treat.

"It still tastes good," Danny said, licking his fingers.

"That's because of the way the cake was wrapped," I explained, wiping my mouth with a napkin to make sure I didn't have crumbs on my face. "It kept the pieces fresh."

"True," Blaine agreed. "That and the preservative crap they loaded in." He pointed to a long list of ingredients printed on the cellophane wrapper.

"We don't have to worry about that anymore," I whispered. "No companies are making cakes with bad stuff in them."

"No companies are making any kinda food," Bobby said.

"No companies are making anything because there's no more companies," Danny added.

"Okay, that's enough," Blaine said, collecting the cake wrappers and tossing them into a big garbage bag. "Dinner table talk's supposed to be fun stuff—like how'd you spend your day?"

I shook my head. I didn't want to think about how I'd spent today—especially this afternoon.

Blaine must have realized his mistake because he quickly

changed the subject. "How about a game of cards?" he suggested. "I found a couple decks."

———

We played poker for over an hour, using toothpicks as chips.

"Any other card game y'all wanna play?" Blaine asked as he scooped up the last pot, which held all our remaining toothpicks. He was a great bluffer and had faked us out again. I'd folded my pair of kings, which would have won.

"Nah," Danny said, stretching his arms and yawning. "You'd probably beat us again. Where'd you learn to play so good?"

"College," Blaine said.

"Oh," I whispered. I'd been trying to stuff the toothpicks back into the box, but stopped when Blaine spoke and I realized I'd never have the chance to go away to school. *No more colleges...*

Blaine sensed my negative thoughts again. "Maybe it's time to go to sleep," he suggested. "It's been a real long day and it's gettin' dark."

"Yeah," Danny agreed. "C'mon." He poked Bobby in the shoulder. "Race you upstairs." Without even saying "good night," the two of them ran up the steps to their temporary bedroom.

That left Blaine and me alone in the kitchen. I stared at my lap and didn't say anything.

"Are you doin' okay?" he finally asked.

"Yes, thank you." I wanted to kick myself for speaking so formally. "How about you?" I asked without looking up. After all, he was the one who'd just lost his friend.

"I'm okay, I guess. There's not much you can do these days except forget all the bad stuff and keep movin' forward."

I raised my head. "That's a real good attitude," I said. "I try to think like that, but sometimes I forget."

"Me too." Then he smiled, his bright blue eyes seeming to sparkle. "So I'll see you tomorrow morning?"

I nodded to him. "I'll be here."

———

I slept pretty well considering I was in a strange house and Blaine was in a room just down the hall. When I woke up, I checked my watch. It was 6:30 and the house was quiet. Trying not to make any noise, I dressed and tiptoed into the bathroom.

When I looked at my hair in the mirror, I made a face. There was no way it was ever going to look good unless I washed it. Then I sniffed my tee shirt. Not bad yet. At least I'd changed into clean clothes before coming here yesterday afternoon. But after today, I'd have to wash everything I was wearing—especially my underwear—or find new stuff. A woman had lived here—the mother of the little girl—and maybe I could fit into her clothes. Either way, I wasn't going to stink.

I took off my bra and tee and ran the water in the sink. Then I washed my hair using shampoo I found in the cabinet underneath and wrapped my wet head in a towel. I was putting on my clothes when there was a series of knocks on the door.

"Get outta there, Erin!" my brother said in a loud whisper. "I gotta go real bad!"

"One second...I'm almost done."

"Now!"

I opened the door and Danny raced past me, locking the door in my face.

Just like home.

———

By seven o'clock, all four of us were dressed and downstairs, ready for breakfast. Danny and I were used to getting up early for Mom School, but I guess Bobby and Blaine were now early risers too. It made sense since we wanted to use as much daylight as we could.

"No school today," I said to Danny as I slid into the kitchen chair next to him.

My brother grinned.

"Me too," Bobby added.

"That's right," I said. "Your mom's been teaching you."

Blaine chuckled as he took out boxes of Cheerios and Frosted Flakes. "Maybe I should make you kids do classwork like you've been doin' at home," he said. "I'm sure I could figure some lessons like..."

When he noticed my scowl, Blaine stopped talking in mid-sentence. I didn't like the "you kids" line—lumped together with a couple of twelve-year-old boys.

"...or maybe we won't do school," Blaine continued, smiling and watching my reaction.

I wasn't sure he understood why I was mad, but I intended to make it clear to him as soon as we were alone. *Alone*. That one little word gave me a tingly feeling.

———

"What do y'all wanna do this morning?" Blaine asked after we cleaned the table, washed and dried the dishes, and again sat in the kitchen. "We already eliminated school." He looked at me, his lips forming a tiny smile.

"Everything's so-o-o boring," Bobby said, leaning back in his chair and glancing at the narrow opening in the kitchen window. A strip of wood covered most of it. "I wish we could go out."

"Well, we can't," I said. It was another beautiful late June day—sunny, with hardly any clouds, and the temperature outside was probably in the upper seventies.

"What about the pool?" Bobby asked. "She won't go in the water."

"But what if she gets us before we go in?" Danny asked.

"Or after we come out," I added. "We don't know for sure that she won't touch something wet. And Zach..." I stopped talking when I remembered Zach's body was still out there and realized it would upset everyone, especially Blaine.

"No swimmin'," Blaine said, standing and resting his arms on the table. "If y'all don't wanna do school, maybe we can play some kind of game."

"Not cards again," Danny said.

"Do they have board games in this house?" I asked.

"I didn't see any," Blaine said. "But we could look through the closets."

"I don't wanna play those dumb games," Bobby muttered. "They're boring too."

Great—stuck here with two whiny boys.

Blaine glanced at Bobby and then at Danny. "How about a scavenger hunt?" he suggested. "We make a list of things to find and form teams. None of us live here so we don't know most of the stuff that's in this house."

"That could be pretty cool," Bobby said, smiling. "Me and Danny'll be a team."

"Sure," Blaine agreed. "Then Erin'll be with me."

————

I felt a little weird at first, nervous about being together with Blaine on a team, so when we all sat around the kitchen table and Blaine started writing a list of things to include on the scavenger hunt, I didn't say anything.

"What's the matter, Erin?" Danny asked. I guess he noticed I wasn't talking.

"Nothing." I smiled and forced myself to get into the game.

"Just trying to think of ideas...How about a red headband?"

"What's a headband?" Bobby asked.

"Something little girls wear around their heads to keep the hair out of their eyes," I explained. "A little girl used to live in the room I'm staying in and maybe she wore headbands. I haven't looked in the drawers so I don't know for sure, but..."

"Sounds good," Blaine said. "I'll add it to the list."

"A green pen or pencil," Danny suggested.

"Does it have to write green or just be green?" I asked.

"Either way is okay," Blaine said as he wrote it on a page of the legal pad.

"How about a yellow tee shirt?" I asked.

"That's good," Bobby said.

"Purple nail polish?" I suggested, the ideas entering my mind now.

"More girl stuff?" Danny complained.

"Why not?" I frowned at my brother. "You can't just have guy things, especially since you two boys are on the same team. We need some stuff for girls too and since a woman lived in this house, she could've used purple nail polish."

"Erin's right," Blaine said, nodding at Danny. "Purple nail polish goes on the list."

———

Blaine stopped writing when we all agreed—or sort of agreed—on thirty things to find. Danny and Bobby still weren't happy with any girl items that I suggested. After Danny copied the list, we were ready to start.

"Okay," Blaine said, reaching into a cabinet under the sink. "Here's a bag for your team and one for us." He gave the boys a large white plastic bag and handed me one. "Any of y'all got a watch?" he asked Danny and Bobby.

Danny nodded.

"Good," Blaine continued. "Meet you back here in the kitchen in exactly an hour and we'll do a count. The team that finds the most stuff on the list, wins."

"What's the prize for winning?" Bobby asked.

Blaine looked at me and I shook my head because I had no idea what we could use for a prize. Money didn't mean anything and the Fishers didn't have any sons so there was nothing special in this house for Danny or Bobby. Besides, if the boys found anything they liked here, they could keep it. The Fishers weren't coming back.

"I know," Blaine finally said. "Whoever wins doesn't have to clean the table and do the dishes for lunch and dinner today. Losin' team has to do all the work."

"You're on!" Bobby shouted. "C'mon team, let's go!" He and Danny dashed up the stairs.

"Good thinking," I said to Blaine. "At least now they want to play."

"Thanks." He gave me that cute smile again. "We should get goin' too. I could use some time off from dishwashin'."

———

Blaine and I started our search in the living room. "What could we find here?" I asked, opening a small wooden cabinet.

"How about a silver photo frame?" Blaine suggested after checking the list.

"That'd probably be on a shelf or a wall." I closed the cabinet and scanned the room, but didn't see any photos on the wall, just paintings of trees and flowers.

"There's gotta be photos," Blaine said. "Of them when they got married or of their daughter."

"Not here though. In their bedroom, maybe? You've been staying up there."

"True," Blaine agreed. "But I don't remember seein' any

photos." He grinned at me. "Of course I wasn't lookin' for them. Let's go check."

We climbed the staircase, passing Danny and Bobby who zoomed by us without saying a word as they headed downstairs.

"Those boys are really into this," Blaine said.

"So I see."

We reached the second floor and entered the Fisher's bedroom. Right away, I saw a silver frame on one of the dressers. After picking it up, I looked at the picture inside. A cute little girl with curly blonde hair sat on a park bench, holding a mermaid doll and smiling like everything was wonderful. *And it was...*

I must have stared at the photo for a couple of minutes without saying anything because Blaine came over to me. "What's wrong?" he asked.

"That's their daughter and she's holding Ariel, one of those dolls that are all over her room."

Blaine took the picture frame and placed it carefully in the plastic bag. Then he took both my hands and held them tightly. "Don't think about that, Erin," he whispered.

"It's hard not to."

"I know...Zach's still out there." Blaine turned towards the window. "But we can't do anythin' about what's already happened."

As Blaine spoke, he pulled me closer to him. And then his hands were holding my face and his lips were on mine. The kiss was soft and gentle. Closing my eyes, I kissed him back, hoping we could just stay like this forever.

Blaine moved away first. "I've been wantin' to do that since I first saw you," he whispered, stroking my hair. "Hope it's okay..."

"It's more than okay," I murmured, closing my eyes. "Kiss

me again."

———

The rest of the scavenger hunt was a blur. Blaine and I must have gone from room to room looking for things on the list, but I don't remember any of it. All I kept thinking about was Blaine kissing me and how it made my whole body feel quivery. *How could shaking all over feel so good?* But somehow it did.

"It's been an hour," Blaine said, glancing at his watch. "Time to see who won." He put his arm around my shoulder and smiled at me.

I snuggled into his arm, feeling better than I had in a long time. I didn't care who won the dumb scavenger hunt and I don't think he did either.

We walked together, his arm still looped around me, till we reached the bottom of the first floor staircase. Then Blaine released me and called upstairs. "Guys!" he shouted. "Come back to the kitchen! Time's up!"

A few seconds later, I heard a pounding noise as Danny and Bobby raced down the steps. "I bet we whooped your asses," Bobby said, grinning at Blaine and me. "We found almost everything."

"Good for you," I said.

"Yeah," Blaine agreed. "Let's go through the list and see if you're right."

The four of us sat at the kitchen table and Blaine took a crumpled piece of paper from our plastic bag. "Okay," he said, looking at the sheet. "First thing to find was a book with the word 'little' in the title or on one of the pages..."

———

Danny and Bobby beat us by a lot: They found twenty-seven of the things on the list and we found just fourteen.

"Ha, ha!" Bobby yelled, pointing his finger at Blaine and

me. "You guys gotta do all the work in the kitchen today!"

"Congratulations," I said, smiling at him. "You two worked very hard and you deserved to win."

Danny gave me a strange look, but didn't say anything. He knew I was usually much more competitive and hated to lose.

"So after lunch, any idea what y'all want to do?" Blaine asked as he lifted the two scavenger hunt bags from the table and deposited them on the floor in the corner of the kitchen.

"I think we should put the things back where we got them," I suggested.

"Why?" Danny asked me. "No one'll miss anything."

"I know, but we don't need stuff piling up in here."

"Erin's right," Blaine said. "We'll return the scavenger hunt things before doin' somethin' else."

"The losers should have to do that," Bobby said. "We found more stuff than you so we got much more to put back. It's not fair." He made a face and folded his arms in protest.

"Not part of the deal," Blaine said, shaking his head. "We're doin' the cleanin', but not puttin' back all the scavenger things." Then he smiled at Bobby. "Tell you what, though. If we get finished before you, we'll help with your bag."

"Thanks," Bobby said.

I guess he felt he won the argument.

———

We ate lunch and when we finished, Blaine and I—the "losers"—washed and dried the dirty dishes. Then, after we put back the scavenger hunt things, the four of us met again in the Fisher's kitchen.

"So what do y'all want to do this afternoon?" Blaine repeated.

"I still wanna go swimming," Bobby muttered.

"You know we can't do that," I said. "Not with Cyndy

Louise out there." *And Zach's dead body.*

"We're not goin' in the pool," Blaine agreed. "We can play cards or...." He raised his finger. "Hey, I got an idea. How about hide 'n seek?"

"Cool," Danny said, nudging his friend. "Whaddya think?"

Bobby shrugged. "Okay, I guess. It's better than nothing."

"Let's do teams again," Blaine suggested, smiling at me. "Same teams as before. Give us a chance to beat you guys this time."

"You can't do teams," Danny argued. "It's too hard to find places to hide."

"Then maybe we can count our points together," Blaine said. "You know, figure you two against me and Erin."

Bobby frowned at him. "But you're still cleaning the kitchen for dinner, right?"

Blaine nodded. "This game'll be for cleanup tomorrow."

"You're on," Bobby said. "What're the rules?"

———

We decided three of us would close our eyes and count to sixty aloud together in the kitchen to give the fourth person a chance to find a hiding place. Then we'd set the timer for five minutes. If the ring sounded before we found whoever was hiding, the person won.

"I wanna go first," Bobby whined.

"No problem," Blaine said, glancing from Danny to me. "Okay with you?"

"Sure," Danny said.

I just shrugged. I wasn't real crazy about playing this game, especially since I wouldn't be able to hide together with Blaine.

Bobby scooted off and Blaine, Danny, and I closed our eyes and counted to sixty.

"Ready or not, here we come!" Blaine shouted as he set the

timer.

Danny immediately sprinted to the staircase and raced up the steps, leaving Blaine and me alone in the kitchen.

"I guess we should start lookin' too," Blaine said, smiling.

"I suppose." I smiled at him.

He reached for my hand and we walked into the living room. I scanned the room, but there wasn't any good place to hide, unless Bobby had wedged himself into the sofa. *No.* We would've seen a bulge.

"Maybe the hall closet," Blaine suggested.

Still holding hands, we strolled to the entrance and I opened the closet. I poked my head inside, but except for a few hanging coats and shoes on the floor, it was empty.

"No one's in here," I said, stepping out.

"You sure?" Blaine whispered as he gently pushed me back inside and after moving the hangers to one end, closed the door nearly all the way. In the darkness, with our bodies pressed close together, he lifted my head and kissed me again. It was a long kiss and it would have been even longer except the stupid buzzer sounded, followed by loud footsteps on the stairs.

"Ha, ha!" Bobby shouted. "You guys didn't find me!"

We wriggled out of the closet and I smoothed my hair as we reached the steps.

Bobby and Danny stood at the bottom of the staircase, both with puzzled expressions on their faces. "Where'd you guys look?" Danny asked. "I didn't see you upstairs."

"We were busy checkin' places down here," Blaine explained.

"But there's no good places to hide downstairs," Bobby said.

"Yeah," I agreed, trying not to smile. "We just figured that out."

After Danny hid in the bathtub and Bobby found him, it was my turn. I ran upstairs as fast as I could and dashed into Blaine's bedroom, planning to hide under the big bed. I was squeezing in there—and hoping it wasn't real dusty—when Danny called my name.

"Erin! Come back down!"

I wondered what was going on, but then I heard the tinkling sound. *Raindrops.* Rushing down the stairs, I met Danny, Blaine, and Bobby at the bottom.

"Let's go," Danny said, tugging my arm. "We don't know how long it's gonna rain."

"Yeah," Bobby said. "See you guys later." He raced to the front door, unlocked it, and left the house.

"Did you check that Cyndy Louise isn't outside?" I asked my brother.

Danny shrugged. "She's never out there anytime it rains."

"Still." I walked to the nearest window and peeked into the street. No Cyndy Louise.

"C'mon," Danny said, grabbing for my arm again.

"Can I at least say goodbye to Blaine?" I asked.

My brother gave me a funny look. "Why? You'll see him again soon."

That was true, but..." You'll be outside later?" I asked Blaine.

He nodded sadly towards the back of the house. "After I take care of some stuff."

Zach. "Do you want us to help bury him?" I asked softly.

"No. It's okay."

"We're outta here!" Danny yanked me with him as he opened the door.

"Bye," I whispered, puckering my lips. Then my brother and I were outside again in the freedom of the rain.

CHAPTER 21 – The Fire

After leaving the Fisher's house, I had trouble keeping up with my fast-moving brother. But I was motivated to run because it wasn't raining hard, just drizzling, and if it stopped...

When I got home, I avoided the smashed CD player on the floor of the porch and raced through the open door. Danny was already inside, standing next to my mother and Muffles. As I stepped into the hallway, gasping for breath, Mom hugged me tightly. Then she smoothed my hair and stared into my eyes.

"How could you run off like that?" she whispered. "Didn't you realize how stupid it was?"

"Danny and Bobby were going anyway," I said, shrugging my shoulders. "I thought I could help."

"Erin, you're fifteen-years-old—not twelve—and you know better. You should've stopped them." Shaking her head, she left me and locked the front door.

"Erin tried, Mom," Danny said. "But me and Bobby wouldn't listen so don't blame her." He hesitated for a moment. "Did you see the note?"

My mother walked into the living room and sat on the sofa, putting her face in her hands. "That made it even worse, knowing what you were doing. I was so scared..."

We followed Mom into the room, Muffles parking himself under my feet.

"But it's okay now," I said, sitting next to my mother and petting the dog. "We're back and nothing bad happened to us." *Just something good happened to me*, I felt like saying, remembering Blaine's kisses.

Mom lifted her head. "Those other two boys, Blaine and Zach. I heard from the neighbors that Cyndy Louise got one of them."

"Zach," Danny said. "He tried to shove her into the pool with a pole, but he couldn't do it and then she touched him."

"Where were you when that happened?"

"In the middle of the pool with Bobby."

My mother turned to me. "And you?"

"Hiding in the bushes."

Mom shook her head and let out a deep breath. "Do you realize how lucky you both are to be alive?"

We nodded and didn't argue. *What could we have said?*

———

The rain stopped soon after we got home so we couldn't go out again. Danny and I were both exhausted so, after an early dinner, we headed to our rooms and I went to bed. I guess I hadn't slept as well as I thought at the Fisher's house.

I dreamt about Blaine. We were trapped together in a narrow tunnel, holding each other tightly, but not kissing because Cyndy Louise was outside, trying to get in. Then we heard her wriggling through the opening and saw her crawling towards us. We backed up as much as we could, but there was no way out the other end. Blaine shoved his body in front of mine and Cyndy Louise stuck out her yellow hand...

"No!" I woke up screaming, my body shaking and covered in sweat. Grabbing a flashlight, I made my way into the bathroom and splashed cold water on my face and neck.

When I lay down again, I felt a little better and tried to sleep. Closing my eyes, I thought about Blaine and me, this time without Cyndy Louise. It was a warm sunny day and we were alone in a meadow filled with beautiful flowers and colorful butterflies, sitting on a blanket and having a picnic. He closed his eyes and I dropped a strawberry into his mouth. Then I closed my eyes and he gently pushed me down on the blanket and we kissed, his lips tasting like strawberries.

I don't know what happened after that because I fell asleep. The next sound I heard was the ringing of Mom's alarm clock.

———

We went back to the same boring routine: school in the morning, homework and free time after lunch, evening together, early bedtime. Danny and I tried to argue that it was the end of June—summer vacation—but Mom insisted on continuing her classes.

"I don't want you two sitting around and doing nothing all day," she explained. "Our school keeps you focused on learning, not worrying."

I looked forward to the twice-a-day telephone with the neighbors, hoping at least to hear how Blaine was doing from Connie, since I was too far away to talk to him directly.

"What's the matter, Erin?" Mom asked the second day home, soon after we'd returned to the bedroom classroom after our morning neighbor talk.

Connie hadn't relayed any message from Blaine and I must have been acting mopey. "Nothing." I lowered my head.

"Are you sure? You've been awfully quiet since coming back."

When I raised my head, my brother was smirking at me. "She likes Blaine," he said. "I saw how she looked at him."

Danny rolled his eyes, opened his mouth, and clutched his heart.

The little rat!

"Is that true?" Mom whispered.

I shrugged, but didn't say anything.

"I see," my mother said, scooting from her desk to my chair. "You miss that boy," she said softly, caressing my shoulders. It was a statement, not a question.

I nodded and looked down again, my eyes filling with tears.

"It's okay, hon," Mom continued. "You'll see him again."

That's when I started to cry. I knew I'd see Blaine again, but that wasn't the problem. Next time, we wouldn't be alone. *When would he have a chance to kiss me?*

I cried even harder.

———

In the afternoon, I escaped to my room, closed the door, and sat by the window with my sketchbook. Of course Cyndy Louise was still patrolling the street. She was bright yellow now, completely bald, with eyes and ears on an otherwise blank face—an unfinished naked and sexless doll. Only her arms and legs still looked human.

Grabbing a pencil, I stopped thinking about Cyndy Louise and drew a portrait of Blaine. He was leaning against a fence, smiling happily with that cute grin. I tried to capture the twinkle in his eyes, but I'm not sure I got it right.

After finishing, I studied the sketch. It was okay, though not my best work. If I asked Mom and Danny who the person in the picture was, they would have figured it out. But I wasn't going to show it to them. I flipped to an empty page and drew another unicorn.

———

When we heard Mr. Douglas' whistle, Mom opened the window for the four o'clock telephone. That's when I smelled it. "Something's burning," I said, pointing towards the right. "Look, there's the smoke."

"Fire," my mother whispered. "It's coming from..."

"Good afternoon!" Mr. Douglas shouted from across the street before Mom finished her sentence.

"There's a fire near here!" Mom yelled to him. "Can you see it?"

"No!" Mrs. Douglas called from another second floor window. "Just the smoke!"

I heard our next-door neighbor's voice and then Danny ran into my room. "Mrs. Perez says the fire's on Hamilton Street," he told us.

That was the block behind the woods.

"Find out if anyone knows more!" Mr. Douglas yelled.

A few seconds later, I heard soft sounds as Mrs. Perez talked to Connie and then told Danny, who immediately relayed the message to Mom and me. "Bobby's mom says the fire's huge and she's afraid it'll spread to the woods!"

No one said anything because we all knew if the fire went through the woods to Walnut Lane, our homes would be next. And I realized something else: Blaine was in the Fisher's house, third from the end.

———

Mom closed the window and I sat on my bed thinking very scary thoughts.

"Erin?" my mother whispered. "You're so pale. Are you okay?"

"I'm worried about the fire," I said softly. That part was true, but I didn't mention Blaine.

Mom sat next to me and held my hand. "It'll be okay," she

said. "We've gotten through everything else and we'll get through this too." She smiled and I forced myself to nod.

I don't think she believed what she said, but it wouldn't have done any good to argue. Also, I didn't want to scare Danny, who'd come into my room. Maybe he didn't understand how bad a fire would be for us.

"Do you think it'd kill her?" my brother asked as he stared at the street. "The fire, I mean. Maybe it could kill all those touchers. Then it'd turn out to be a real good thing."

Mom shrugged. "I don't know about that," she said. "But let's not talk about the fire anymore. How about a game of cards? Gin anyone?"

Danny shook his head.

"No," I said.

My mother looked at both of us. "I'm not going to lie to you," she began. "Fire could be a big problem if it spreads into the woods. But even if that happens, we'll find a way to survive. I don't want you two to worry about it now. We still have time and the fire may die down, the wind could shift, or it could even rain."

She turned towards the window. "In fact, it's cloudy right now so we might get some rain tonight."

I closed my eyes tightly and prayed hard to the rain gods.

———

I guess the gods weren't listening because it didn't rain that night. When I woke up and opened my window, it still smelled like smoke. But when I poked my head outside, I couldn't see any fire. The only good thing was it didn't seem very windy.

We didn't talk much at breakfast. I could tell that Mom and Danny were thinking about the fire too. Although I couldn't answer most of Mom's questions during school, she didn't push me like she usually did.

Just before the ten o'clock telephone, Mom and I dashed into my room and I opened the window again. It was even smokier than before.

"We still smell the smoke!" Mr. Douglas hollered after greeting us. "Norma, call down the street and find out if the fire has spread!"

We waited for the report from Bobby's mom, whose house was next to the woods. I ran into Danny's room so I could hear Mrs. Perez.

The message relayed from Mrs. Mitchell wasn't good: The fire was spreading and it was closer to the woods. She thought it could reach her house before the end of the day.

"They have to get out!" Mr. Douglas shouted to us. "How can we help them?"

Danny and I looked at each other. What could we do? Cyndy Louise was still outside, a yellow faceless blob thing. I didn't know if the fire would hurt her, but she didn't seem to mind the smoke.

And if the fire spread to the Mitchell's house, it would continue through the rest of the block. I turned from the window as my eyes started to water.

———

After the telephone talk, Mom cancelled the rest of school. We were all too upset to concentrate on anything but the approaching fire. The three of us sat around the kitchen table trying to come up with a plan.

"There must be something we can do," Mom said.

"Bobby's over there," Danny whispered, lowering his head.

I felt bad for my brother. But I also felt bad for Blaine and the rest of us. Even if our block escaped the fire, what did we have to look forward to? We were still trapped like rats in our house cages. The only difference was that right now our cages were about to go up in flames.

"What about using the water hydrant and the hoses?" Mom suggested.

"Didn't Cyndy Louise rip the hoses apart?" I asked.

"Not all of them," Danny said. "Just the ones attached."

"But we can't get to the hydrant unless it rains," I pointed out.

"If it rains, we may be okay anyway," Danny said.

"The hydrant's too far away from the houses by the woods," Mom said. "And we couldn't set up enough hoses."

"Unless it rains," I repeated.

As we sat quietly, Muffles waddled over to each of us and nuzzled our knees, hoping for a little attention. But we ignored him, focusing on the fire.

"They're gonna have to run," Danny whispered.

"No." I shook my head. "They can't run fast enough. She'll touch them."

"Maybe not," he said, smiling at me.

———

My brother is a pretty smart kid. After he told Mom and me his idea, I felt a little hope for the Mitchells. It didn't solve the problem of the fire spreading, but if that happened, we'd all die anyway. For now, maybe Bobby and his mom could escape to another house further up the block.

Just before the four o'clock telephone talk, I opened my window and the smoke was thicker. When Mrs. Mitchell reported that the fire had spread into the woods, we relayed Danny's idea to her.

"They're going to try it!" Mr. Douglas yelled to us. "Rhonda and Blaine will both be ready to take them in, depending on where Cyndy Louise is!"

Their escape was set for five o'clock, giving them enough

time to apply Danny's plan and also pack a couple of things to carry in backpacks. They couldn't take much because they would have to move quickly, only they weren't planning to outrun Cyndy Louise. We all knew that was impossible.

Just before five o'clock, Mom, Danny, and I gathered in my room to find out if the escape plan worked. When I opened the window, it still smelled very smoky.

The Douglasses waved to us from their second floor windows across the street and Mrs. Douglas held up both hands with her fingers crossed. Then we waited. It seemed like hours before we heard anything, but it probably wasn't more than five minutes.

"They made it!" Mr. Douglas shouted. "Thank you, Danny! Your plan worked!"

"Way to go, kid!" I said, pounding my brother on his back.

"It wasn't that hard to figure out," Danny said, grinning. "You just gotta remember that she doesn't like water."

Danny's idea had been for Bobby and his mom to soak their clothes, put them back on, and soak their hair, faces, hands, legs, shoes—everything they were wearing, including the backpacks they would carry, and go into the street like that, soaking wet.

The Mitchells had walked quickly—not run—and when Cyndy Louise got near them, she had seen the dripping water and backed away, not trying to touch them. Bobby and his mom crossed the street and went into the Fisher's house. Now they were with Blaine.

I closed my eyes. *With Blaine...Where I wanted to be.*

CHAPTER 22 – Fire Starter

The fire continued to spread. At the next morning's neighborhood talk, we learned flames were halfway through the woods and heading for Walnut Lane. We'd all been dumping our garbage back there so those filled plastic bags would probably make the fire even stronger.

"The Mitchells will have to move again and so will the Weisses," Mom said as we returned to her bedroom for school. "After the empty houses, Rhonda and her son and the people in the Fisher's place are the closest to the fire."

People in the Fisher's place. That included Blaine. "But if the fire keeps coming..." I started to say.

"We'll take this one step at a time, Erin," Mom said, interrupting me. "The wind could shift, it could rain..."

"...or the fire could keep growing till we're all trapped," I added. "Then running outside soaking wet won't help us 'cause we'll have no place to run to and when we dry off, Cyndy Louise or one of the other touchers will..."

"That's enough," my mother whispered, nodding towards Danny, who sat next to me, staring at the unopened textbook on his lap. Mom glanced at her notes. "Okay, back to class. Both of you had science homework. Erin, you go first."

———

We had better news in the afternoon's telephone talk. The wind had died down and the neighbors at the end of our block thought the fire had slowed too. Although it still burned in the woods, the flames hadn't spread into the Mitchell's house or what used to be the Santangelo's house.

"Do you think we're gonna be okay?" Danny asked when the talk was over.

"I hope so," Mom said. "At least everyone down the street should be all right for the rest of today." She smiled at us. "Do you two want to play a game of poker or gin?"

"Not me," Danny said, racing out of my room.

I shook my head.

As she headed for my door, Mom turned and looked at me sadly. "Please, Erin," she said. "Try not to worry about the fire."

I shrugged and glanced out the window. Like usual, Cyndy Louise walked along Walnut Lane, moving towards us, the smoke not bothering her at all. But something was different: She carried a long branch and half of it was burning.

"Mom! Danny!" I shouted. "Come back here!"

My mother and brother rushed into the room.

"What's wrong?" Mom asked.

"Look at her!" I pointed out the window.

"Oh, my God," my mother whispered. "She's going to start a fire."

———

Cyndy Louise reached Mrs. Perez's house, waving the burning stick like it was some kind of new toy.

"Danny," Mom said, grabbing my brother's arm. "Put Muffles outside. Maybe he can distract her." Then she faced me. "Come into Danny's room. If we both yell real loud, maybe Norma'll hear us." We opened the side window and shouted.

A short time later, Mrs. Perez opened her upstairs window. "What's the matter?" she called.

"Cyndy Louise's in front of your house with a burning torch!" Mom hollered. "Do you hear Muffles barking? We sent him out to bother her and buy us some time!"

"Time to do what?" Mrs. Perez asked. "If I run out, she'll touch me!"

Just then, I remembered something. "Don't you have a water sprinkler system?" I shouted. "Can you turn on the water without going outside?"

"No!" Mrs. Perez yelled. "Not without electricity!"

"Is there any other way to turn it on?" I asked.

"The valves are behind the house in a box on the ground to the left of the garage!" she called.

"Erin, you can't go outside," my mother said, clutching my arm.

"We can't just let her burn down our houses."

"Cyndy Louise is..."

"...in front of Mrs. Perez's house dealing with Muffles," I said, finishing Mom's sentence. "I still hear the barks. I've got to go out and turn on the water. I'll wet myself first like the Mitchells did."

"You're not going alone."

Shrugging, I stuck my head out the window again. "How do you start the sprinkler?" I shouted.

"Turn the valves counterclockwise—and you may need a wrench!"

I rushed into the bathroom and quickly splashed water all over my face, body, arms, and legs.

Danny, who had been in my room watching Muffles battle Cyndy Louise, came to the bathroom door.

"You're going out?" he asked.

"Yeah. I'm turning on Mrs. Perez's sprinkler system by

hand. There's a box outside, next to the garage."

"I'm going with you," he said, pushing me away from the sink and wetting himself.

I heard Mom's voice behind us. "You're not going anywhere by yourselves. I'll meet you by Norma's garage. Be careful. If Cyndy Louise comes close, don't rely on the water protecting you. Run away."

Danny and I moved as quietly as we could from the rear door through our yard to Mrs. Perez's garage. At least the sprinkler valves were in the backyard. In front of the house, Muffles was barking and growling, hopefully keeping Cyndy Louise busy.

"Here it is," Danny whispered, opening a rectangular plastic box with eight valves inside.

"Which one works the front sprinkler?" I asked.

"We gotta turn them all till we find it." Danny twisted one of the knobs, but it didn't budge.

"Let me try," I whispered, shoving his hand away. But I couldn't turn the valve either.

I heard footsteps and jumped up as Mom approached, soaking wet and holding a wrench. Kneeling on the grass, she used the wrench to twist one of the knobs. Water sprayed somewhere nearby, but I couldn't see where it was coming from.

Then I heard a thump in the front yard, followed by whimpers from Muffles.

"She must've hit him," Danny whispered. "Poor brave dog."

"I hope she didn't burn him," I murmured.

Mom turned another valve with the wrench and I heard more water shooting up somewhere in the yard.

Danny poked my arm. "Cyndy Louise," he whispered.

I looked up and saw the toucher about twenty feet from us, near the front of Mrs. Perez's garage. As I watched, she lifted her fire stick toward the siding.

At that moment, another sprinkler shot up and sprayed water in a large semicircle that included where Cyndy Louise was standing. Dropping the flaming branch, she stepped back, wiping the water from her yellow body with both hands and staring at the spouting liquid. She must have been too hypnotized by the water to notice the three of us lying flat in the grass.

Cyndy Louise stood there for a few minutes, out of the path of the sprinkler, rubbing her arms and legs until she was completely dry. Then she turned from Mrs. Perez's house and walked away.

———

"She didn't take the stick," I whispered when Cyndy Louise was out of our sight.

"It's still burning a little," Danny said. "See the smoke?"

I got up slowly, looking at the stick on the ground. It sizzled, but with the sprinkler spraying it lightly with water, it wasn't setting fire to the grass.

Then I heard a patter of small steps, followed by several loud barks as Muffles joined us, leaping at our legs.

"I'm so glad you're okay," I whispered, patting the brave dog. "Let's move."

After we all made it into the kitchen, Mom quickly locked the door and we rushed upstairs to my room. "She's heading the other way," I said. "And if she goes into the woods, she can get another fire stick." I turned to my mother. "We don't have a sprinkler set-up, right?"

My mother nodded.

"So if she comes back here with more fire, what do we do?"

Mom shook her head sadly. "I don't know," she whispered.

———

Mom and Danny went back to their rooms, Muffles scampered away, and I grabbed my sketchpad and started a new drawing of Blaine, this time standing in front of the pool. But I couldn't concentrate because I kept watching for Cyndy Louise. I hadn't seen her since she left Mrs. Perez's house. *No good.*

Even with the window closed, I smelled more smoke. Opening my window, I stuck out my head. High flames were shooting out from somewhere at the end of our side of the block. *Not Blaine's house!*

"Mom! Danny!" Again I called them into my room and had both lean out the window.

"I think it's the last house that's on fire, the one right next to the woods," Danny said.

"The Santangelo's house," Mom whispered.

"But the family moved into Mr. Ortega's," I reminded her. "So no one's inside there now."

"Thank goodness," my mother murmured as she closed the window. My room stunk of smoke.

"That fire can spread to the other houses," I said.

"Or she can come here again," Danny added. "I'm gonna get the water guns and look for balloons." He ran out of my room.

I glanced at my mother and shrugged. "What good will that do? He won't be able to squirt enough water or throw enough water balloons on Cyndy Louise to stop her. She'll just move to a different side of the house." Then I had another thought—a really bad one. "What if she comes back at night, when we're all sleeping?"

My mother smiled at me. "We won't all be asleep. We'll take shifts tonight like soldiers, watching for Cyndy Louise." Reaching over, she grasped both my hands. "It'll be okay, Erin. We've gotten this far and we're not going to let her burn down our house. I promise."

"How can you be so sure?"

"Trust me on this."

I didn't believe Mom was confident about her promise. She was just trying to be strong for us so I didn't say anything and hugged her tightly.

———

We divided the night into eleven hours—from eight p.m. till seven in the morning—and each of us got three or four hours of guard duty. Danny had the first shift, Mom took the four hours in the middle of the night, and I got the end, from four a.m. till seven. Mine was the best deal: It was the shortest, I'd get to sleep most of the night, and we were up by seven anyway. Of course my reasoning only made sense if nothing happened.

And something did. "Get up, Erin!" my mother shouted sometime in the early morning. "She's here with more fire!"

I shot out of bed immediately. Hearing that someone is trying to burn down your house will make a person move real fast.

Mom had called me from Danny's room. I turned on the flashlight, stepped into a pair of jeans, tucked in my nighttime tee, and ran into my brother's room.

The window was open and Cyndy Louise stood below, holding another fire stick. Danny leaned out the window and squirted at her with two water pistols. But even with my brother's great aim, he couldn't reach her. "It's too far!" he yelled. "I wish I could've found some balloons."

Using the flashlight, I made it to the kitchen as fast as I could, grabbed a pot and two water bottles and rushed back upstairs. The commotion woke Muffles from his kitchen doggy bed and he followed me.

"Here," I said, giving the pot to Mom. "Let's fill up these and throw water on her."

My mother and I raced to the bathroom. I filled the bottles in the sink while Mom used the tub.

"Hurry!" Danny shouted. "I'm not getting her wet and she's burning the house!"

I ran into his room with the filled bottles and gave them to Danny, figuring he had a better chance of hitting her. He dumped the first one, but it just grazed her arm. He had better luck with the second bottle—the water splashed all over her face.

Cyndy Louise moved away from the house, rubbing her face hard with both hands as if she'd been contaminated. But she didn't pick up the burning stick so flames were shooting up from the ground onto our house.

"We have to put out the fire!" Mom yelled. "Fill the bottles with more water and I'm taking this pot downstairs."

Danny and I rushed to the bathroom. My brother filled his water pistols and I filled the two bottles. Then we followed Mom to the first floor.

———

The fire outside lit up the sky so when I peeked through the side of our boarded up living room window, I got a clear view of Cyndy Louise a couple of feet away, still trying to wipe the water off what was left of her face.

Smoke was filtering into the house and I felt the wall next to me—it was getting hot.

"Come!" my mother commanded, waving her flashlight at Muffles.

"What are you doing?" I asked.

"Maybe the dog can get her away from here like at Norma's house," she said.

I heard the back door open, followed by Muffles' loud

barks.

"Both of you!" Mom called from the kitchen. "Fill up the water guns too!"

Danny and I loaded our weapons at the sink, coughing because the smoke was real bad.

"Danny, see if she's still there," Mom said.

My brother rushed into the smoky living room and then back to the kitchen, choking. "She's standing by the fire and Muffles is barking at her," he said between gasps.

"We don't have a choice anymore," my mother whispered, waving away the smoke. "We can't stay here so we have to go outside."

———

We used Danny's idea again: wetting our bodies—especially the areas Cyndy Louise could easily touch. Then with our supply of water weapons, we walked out the kitchen door with Mom leading the way. Even though it was the middle of the night, we didn't need our flashlights to see.

"If you dry off before we chase her away, run inside or to the sprinkler," my mother said, indicating the water that still sprayed in a semicircle near Mrs. Perez's garage.

When the three of us reached the burning side of our house, we saw Cyndy Louise lunging at Muffles. The dog gave a happy yelp and ran to meet us.

"No, Muffles!" Mom shouted. "Go get her!" She pointed at Cyndy Louise, now rushing our way.

Danny fired both water pistols, hitting her in the face and arm. Cyndy Louise backed away and again did her rubbing act as Muffles stood nearby, barking and nipping at her yellow skin. But she ignored him, concentrating on drying herself.

Mom threw the pot of water on the fire and I heard a hissing sound as smoke shot up and some flames disappeared.

But the side of our house was still burning.

"We're going inside!" my mother yelled. "We need more water."

Since I still had two full bottles, I poured them on the fire and then we all headed back into our burning house.

———

The kitchen was smokier than before. After we splashed water on ourselves again, we refilled the pistols, bottles, and pot and returned outside.

Cyndy Louise must have dried herself—and we weren't soaked enough—because as soon as she saw us coming, she lunged forward, arm outstretched and ready to touch Danny, who was in front.

"Get back!" he yelled, squirting her face once more.

She followed his order and jumped away, yellow hands pawing at her eyes and the empty parts of her face.

Meanwhile, Mom and I again poured water on the fire. Although it hadn't spread, it continued to burn the side of our house.

"She's coming!" Danny yelled as he dashed for the rear door. Mom and I followed and this time, so did Muffles.

Just seconds after we were all inside, we heard heavy pounding on the door combined with the shuffling sound of the knob being turned. Thankfully, Mom had locked the door.

"Must...put...out...fire," she said, gasping between each word. Using her flashlight, Mom pointed to the cabinet holding the pots and pans. "Take...up...fill...pour."

I connected the dots: We should take more pots upstairs and fill them with water. Then we were supposed to dump the water on the fire below.

"C'mon!" I poked Danny's side and we each grabbed a pot and ran upstairs as quickly as we could. I heard paw steps behind us as Muffles followed. In the bathroom, I filled my pot in the sink and Danny used the tub. Then we ran to Danny's room and opened the window. It was very smoky, but at least some fresh air entered the house too. Muffles watched us; I heard his heavy panting.

Danny and I poured our pots down the burning side of the house, watching as streams of water reached the fire. This time it helped, the flames becoming small flickers.

"One more," I said as I returned to the bathroom and refilled my pot. Danny did the same.

After we dumped our second pots of water, I didn't see any more fire. But it was still smoky. Danny popped his head out the window, swatting away the smoke, and then turned to me. "Where's Mom?" he asked.

I looked at my brother and then rushed down the steps with Danny and Muffles on my heels. Shining my flashlight into the kitchen, I saw my mother lying on the floor, face down.

————

Danny and I turned Mom around. "Is she alive?" he asked, sounding really scared.

Putting my head against her chest, I heard a faint heartbeat. "Yes, thank goodness, but we've got to get her outside."

"Water first," Danny said, moving to the sink. He filled the pot Mom had been using and poured water all over her face and body. She didn't stir. "Now us."

After we wet ourselves again, Danny loaded his water pistols and together we dragged Mom through the door, Muffles trailing behind us. With the fire out, the night was dark again so I shined the flashlight in front of us.

"Bark at Cyn...!" Before I finished the order, Muffles rushed at the approaching toucher, yelping and snapping. Cyndy Louise swatted the dog out of her way and since I was the closest, extended her arm towards me.

Although I was wet, I didn't want to test whether I was wet enough to keep her from touching me. "Danny!" I yelled.

"Got it!" My brother squirted his gun, hitting her yellow nippleless chest and she backed away, rubbing what used to be her breasts to wipe away the water.

Mom still lay on the ground next to us, eyes closed and not moving. Kneeling, I gently wiped her wet face. "Please wake up," I pleaded. "You've got to wake up." I shook her body a little, trying not to be too rough.

"Danny, what do we do now?"

"Try mouth-to-mouth."

I wasn't sure how to do that, but I put my lips against Mom's and breathed into her mouth. Out of the corner of my eye, I saw Cyndy Louise heading back to us, both arms outstretched. Danny squirted her again, this time hitting her ear and head. She stopped moving and concentrated on removing the water.

"Mmmm."

The mumbling sound came from my mother. I pulled my mouth away and looked at Mom's face. Her eyes were open and she smiled at me.

"Honey," she whispered. "Where am I?"

"Outside and Cyndy Louise is here. Can you sit up? We've got to go back in."

"I'll try." She lifted herself into a sitting position.

"Mom's okay!" I called to Danny who was watching Cyndy Louise dry herself.

"We gotta go," he said. "She's coming again and I'm out of water."

We each grabbed one of Mom's arms and, half pushing her, raced to the door. Muffles, still barking at Cyndy Louise, covered our backs. When we were all inside the kitchen, I locked the door. There was a heavy pounding and the knob was twisted a couple of times, but then it became wonderfully quiet.

CHAPTER 23 - Reunited

Danny and I opened all the upstairs windows and while I shined the flashlight, he leaned out to squirt the windows and sides of our house. That was my idea—just in case Cyndy Louise noticed the open windows and tried to climb in.

"How could she get up here?" my brother asked as he dangled out my window to finish spraying. "Does she have a ladder? She's never used one."

"She could go into the garage of an empty house and find a ladder," I said. "We need fresh air in here and can't take that chance."

When we finished, we walked into Mom's bedroom. She was resting on top of the covers, but her eyes were open.

"How do you feel?" I asked, taking her hand.

"Tired, dry throat, but not bad." She spoke in a raspy whisper and smiled at us.

"I'll get you water," Danny said, grabbing my flashlight and racing into the bathroom. He returned with a small cup of water and gave it to Mom.

"Thanks." Pushing herself up, she took a small sip. "The fire?"

"We put it out," I said. "We did what you said and poured

water on it. And just now we opened all the windows upstairs, wet them, and Danny sprayed the outside of the house so Cyndy Louise won't try to climb up and get in."

"Good." Mom put the water on her night table and lay back on the pillow. I think she was too weak to talk much.

"Try to get some sleep," I said, stroking her hand. "We'll keep watch the rest of the night."

She nodded and closed her eyes.

———

There wasn't much nighttime left so it didn't pay for Danny and me to take shifts. For the next couple of hours, I sat in my room and Danny sat in his.

I looked out the window, breathing mostly fresh air, and watched Cyndy Louise walk up and down the block. *Boring!* But at least she wasn't carrying any new fire sticks. Twice I checked on Mom to make sure she was okay. Both times, she was asleep.

I was really glad when it started to get light outside and the alarm clock finally sounded. I raced into my mother's room. "Did you sleep well?" I asked.

"Yes, thanks." She studied me. "Erin, you look beat. You must be exhausted after last night." My brother entered the room. "...and you too, Danny."

Mom shook her head. "No school today," she said. "Go back to bed and I'll watch out for Cyndy Louise. You didn't see her setting any other fires late last night, did you?"

"No," we both muttered.

"There's not much smoke anymore," Danny said. "Maybe the fire's out."

"Let's hope so," Mom said.

After Danny resprayed the outside of the house and the upstairs windows, we closed them part of the way. Then my brother and I went to bed, leaving Mom in charge of monitoring Cyndy Louise's activities. I don't know about Danny, but I fell asleep as soon as my head hit the pillow.

———

I woke up to the wonderful pattering sound of rain on the roof. When I glanced at my watch, I saw it was 12:30. After taking a cold shower, I dressed and went downstairs, feeling really hungry.

Mom and Danny were in the kitchen with Muffles, having lunch.

"Hi, sleepyhead," Mom said smiling.

"Sorry." I scooped powder and added water to make a glass of milk.

"I was just kidding, hon. After last night, you needed the rest. Danny only got up a few minutes ago."

"The air's much better in here," I said, changing the subject. It seemed less smoky.

"Yeah," Danny agreed. "The fire's out."

"How do you know?" I asked.

"From Jennifer Mitchell at this morning's telephone," Mom explained. "I couldn't talk to the neighbors, but I listened in my room and just told Danny the news."

"We're very lucky then," I said, pouring Rice Krispies into a bowl and adding some of my milk to it.

"Yes," Mom agreed. "I checked the damage when it started raining and it's not too bad. The side's a bit soft, but I don't think it's weak enough for her to push it in and get into the house."

"Good." I finished my cereal and reached for a box of crackers.

"Erin," Mom said quietly. "We weren't the only house that burned last night."

I stopped chewing and stared at my mother.

"The Santangelo's house," she continued. "We don't know if Cyndy Louise started the fire or if it spread from the woods." She shrugged. "In any case, Mrs. Mitchell said the house is completely gone."

"But the Santangelos weren't in there, right?" I asked.

My mother nodded. "The family is still in Ramón Ortega's house."

I continued eating crackers and thinking about the fire—and what could have happened to the Santangelo family. They'd been lucky twice. How long could their luck—and ours—continue?

———

After lunch, we opened the upstairs windows wide. Then we got into our raingear and hit the street with Muffles. It had just been four days since we'd seen our neighbors, but it seemed much longer. Mrs. Perez must have turned off her sprinklers because no water was spraying in her yard.

"Mom, can I please go down the block by myself?" I asked.

She looked closely at me. "I don't want you to get trapped again."

"It's pouring right now and I have a water gun just in case. I'll make sure I'm wet so I can come home even if it stops."

My mother gave me a funny little smile and then looked at her watch. "You've got fifteen minutes. Then find Danny and me. We'll probably be outside with the Mitchells."

Nodding, I grabbed my umbrella and ran. I passed the Santangelo family, standing in front of Mr. Ortega's house with Mrs. Perez. Maybe they were talking about last night's fire, but I didn't stop to find out. After waving to them, I continued down the street, rushing by the Chou's house. I didn't see Connie and Emily.

I slowed to a walk when I neared the Fisher's house. Then

I reached under the umbrella and patted my hair, hoping the wet ponytail didn't look too awful. When I didn't see Blaine outside, I rang the doorbell.

He opened the door and gave me a big smile. "I guess it's rainin' out."

I returned his smile. "I guess it is."

"Can you come in?" He moved aside and gestured to the living room.

Mom hadn't said anything about having to stay outside. "Sure." I closed the umbrella, hung my raincoat on the hall closet's doorknob, and stepped into the living room.

Blaine shut the door and followed me. "Man, I missed you," he whispered, grasping both my hands and nuzzling my hair with his mouth.

"I missed you too," I said softly. "I thought about you all the time, even with the fire."

"Yeah," he murmured, his mouth still on my wet hair. "It was close."

"She set our house on fire too," I whispered.

"Really?" He stepped back, studying me.

Blaine said he'd been up late checking the fire in the Santangelo's house—watching that it didn't spread—and missed the morning's telephone talk. I told him what had happened to us.

"You could've died." He lifted my chin and stared into my eyes. Then, placing his lips on mine, he kissed me tenderly. I closed my eyes and felt his hands travel along my tee shirt, lightly touching my breasts.

Opening my eyes, I gazed at his face.

"Should I stop?" he whispered.

I shook my head and closed my eyes again.

He was very gentle, fingering the top of me as if I was some kind of delicate flower he was exploring. I kept my eyes closed as his kiss became stronger and he prodded inside my mouth, his tongue searching for mine.

He smoothed my hair and lowered me onto the couch so I was lying face up. "Erin," he whispered as he finally ended the kiss and caressed my arms. My eyes were still closed as he touched them lightly with his fingertips. It all felt so good...

There was a loud knock on the door.

"Damn," Blaine mumbled, moving away from me. "Why now?"

I sat up as Blaine opened the front door.

"Hi," my mother said. "Is Erin here? I gave her a time to meet me and it's past that...Oh, there you are." She poked her head inside, holding Muffles on his leash.

I reached the entrance hoping I didn't look too disheveled. "Sorry," I murmured, grabbing my raincoat and umbrella. "We were talking about yesterday's fires and I lost track of time." I turned around, trying to sound casual. "Bye, Blaine. It was nice seeing you again."

"Same here."

Then I walked into the rainy street with my mother and Muffles.

———

Mom didn't say anything when we left Blaine's and I wasn't in any mood to talk. But the silence felt uncomfortable. "Where's Danny?" I finally asked.

"At the Mitchell's. I left him with Bobby when I had to come and get you."

Bad topic. "What did you find out about the fire in the Santangelo's house?" *Much safer topic.*

"Jennifer thought it spread from the burning woods and Cyndy Louise didn't start it, but she's not sure." Mom shrugged. "That house is totally destroyed...See?"

We stopped in front of piles of twisted black pieces of wood that were still smoking, even in the steady rain. Muffles sniffed at several of the burnt chunks and then backed away.

It could've been us...

Mom must have read my thoughts. "Don't think about it, Erin," she said, taking my arm and gently pulling me away from the blackened ruins. "All the fires are out now so we're not in that kind of danger."

Not fire danger, just normal Cyndy Louise toucher danger. Normal? What was normal anymore?

―――――

As Mom, Danny, Muffles, and I walked up the block in the rain, we met Connie and Emily, who were talking to Mrs. Weiss and her son, Jake.

"Rin! Rin! Rin!" Emily hollered, opening her arms wide when she saw me.

"Hi, Emmy." Rushing over, I hugged the little girl. "How're you doing?"

"Wanna out," she said, pushing at the buckles that locked her into the stroller.

"No, sweetie. It's raining and you can't run around."

"Out!" she shrieked. "Wanna out!"

I backed away as Emily's yells became louder. "Sorry," I whispered to Connie. "I didn't mean to start trouble."

"It's not your fault," Connie said as she comforted her daughter. "She's been cooped up in the house for so long and now she's stuck in the stroller."

"What's goin' on here?"

When I heard the familiar drawl, I turned—and there was Blaine, standing in the rain without an umbrella and smiling at me again.

"Emmy doesn't like being strapped in her stroller," I

explained.

"Can't blame her," he agreed.

Connie unfastened the straps. "I'm taking her out of jail and we'll walk in the rain together...How's that, honey?" She smiled at the little girl. "Want to go for a walk with Mommy?"

Emily beamed and clapped her hands. "Rin come too!" She clutched at my arm.

"Can I?" I asked Mom.

"Not for too long. Be back in ten minutes."

I nodded.

"Do you want to walk with us?" Connie asked Mrs. Weiss, who had been talking to my mother while Jake petted Muffles.

"No," Connie's friend replied, pointing to the little boy in the stroller with the makeshift cover. "He's too wet so we're going inside to dry off."

Blaine, water dripping from his hair into his face, grinned at Connie and me and shrugged. "I kinda like the rain. Is it okay if I tag along with you ladies?"

"Sure," Connie said, smiling. "You can even wheel the stroller, just in case my little walker gets tired."

We stepped into the street and headed slowly up the block towards my house, Connie and Emmy on one side, then Blaine next to me, wheeling the stroller. I held my umbrella over the two of us.

"Was your mother mad?" Blaine whispered.

"Yeah, but she didn't say anything."

He was quiet for a moment.

"House!" Emmy shouted, pointing to her home.

"Do you want to go inside?" Connie asked. "Are you getting too wet?" She was trying to keep the umbrella over her daughter, but water was seeping through.

"Wet," the little girl said, sticking her arm into the rain. "Wet!" she repeated, giggling happily.

"I'll take that as a 'no,'" Connie said. "But we'll stop here anyway. Thanks for the company." Smiling at Blaine and me, she took the stroller from him.

———

As the two of us walked together on the rainy street, I peeked at my watch. *Five minutes left...*

"Why'd you go to school here instead of closer to home?" I asked.

"I always rooted for the Patriots," Blaine said. "Besides, UMass has a good sports management program—or at least, had one..."

"Was that your major?"

"I was a freshman so I didn't choose a major yet, but that was my plan."

"How about your family?"

"I've got my mom and a younger sister, Maddie, who just turned thirteen. My dad's not in the picture—he left us when I was eight."

"I'm sorry."

Blaine shrugged. "Thanks, but he wasn't the best father so I don't miss him."

"Oh." *I missed my Dad—very much.*

We walked quietly until Blaine spoke. "When will I see you again?" he asked.

"I don't know." I glanced at him. "Are you still planning on leaving here and trying to get home to Atlanta?"

"It's goin' to be much harder without Zach. I miss him a lot." He shook his head. "I can't get there all by myself...Know anyone that'd want to come with me?"

I hadn't expected that question and I didn't have an answer so I glanced at my watch. "Sorry," I said. "My walking time's up."

CHAPTER 24 – Scouting Party

We spent the rest of the afternoon outside in the rain, talking to everyone. I didn't see Blaine again, but that was okay because I still didn't know what to tell him. How brave was I? The touchers were everywhere. If I went away with him, I might never see Mom and Danny again. And of course, I could die. Or what if I went with Blaine and he died?

I tried to shove those questions into the back of my brain and concentrate on the present, which, as Mr. Douglas reminded me, wasn't so wonderful. "How're you doing with food, Maura?" he asked my mother.

"Not great. We've only got about a week or two left. How about you?"

Mrs. Douglas shrugged. "We'd put aside so much, I thought we'd never run out. But after a month and a half, we're getting low. What are we going to do?"

"Not the supermarket again?" I asked, remembering that disgusting place.

"No," Mom said. "We can't go back there. All the food stores have to be crawling with rats, bodies, touchers, and Lord knows what else."

"What about other empty houses?" Danny asked. "Like on

our block."

"Good idea," Mr. Douglas said. "If we can stay away from the touchers."

I shook my head. "Shouldn't the empty houses belong to the people who are still alive on that street?"

"You're assuming every block has people—and I don't think that's true," my mother pointed out.

"So how do we find a block near here with no people?" I asked.

Danny pointed to our garage. "We go for a car ride and check out neighborhoods."

"We have to do that in the rain," I said. "That's the only time regular people will be outside."

"Only if they've figured out that touchers don't like to get wet," Mr. Douglas said.

His wife grabbed his hand. "Harold, wouldn't everyone still alive know that by now?"

"Not necessarily," he said, shrugging.

"But what about the touchers?" I asked. "They're inside when it rains."

"We should scout a block in the rain and if no one's out, go back when it's not raining," Danny suggested.

"But then Cyndy Louise and the touchers that live there will be outside," Mom said.

"Yeah," Danny agreed. "We'll have to be real careful and..."

"...we could get trapped," I interrupted. "Or killed."

My brother shrugged.

"Let's think about this," Mr. Douglas said. "We'll mention it to the others and maybe we can come up with a better plan."

We agreed, but I didn't have much hope. If we needed food, we couldn't go to a supermarket so we'd have to find empty houses and take our chances with the touchers. Rain or shine? Neither time was good.

———

When we went home for dinner, we closed the upstairs windows. Getting fresh air into the house all afternoon had worked. Now when I took a deep breath, I didn't smell as much smoke. After eating, I peeked through the opening in the living room window and knew it was no longer raining because Cyndy Louise was back outside.

The next morning, it was life as usual: Mom School in her bedroom. I tried to concentrate on the reading assignment, but my mind drifted to Blaine and the last thing he'd said to me. *Did I want to travel with him?* I still didn't know the answer.

"Erin?" Mom looked at me, a puzzled expression on her face.

"What?"

"Are you reading? Your eyes are staring into space, not at the book."

"Sorry. I was thinking about something else." Lowering my head, I tried to focus on the open page on my lap. But every time I started reading the printed words, I heard Blaine's voice asking, "Know anyone that'd want to come with me?"

Finally I closed the book and shook my head. "Sorry, Mom. I have a headache and can't concentrate right now. Can I be excused?"

She stared at me for a moment. "Okay. Take a ten-minute break."

As I rushed out of the room, I heard Danny's whiny voice. "What about me? How come she gets a break and I don't? That's not fair!"

"All right, you can..."

I closed my door so I didn't hear the rest of their conversation. But I could tell my brother won the argument.

———

Soon after I returned to class, it was time for the morning telephone talk. When Mr. Douglas relayed our idea of checking nearby streets during the next rain to see if any homes were empty, the response from our neighbors was positive.

"Who should go?" I asked Mom while she closed my window.

"Not you."

"Why? It'll be safe outside if it's raining."

"What if the car breaks down? We only drove ours once since the bubbles and I don't think any other cars on the block have been driven at all so we don't know how they'll run."

"Blaine used his car more recently," I pointed out.

"Then maybe he should be the one to go."

"But he's not from around here so he doesn't know where to look—and he could get lost." *Scary thought*.

Mom nodded. "That's true. So if he scouts our streets, someone has to go with him—but not you."

"I guess that means I can't go either," Danny said as he came into my room.

"You've got that right," my mother said.

———

In the afternoon telephone talk, Mr. Douglas asked for volunteers to check the neighborhood for empty streets during the next rain.

Mom wouldn't let me or Danny say anything.

"We have our volunteers!" Mr. Douglas shouted to us. "Blaine is taking his car and Lynne and I will go with him!"

"They're too old," I muttered. "What if they're attacked?"

Mom shrugged. "The Douglasses both walk fine and most everyone else has children to take care of."

"But your kids are older and can take of themselves," Danny said as he left his next-door post and entered my room.

194

Mom studied him for a moment. "So you think I should offer to go?" she asked.

"I didn't mean that," my brother said. "I meant you should let Erin and me go with Blaine because I'm the best shot with the water gun and we can both run real fast. Mr. and Mrs. Douglas can't."

"No," Mom said, shaking her head emphatically. "That's not happening."

———

My mother was wrong. When it rained after lunch two days later and the Douglasses weren't outside, we knocked on their door and found out Mrs. Douglas was sick and Mr. Douglas was taking care of her.

"Danny and I have to go with Blaine now," I said to Mom, who was holding Muffles on his leash.

"No. We'll wait till the next time it rains."

"We can't," I argued. "Everyone's food is running out, even the moms with young kids. You heard that yesterday from Connie and Mrs. Weiss."

"Yeah," Danny said. "We gotta do this now."

Mom sighed and looked first at my brother and then at me. "All right," she said. "But I'm going with you." She turned to my brother. "Danny, please tell Blaine that the three of us will scout the neighborhood with him whenever he's ready."

"Let me tell him," I offered. "Give me Muffles and I'll race down the street. It'll be good exercise for both of us."

My mother smiled at me. "Here, Erin," she said, handing me the leash. "Get your exercise—but this time, come right back."

I ran along the street holding my umbrella and Muffles' leash, not even stopping to talk to Connie, who stood in front of her house with Emily and Mrs. Perez. I just waved as I rushed past them.

Blaine wasn't outside so I closed the umbrella and rapped heavily on his door.

"Coming!" he called and seconds later swung the door wide open and smiled. "Erin! I didn't expect to see you here." Muffles nuzzled Blaine's leg and he reached down to pet the dog, glancing behind me. "I thought you were the Douglasses. Where're they? We're supposed to be leavin' soon."

"Sick," I said, catching my breath. "Mrs. Douglas...so we're going with you instead—me, my mom, and brother." I grinned at him. "If it's okay with you."

He grasped my free hand and stared into my eyes. "It's much more than okay...I missed you."

"I missed you too," I whispered, releasing my hand. "But I've got to get right back. I promised my mother I'd just tell you we'd be the ones riding with you today and then go home. And after last time..." My voice drifted off.

"I remember." He smiled at me again and then shrugged. "I gotta finish gettin' ready anyway. I wondered why the Douglasses were so early. They weren't supposed to be here till one."

I checked my watch. It was 12:50. "Okay, then," I said. "We'll all be back in ten minutes, ready to go."

———

At one o'clock, I sat in the front passenger seat of Blaine's blue Honda Civic, with Mom and Danny in the back. Although it was still raining, my brother and I each carried a water gun—just in case—and Mom had two bottles of water in her raincoat pockets.

"Where do you want to go first?" Blaine asked as he drove slowly to the corner.

"Make a right on Barker Street," Mom said. "Then go two

blocks and make another right on Curran Road."

The streets were eerily quiet as Blaine drove past my deserted high school, abandoned cars, and decaying dead bodies. Then from somewhere behind us, I heard sounds of galloping footsteps. "What's that noise?" I asked, turning around.

"It's a bunch of dogs," Danny said. "And they're coming this way."

As Blaine turned into Odell Court, the first street Mom wanted to check, the dogs reached the car and surrounded us, leaping at the windows, barking and snarling loudly.

"Good thing we left Muffles with Norma," Mom said. "He'd be going crazy...Poor dogs, they look so thin."

There were five of them, all so skinny you could see their bones. I don't think they wanted to hurt us; they were just so hungry.

"What'll we do?" I asked Blaine. He had stopped the car, but the dogs continued to try to get at us. One little gray and white mutt stood on the hood, scratching at the front window.

"We sure can't get out," he replied.

"I wish we could feed them," I whispered.

"Honey," Mom said, leaning forward and rubbing my shoulder. "We don't even have enough food for ourselves. That's why we're here."

"I know, but..."

"Did you notice though," Danny interrupted, "there's no one outside now so maybe this block is empty."

"Or maybe they heard the dogs comin' and ran inside," Blaine pointed out. "Anyway, we can't check this place now."

"They don't look like they'd hurt us," I whispered. With its sad black eyes, the little mutt on the hood seemed to be staring right through me.

"They're starving animals and we don't have any food for

them," Mom said. "Who knows what they'd do. Blaine, please go...now."

As he made a U-turn, the little mutt jumped off the car. Then Blaine drove as quickly as possible back to Curran Road. The dogs tried to follow the car, but even though we weren't going fast, they couldn't keep up. Then, finally, they were gone.

———

Blaine reached Curran Road and stopped. "Where to now?" he again asked my mother.

"Let's try the other direction," Mom said. "There are bigger homes on the west side."

"Yeah," Danny agreed. "The rich people lived there."

Blaine drove and we were quiet, each of us staring at the depressing wet roads filled with deserted cars, dead bodies, and messed-up stores—rats jumping in and out of the broken windows. Once or twice, I saw some people walking along side streets. But I couldn't see what they were doing.

A few times, we couldn't continue along Curran Road because cars or trucks blocked the way so Blaine detoured around them. It was like playing a video game in a war zone.

"Make a right here," Mom said and Blaine drove through the smaller street till he reached another intersection. "Turn right," she ordered. "Then go two blocks and make a left."

When we reached Mom's destination, the street sign said "Redleaf Way." I'd never been here, but I could see it used to be a rich neighborhood. The houses were huge, surrounded by large lawns, and they all had lots of windows. Only now, many of the once beautiful windows were broken and the wet road was filled with sharp pieces of glass.

"Be careful," Mom warned as Blaine drove slowly along the quiet street. "We don't want to cut the tires."

"I'm tryin'," Blaine said. "Do you guys see any people here?"

"Nope," Danny replied. "Nobody."

"They could be inside, too scared to come out," I said. "Or maybe someone's watching us from the window...That's what we did when you drove into our street."

"Okay," Blaine said. "Everyone check the windows."

Although I didn't see any movement from behind the windows, the place was giving me the creeps. I shuddered.

"What's wrong?" Blaine asked me.

"It's so spooky here. I don't see anybody, but I still feel like someone's watching."

We reached the dead-end part of the street and that's when I saw them—the bodies—in the tall unmowed grass of a front lawn. There were three people—a man, woman, and boy. At least they were all facedown. *Dead on the dead-end*.

Blaine stopped the car while we studied the bodies, which were partly covered by the grass.

"If people were still living in some of these houses, don't you think they would have buried them?" Mom asked quietly.

"Yeah," Blaine agreed. "It doesn't seem like anyone's here."

"So if no people are alive, then maybe the touchers don't stay here either 'cause there's no one left for them to kill," Danny said.

I nodded and turned to my brother. "That's a good point. Cyndy Louise stays on our street because we're there. If no one's here..."

"Yes," Mom interrupted. "But if we come back for food, one of those toucher things can notice us, even if it's not staying here. You know they're somewhere near, watching."

"We'll have to take that chance," I said.

CHAPTER 25 – Redleaf Way

The rain stopped overnight and by morning the sky was sunny. Judging from the temperature inside our house, it was also real warm. We ate breakfast and had classes until our break for the ten o'clock telephone talk.

Mr. Douglas blew his whistle and waved to Mom and me.

"How is Lynne feeling?" my mother called.

"A little better!" he shouted.

"Tell him about yesterday," I whispered.

My mother nodded. "We found a street we think is empty and may have food!" she hollered. "We want to go back and search the houses there!"

"That's great!" he shouted. "But I still can't leave Lynne!"

"We'll do it!" Mom yelled. "After lunch at one o'clock here! Please pass the message to Blaine! Tell him to be wet!"

"Do you think he'd forget that?" I asked.

Before she had a chance to answer, Danny rushed into my room. "We're all goin? Great!"

"That's not the word I'd use," Mom said. "But we need the food so we can't wait for the Douglasses."

———

Mom, Danny, and I were soaking wet and ready. As they waited behind the front door listening for Blaine's car, I sloshed into the kitchen, grabbed Muffles' two plastic bowls and filled them with dog food and water, which immediately got his attention. Then I walked to the kitchen door, followed by the dog, who sniffed curiously at my dripping clothes and water trail.

"Bye," I said, ruffling Muffles' soft head as I opened the rear door. He dashed into the yard and I quickly placed the bowls outside. "I hope we'll see you soon," I whispered. But Muffles paid no attention to me and ran to the food dish for his unexpected meal.

A few minutes later, Blaine's dented Honda pulled up to our house. After Mom locked the door, Danny and I raced from the porch and I again sat in the front passenger seat.

"Where's Cyndy Louise?" I asked Blaine as Mom joined Danny in the back.

"Down the block. She came after me till she saw I was wet."

As Blaine drove, somehow everything—the bodies and the wrecked cars—looked worse today in the sun. Rats and bugs feasted on the corpses, along with some mangy-looking cats, but no dogs. Blaine honked the horn, trying to get the animals to move. They ignored the sound so he drove slowly, weaving to avoid all the obstacles, alive and dead.

"This is so gross," I mumbled. Then I saw two touchers, both running fast from opposite blocks, zeroing in on us. "Blaine!" I yelled.

"I see them," he said, making a left from Barker into the next side street.

"They're still following," Danny reported.

"Keep going straight," Mom said. "This road connects to Spring Street and we can take it north to Redleaf."

Blaine drove as quickly as he could, swerving around

several cars and bodies.

"I don't see them anymore," Danny said. "I think they're gone."

"That's good," Blaine said. "Then maybe..."

There was a loud thump on the hood as another toucher threw itself onto our car. A bald yellow head leaned against the front window, staring at us.

"Can you see the road?" I asked Blaine.

"Enough, but I'm gonna try to get it off." He zigzagged along the street as the toucher pounded heavily on the glass. If the creature had had a mouth, it probably would have been snarling at us, but all it had were two angry-looking eyes. Unfortunately, it still had two hands, which gripped the hood of the car.

"It's not working," I said.

"Hang on, everyone. I'm gonna make a sharp left." Blaine reached Spring Street and swerved into the larger road, knocking the toucher off the hood and onto the ground. Blaine continued straight as fast as he could.

"It just got up and is chasing us," Danny reported.

Blaine drove even faster.

"It's gone," Danny said.

———

We reached Redleaf Way without any other incidents and Blaine drove slowly along the silent street, again avoiding the broken glass.

"It still looks empty except for the dead people in the back lawn," I said when he returned to the beginning of the block.

"Yeah," Danny agreed. "No toucher either."

"We don't know that for sure," Mom pointed out. "We just don't see any of them outside."

Blaine turned to me and then to the back of the car.

"Everybody still wet?" he asked.

"Yes," I said and Danny and Mom nodded.

"Okay." Blaine parked in the driveway of the first house on the corner, a huge colonial with only one broken window in the middle of the second floor. "Y'all take your water and bags. We're goin' in."

The front door was locked so Blaine found a rock, which he used to smash one of the ground floor windows.

"I hope that noise doesn't bring a toucher," Mom said.

"Me too," Blaine agreed. "But we gotta get in. We don't want to be walkin' around outside here in dry weather." He climbed through the broken window, pointing a loaded water gun.

"It seems clear," Blaine said, opening the front door for us.

We all stood in a large formal dining room with a long rectangular table and twelve black chairs. It was totally quiet except for the sounds of our breathing and the occasional drips of water from our wet clothes onto the wooden floor.

"The kitchen must be in the back," Mom said, walking toward the rear of the house.

We followed her through a wide hallway until we reached a kitchen that covered the entire length of the house.

"Wow!" Danny said. "Some kitchen!"

"I wonder how many people lived here," I said. "There's room for thirty or more."

"I hope they kept food for thirty people," Blaine said as he started opening cabinets. "Let's find it."

We opened and closed all the cabinets, but didn't find much food. There were a few cans of tuna and peanut butter, some bags of chips and pretzels, paper plates and cups, and not much else. Most of the cabinets held fancy plates and dishes.

"It doesn't make sense," Mom said. "It doesn't look like anyone else has been here so there's got to be more..."

"Downstairs," Blaine interrupted. "Dry food's gotta be

stored in the basement."

————

We found a door in the kitchen that led downstairs and stood in front of it for a few seconds, no one saying anything until finally, I spoke. "I don't want to go down there. It's dark and creepy and we could get trapped like the Santangelos."

"I was just thinking the same thing," my mother whispered.

"How about if I go first, by myself, just to check it out?" Blaine asked. "Then if I find food, someone can come down to help load it and two of you can stay up here to keep watch."

Mom nodded.

Blaine opened the door and shined his flashlight past the concrete steps and into the blackness. "Dark and quiet," he said softly.

"Are you sure you're okay with this?" I asked.

"Yeah."

"Lemme go with you," Danny offered. "I'm not scared."

"No," Blaine said. "You're the best shot with the water gun so you stay here and take care of the ladies."

Ladies? How'd I become someone weak who needed protection? I looked questioningly at Blaine, but he smiled as he headed down the stairs to the basement.

"What's it like?" I called when the footsteps stopped.

"Lots of storage cabinets."

We heard the clanging noises of metal doors being opened and closed.

"So?" I asked when Blaine didn't say anything.

"No food yet," he said. "But this place's huge."

We heard footsteps as Blaine moved around below. Then he called to us. "I just hit the mother lode! Send someone down with a bunch of bags!"

Mom looked at Danny and me. "I'd go, but then the two of

you'd be up here all by yourselves."

"Let me go down," I said, reaching for the large black plastic bags my mother carried. "Like Blaine said, Danny's the best shooter."

Mom reluctantly gave me the bags. "Be careful, Erin," she whispered.

I nodded, shining my flashlight on the top step. Then I closed the door and slowly walked downstairs into the creepy basement.

It wasn't completely dark when I reached the bottom because Blaine had propped his flashlight on the floor in the back of the large storage room. I could see him tossing boxes of food into a bag.

"Glad you could make it," he said, giving me a big smile and pointing to an open cabinet a few feet away. "That one's full of paper towels, tissues, toilet paper, and other stuff like that. This place's like a goddamn warehouse. I can't believe one family stored all this."

"It works for us." I began filling a bag with rolls of toilet paper. "Maybe we can get everything we need here so we won't have to check the other houses."

"Maybe...How many bags did we bring?"

"I don't know—ten or twelve."

"Ten full bags is probably all the car can..."

That's when Blaine and I heard the shattering glass upstairs, followed by my mother's scream.

———

For a moment, neither of us spoke. Then Blaine grabbed his flashlight and dashed to the steps. "I'm goin' up," he whispered.

"You're not leaving me down here by myself." Dropping the half-filled bag, I rushed after him.

When we reached the top of the stairs, Blaine took out his

water pistol and slowly twisted the doorknob, opening the door just an inch or two. After taking a quick peek outside, he closed the door.

"Nothing's there," he whispered.

"Where're Mom and Danny?"

"I didn't see them."

"Look again."

He opened the door a little wider and rechecked the room. "I think it's empty so I'm goin' out...Wait till I tell you it's clear."

He stepped into the kitchen and closed the door, leaving me in darkness. It seemed like forever before I heard Blaine's voice. "Okay, Erin."

"Where are they?" I asked again as I entered the empty kitchen.

"It sounded like some glass broke," Blaine said. "Let's find what made that noise." Still holding the water guns in front of us, we left the kitchen and walked through the hallway to the front of the house. When we reached the living room, we found the source of the noise. A window had been broken by a large rock, which lay on the floor along with many pieces of glass.

"The next question we have to answer is, 'Who or what did this?'" Blaine said, pointing to the shattered window. "A person or a toucher?" He moved carefully to an undamaged window and opened the curtain a couple of inches.

"That answers my question," he said, signaling me to come closer.

A big yellow toucher—a man-thing—stood next to Blaine's car, holding another rock.

"Can we chase it away?" I asked.

Blaine shook his head. "Then it'll come after us. Right now, it doesn't know we're here."

"But it could know about Mom and Danny. It could've heard Mom's scream."

"Maybe not, especially if it threw the rock from the street."

"It knows about the car."

Blaine nodded. "It must've figured somethin's happenin' here."

"So where'd Mom and Danny go?"

"Probably upstairs." He took my arm. "Let's find them."

"What if another toucher's sleeping in the house?" I said softly as we walked up the staircase.

"It's not rainin' so they're all outside. Besides, we'd have heard it by now."

"How? They don't talk."

"But they're real noisy when they move."

We reached the second floor and entered the first bedroom on our left. "Mom? Danny?" I called in a loud whisper. "Where are you?"

No answer.

The next door was closed so Blaine knocked on it. "It's me and Erin," he said, again whispering loudly.

The doorknob turned and Danny, holding the water gun in front of him, slowly poked his head out.

My mother ran past him and hugged me tightly. "What happened? When the window broke, we ran up here as fast as we could."

"It's a toucher," I said. "A big man-thing. It threw a rock into the window and now it's checking our car."

———

We all walked into a bedroom that faced the front of the house and I peeked through one of the windows, being careful not to be seen. "That toucher's still out there," I said. "It's opened all the car doors and is looking inside."

"It won't find anythin'," Blaine said, shrugging.

"What do we do now?" I asked.

"We go back to the basement and finish packin' the food," Blaine said.

Mom shook her head. "We should get out of here."

"Not with that toucher thing poking in the car," Danny said.

"Yeah," Blaine agreed. "We can't go anywhere right now so Erin and I should finish loadin' up. You two stay here and check on that toucher outside. Let us know if anythin' changes."

"How?" Danny asked.

"Do three loud taps with..." Blaine scanned the bedroom and then pointed to a frilly lamp on the end table. "Bang with that."

Danny nodded.

In the quiet that followed, we heard a strange new sound.

"What's that?" Mom asked.

Rushing to the window, I peeked outside. "Oh no! The toucher's slashing the tires."

"Quick," Blaine said, waving his arms. "We all gotta get back into the basement before it finds us."

"Why there?" I asked, remembering the creepy darkness.

"Food," Mom said. "And no windows so it can't get in."

"Yeah," I agreed. "And we can't get out."

―――――

We made it downstairs to the kitchen, hurried into the basement staircase, and quickly locked the door. Then, with Blaine shining his flashlight, we tiptoed down the steps.

"When the batteries run out, we'll be stuck here in the dark," I whispered.

"That's only true if we can't find more flashlights or batteries," Blaine pointed out.

"There's gotta be batteries down here," Danny said, surveying the gigantic basement. "This place is huge."

Blaine nodded. "And there's a ton of food so we won't

starve."

"Is there a bathroom?" Mom asked softly.

"Has to be one." Blaine shined the flashlight along the wall. "We were busy lookin' for food before." He walked around the edge of the room and opened a door. "Closet," he said, closing it.

I heard another door open and then shut. "This one's for the furnace," Blaine called in a loud whisper. It was quiet until he opened another door, further away. "Found it," he said.

When Blaine returned, he and Danny went on a search for flashlights and batteries. Meanwhile I sat on the floor, closed my eyes, and tried to get comfortable in this new dark prison.

Mom sensed my mood. "It's not so bad here, Erin," she said, sitting next to me. "The floor's even carpeted."

That was true. We were in a basement, but it was a big and fancy one. "I don't like being in the dark," I grumbled.

"I know. Let's hope they find batteries or new flashlights."

I shrugged and said nothing.

A beam of light shined on me as Danny and Blaine returned, both smiling. "Look what we got," Blaine said as Danny hoisted two large flashlights and turned them on.

"And there's more too," my brother said as he handed me one of the new bright lights.

"Feel better now?" Blaine asked me.

"I guess."

"Good...So how about we finish packin' the food? Then we'll be ready to leave here soon as we can."

With all four of us working, it took less than a half hour to fill ten big garbage bags.

"What now?" I asked when we finished. "We can't see what's going on outside so how do we know when the toucher's gone?"

"We'll wait a little longer and then I'll go up and check," Blaine offered.

"But even if it's gone, we can't use your car," I continued.

"There're other cars on the block."

"But they haven't been driven since the bubbles fell and that's nearly two months ago. How do you know a car'll still work?"

"I'll keep tryin' till I find one that starts up."

I shook my head. "You'll never make it out there by yourself. The motor's loud and they'll hear it."

"I'll go with him," Danny said. "I can shoot the toucher, keep it away."

"No." Mom spoke quietly, but firmly. "You're not going."

"We'll get ourselves wet before we go out," Danny persisted. "Then they won't wanna touch us."

My mother frowned at him. "There's no shower down here so you can't get wet enough."

I stood and pointed my flashlight at everyone. "I think we should all go outside together. We'll wet ourselves in the sink like Danny said and fill up the water guns. It's better than just staying down here."

Mom studied me and then she nodded. "You're right, Erin."

———

We sat quietly in the basement for more than an hour, but at least it wasn't in the dark. I'd found a bunch of old magazines in the bottom of one of the cabinets so I skimmed through a few copies of *People*. Actors, singers—it was like reading fairy tales—stories and photos of a world that no longer existed.

I glanced at Danny. His eyes were closed, but I couldn't tell if he was napping or only resting. Mom was busy writing stuff on a piece of paper. And Blaine? I'm not sure what he was doing. Every time I looked at him, he was staring at me and smiling.

"What're you looking at?" I finally whispered.

"Just watchin' you read," he said.

"What's so funny about that?" I asked.

"Not funny, just cute."

"Thanks for the compliment. But how come you're not doing anything?"

He shook his head. "Oh, but I am doin' somethin'. I'm listenin' for sounds upstairs in the house or outside and I haven't heard anythin' for the last twenty minutes."

"Do you think it's gone?" Mom asked.

Blaine shrugged. "Can't be sure, but maybe." He switched on his flashlight and checked his watch. "It's four-fifteen now so if we're leavin' today, we should go upstairs soon. We don't want to be stuck outside in the dark and we don't know how long it'll take to find a car that works."

"What about all this?" my mother asked, pointing to the pile of filled garbage bags.

"Let's each carry one bag up," Blaine said. "Wet the outside of it too. If everythin' works out, we'll come back for the rest."

———

Blaine walked up the steps first, shining a flashlight and dragging the heaviest wet bag. We lined up behind him, each of us lugging a bag. Blaine unlocked the basement door and opened it slowly, signaling that we should wait. Then, leaving the bag on the steps, he closed the door and tiptoed into the kitchen while we stood in the darkness, listening to the steady dripping of our wet clothes on the concrete stairs.

A few minutes later, Blaine opened the basement door and whispered, "I don't see a toucher outside. Come out, but try not to make any noise." Hoisting his bag of food, he carried it into the room.

I entered the kitchen, followed by Danny and Mom. Then we all went back downstairs for the other bags, which we dragged through the hallway to the front of the house. When I looked outside, I saw our busted car with its open doors and slashed tires.

Blaine pointed across the street to his left at a white SUV parked in the circular driveway of another huge house. "I'm gonna try that one first 'cause it's big and it's so close," he said softly.

"Let me go so I can cover you," Danny whispered, lifting his water gun.

Mom shook her head.

"We should all go," I said softly. "This way we'll be together and ready to leave if the car starts up. Also the noise of the motor could bring the toucher back here."

"She's right," Blaine said. "We're safest now since we're real wet and the guns and bottles are fully loaded."

My mother looked at him for a moment. "Okay," she whispered. "We'll go together."

―――――

We walked outside, each of us dragging the wet bags and again trying to avoid stepping on the pieces of glass all over the street. It was creepily quiet; the only sounds were the soft thuds made by our bags scraping the ground. Blaine moved the fastest and as soon as he reached the SUV, he dropped his bags and rushed to the car door.

"It's locked," he whispered.

"Should we break a window?" I asked.

Blaine shook his head. "Too much noise." He pointed to the house. "I'm goin' in there. Gotta be a car key hangin' somewhere."

None of the ground floor windows were broken so Blaine moved along the outside tugging at the sills, searching for one that wasn't locked. Without saying a word, Danny scooted behind him, crouching with his water gun.

"Danny!" Mom called in a loud whisper as she tried to grab my brother's wet shirt.

"Let him go," I said softly, pushing her arm away. "They'll be okay."

My mother and I waited together in silence. At first, I kept shifting my eyes from the house to the street. But when Blaine and Danny were out of sight, I focused my full attention on the road.

Although I didn't see anything, I heard a faint sound coming from the open end of the street. "What's that noise?" I whispered.

"It's footsteps," Mom said softly and indicated the back of the house. "Take the bags."

We dragged all the bags into the overgrown grass and moved close to the house, hugging the edge of the building. When we reached the back, we peeked into the street. The big man toucher stood in the road, again examining our busted car.

"What'll we do?" I asked.

"We've got to find Danny and Blaine. If they run out there..."

She didn't finish the sentence, but she didn't have to.

———

"Danny!" Mom called in a loud whisper.

There was no answer.

She called my brother's name again.

"They must be inside," I said softly. "I'll check for an open door or window." I sidled towards the other end of the house, tugging on windowsills along the way. They were all locked.

But when I reached the sliding door and pushed the handle, the door opened. After sashaying back to Mom, I grabbed two of the bags.

"Follow me," I whispered. We dragged the rest of the bags through the high grass and into a gigantic rec room.

"Danny!" Mom called again, louder than before. "Where are you?"

We heard running footsteps and then my brother appeared in front of us, a huge smile on his face. "I'm right here," he said. "Blaine just found the keys."

"Yup." Blaine surfaced behind Danny, dangling a set of car keys above his head. "It's for a Lexus SUV LX so it should be good."

"That's great news," I said. "But we can't go outside now because the toucher's back in the street."

Blaine studied the room we stood in. It had a pool table, ping-pong table, four comfy recliners, and two huge TVs. "I wouldn't mind just stayin' here—nice house with plenty of room." He nodded at the garbage bags. "We've got plenty of food and there's probably more here."

I shook my head. "What about Muffles and our neighbors? They're counting on us."

"Just kiddin'." He gave me a sheepish look.

"After we deliver the food, you can come back to this house," Mom said.

Blaine shrugged.

I looked at him and wondered if he had been kidding or really wanted to live here—away from me. *Was it over with us?* Of course this wasn't exactly the best time to be worrying about my love life. "What do we do now?" I whispered.

Mom pointed towards the front of the house. "We should see what that thing outside is doing now...Leave the food."

"Even if the toucher's there, we should still try the car,"

Danny whispered as we followed my mother down the hallway. "We're wet enough so he won't bother us."

"You can't be sure," Mom said.

"I don't wanna be stuck here," Danny whined.

"It's better than that basement," I pointed out. Thinking about being trapped in the darkness still gave me goose bumps.

We reached the living room, which faced the street, and Blaine carefully opened a fold of the fancy purple curtains. "Toucher's still down the street by the other house we were in," he reported. "I think Danny's right and I should try to start the SUV." He looked up, jingling the set of Lexus keys.

"Lemme go with you," my brother said.

"No." My mother grabbed his shirt by the back of the neck and held on tightly. "You're not going."

I looked at Blaine, but didn't smile or volunteer to go with him. I was still pissed.

"Wish me luck," he whispered, smiling at me.

"Good luck," I said, not returning his smile.

———

Holding a water gun, Blaine quietly opened the front door of the house. Then I watched from the window as he crept outside, crouched against the white SUV, and pressed a button.

I heard the familiar "ding ding" signaling the door opening. "He's in," I announced.

Blaine put the key into the ignition and turned it several times. But nothing happened.

"The car's not starting," I said.

After twisting the key twice more with no success, Blaine stopped trying. He'd left the front door open—I guess it was hot inside—so I could see him sitting in the car and doing nothing.

"He's just sitting there," I reported.

"He's waiting before turning the ignition again," Mom explained. "Sometimes that works."

It seemed like hours—but it was probably only a few minutes—before Blaine tried the key again. This time there was a soft humming sound and the engine roared to life. But the motor seemed real loud, especially on this quiet street. The toucher must have heard the noise too because the big man-thing immediately raced towards the white SUV.

"It's coming!" I yelled. "Grab some food and let's go!"

Blaine either heard me or saw the toucher because he honked the horn. Mom closed the door of the house and we all dashed to the car, each of us lugging one of the food bags. Blaine had left three of the doors open—all but his—so I got into the front seat with my bag and Danny jumped into the back seat behind me. Then he scooted over to make room for Mom to slide next to him.

But the toucher got there first and I guess we weren't wet enough because it reached for my mother with a deadly yellow hand.

"Watch out, Mom!" I yelled.

Danny leaned over and squirted the man-thing squarely in its ugly face. "Go away!" he shouted.

The toucher immediately withdrew its arm and moved a few feet from the car, frantically rubbing its eyes and the smooth lower part of its face.

"Quick!" I yelled. "Get in!"

Mom tumbled into the car with her bag of food.

Having wiped away all the water, the toucher rushed back to our car. But by then we were all safely inside.

CHAPTER 26 – Mean Streets

Maybe it was the time of day—early evening—but the streets were worse driving home than when we'd started out. There seemed to be more bodies, although that was probably just my imagination. But I know there were more touchers.

We'd just turned onto Curran Road when a woman toucher with a few strands of red hair jumped on the back of the SUV and held on.

"She's trying to open the rear window and come inside!" Mom shouted.

"Hold on, y'all," Blaine said as he zigzagged the car like an Olympic skier racing around flags down a mountain. Unfortunately, our racer was avoiding dead people and wrecked cars so it was more like a demolition derby.

"She's still banging on the window!" Danny hollered.

"You gotta shoot her," Blaine said.

"No! I'll do it." That response came from my mother.

"Both of you use the guns!" Blaine ordered as he stopped swerving and drove straight. "Do it fast!"

I turned to watch Mom and Danny open their side windows and squirt the redheaded toucher. Mom just hit the thing's leg, but my sharp-shooting brother sprayed it right in the face.

The toucher rolled off the car and onto the street, rubbing its wet face with yellow hands.

"One down," Blaine said.

———

Danny and Mom had just finished reloading their guns with water from bottles we'd filled before leaving the last house when I spotted the next touchers. "Two of them!" I yelled. "On both sides of the street!"

A man toucher and boy toucher rushed at our car from opposite directions. Although Blaine drove faster and made a left into the next side street, his maneuver didn't work because the smaller street was completely blocked by wrecked cars.

As the two touchers neared our SUV, I aimed my gun at the man-thing. But I missed.

"I'm gonna back out," Blaine said.

Before I squirted again, the boy toucher reached down and picked up a large stone. "Watch out!" I yelled. "He's got a rock!"

I felt a strong jolt and heard a loud shattering noise in the back of the car.

"What happened?" Blaine asked.

"The window's busted," Danny said.

When I turned around, I saw the man-thing standing on the SUV, smashing its fists against the cracked window. The toucher had made a small hole and two yellow fingers dangled through the glass, reaching for my mother, who leaned forward against Blaine's seat.

"Get outta here!" my brother shouted, squirting the thing's fingers. The toucher quickly withdrew its hand, but stayed on the SUV. Opening his window, Danny fired at the toucher's face. Bull's-eye! The man toucher jumped off, now focused on getting rid of the water.

"Erin!" Blaine shouted. "Duck!"

I crouched low just before a rock smashed my window. When I looked up, I couldn't see anything through the shattered glass.

"Danny, what's happening out there?" I shouted.

"Lemme finish this first," he said.

"Finish what?"

"The boy toucher. I gotta shoot it before it throws another rock at us."

I heard the spray of water.

"Okay," Danny said. "We're good now."

That's when I realized my mother hadn't spoken in a long time. Turning around again, I looked at her. She still sat with her head tilted down. "Mom?" I said quietly.

My mother didn't respond.

"Danny...Is Mom okay?"

My brother gently lifted my mother's head. Her eyes were closed, but she wasn't sleeping. He put his head against her chest and listened. "She's alive, I think," he whispered.

"What happened to her?" I asked.

Danny pointed to a reddish bruise on her head. "This," he said.

My brother and I didn't say anything else. I just kept looking at my mother and wondering how badly she'd been hurt.

Blaine finished backing out of the side street and was moving forward again. "Does one of you know how to get to your house from here?" he asked.

I glanced at the road sign: Thornwood Street. "You're going the right way," I said. Then I tried to stop thinking about my mother so I could direct Blaine.

He steered the SUV past a pack of dogs sniffing two rotting bodies covered with flies. After that, he zigzagged around three wrecked cars and a bus, finding just enough room to squeeze through.

"Turn here," I instructed.

Blaine drove along Needham Road, which was free of bodies and wrecked cars. *Better*, I thought. But I was wrong.

———

"Toucher!" Danny yelled. "On your side, Erin!"

"I can't see it clearly!" I hollered as a yellow blur rushed to the car.

"Watch out!" my brother shouted. "She's gonna throw a bottle!"

As I ducked, I heard Danny lower the window and squirt his water gun. "Got her!"

From my crouching position, I looked through the good window behind Blaine and saw the toucher standing in the street, poking at its wet face with both hands. The bottle was gone.

"How much further?" Blaine asked, his eyes focused straight ahead on Needham Road.

"We're almost there," I said. "Make a right at the next block."

He turned and traveled slowly along the street, avoiding the smashed cars. I saw arms dangling out of a silver van, but tried not to think about whom they might have belonged to.

"Make a left onto Barker," I said. "Then the next left is Walnut Lane."

He entered our street and parked the SUV in our driveway. But we couldn't get out. Though it seemed like we'd been away for a long time, it had only been a few hours and things hadn't changed: Cyndy Louise was still patrolling the block.

"What now?" I asked Blaine.

He turned to Danny. "Do you have any water left?"

My brother shook his head. "Used it all up on the way

back."

"I don't think we're wet enough either," I said, feeling my barely damp tee shirt.

"We can't just sit and wait in the car." Blaine nodded at the hole in the back windshield. "She can get in through there—or bust through your smashed window, Erin."

"And she's faster than us so if we run to the house..."

"Mom's still not awake," Danny said, interrupting me. "How'll we get her inside?"

"Let me think." Blaine closed his eyes in concentration.

"You better think fast," I told him. "Cyndy Louise is coming."

———

"The bags..."

"What about them?" I asked Blaine.

"Do we have any drinks—any liquids?"

I shuffled through the food I had taken and I could hear Danny going through the plastic bags in the back. "I don't have anything," I said.

"I found one bottle of Coke," Danny said. "Lemme load the gun."

"Do you think that'll work?" I asked Blaine.

"Coke's mostly water."

Cyndy Louise had reached Mrs. Perez's house. "She's almost here," I said.

"You both be ready to run," Blaine told us.

"What about my mother?" I asked as I took out the key to the house.

"I'll take care of her."

As Cyndy Louise walked up our driveway, Danny leaned his gun through the hole in the back windshield and squirted her face with the soda. "Got her!" he yelled.

Cyndy Louise dropped to her knees to wipe off the brown liquid.

"Now!" Blaine shouted. "Go!"

Jumping out of the car—Danny right behind me—I raced to my front door, trying hard not to fumble with the key. Then I heard barking and Muffles was there too.

I unlocked the door and the three of us ran inside. "Where's Blaine?" I asked as Danny slammed the door shut and I locked it.

"Still in the car with Mom."

My brother and I, followed by Muffles, ran upstairs to my room so we could watch from the window. But there was nothing to see. The SUV was gone.

———

"Where'd he go?" I whispered, sitting on my bed and petting the dog.

"Away from Cyndy Louise," Danny said. "He couldn't sit there."

"But Mom..."

Danny leaned against the wall and I sat on my bed, neither of us talking. "He can't just drive around with nothing to squirt at the touchers," I finally said.

"He should be good. He's got lots of food."

I glared at my brother. "That's a dumb thing to say. You make it sound like he can just stop somewhere and have a picnic."

Danny shrugged.

"And what about Mom?" I asked. "How bad do you think she's hurt?"

"I dunno. Maybe she just banged her head."

I jumped off the bed. "Let's go downstairs and plan what we should do next."

"There's nothing we can do," Danny said. "We gotta wait for Blaine."

"That's not true. We can be ready."

———

I ran to the bathroom. "Quick...In the shower," I ordered Danny, turning on the water. Muffles watched the cold spray cover our clothes and bodies, wondering what was going on. Afterwards we squished down the steps, trailed by water and Muffles.

"We're making a mess," my brother said.

"I only hope Mom's okay enough to be mad," I whispered.

While I loaded the water pistols, Danny checked the dining room window. "Is anything happening?" I asked.

"No."

We waited quietly, watching the street and dripping water all over the wooden floor until I heard a loud honk outside. "Do you see the car?" I asked.

"Uh, uh." Danny shook his head.

"Maybe Blaine's just signaling us to get ready," I suggested.

"Probably. He couldn't stay in the driveway and wait for us with Cyndy Louise out there."

"Let me know when you see the car," I told Danny.

Several minutes later, I heard the sound of a motor. "Danny..." I started to say.

"Yeah, it's Blaine. He's pulling into the driveway right now."

"Cyndy Louise?"

"I don't see her."

"C'mon." I opened the front door and immediately closed and locked it before Muffles could escape.

———

"I see you got the message," Blaine said as I slipped into the front seat and Danny again sat in the back next to Mom, who still wasn't moving.

"You should go into the house now," I said, shoving my keys at him. "It's the silver one."

"No." He pushed the keys away.

"Danny and I are wet so we're safer out here."

"True, but you two don't know how to drive the car."

"We'll hold her off until you shower and get wet."

Blaine shook his head. "That'll take too long." He looked through the rear-view mirror. "Anyway, she's already here."

When I turned, I saw Cyndy Louise rushing towards the driveway.

"I'll shoot her," Danny said, shoving his pistol through the broken window.

"Let's get your mother out while he's keepin' her busy," Blaine said.

I looked at him. "But you're not wet."

"I'll be okay...Gimme your gun."

I handed him my water pistol.

Blaine and I opened our car doors. As I dashed around to my mother's side, he stepped out, opened Mom's door, and squirted Cyndy Louise. She had moved out of Danny's range and now crouched near us, concentrating on removing the water from her legs.

"Cover me," Blaine said, tossing me the gun. Then he lifted Mom under her arms and dragged her to the house.

I stood behind Blaine, walking backwards so I could monitor Cyndy Louise's movements. When I glanced at the SUV, I realized my brother was still inside. "Danny!" I yelled. "Get out of there!"

After squirting Cyndy Louise once more, Danny opened his door and ran to our house, reaching us in time to lift Mom's legs as Blaine climbed up the porch step.

We were nearly at the front door when Cyndy Louise—moving faster than any person—lunged for Blaine's left shoulder. Just before her yellow hand touched him, I sprayed her arm as much as I could. She backed away, trying to rub off the water.

"Key!" Danny yelled, holding out his hand.

I had been clutching the key ring in my left hand, even when shooting the water pistol. As I tried to stop shaking, I gave Danny the keys. I heard the door open and continued walking backwards until I made it into the house, closing and locking the door about two seconds before Cyndy Louise smashed against it.

She was super fast and super strong, but she wasn't strong enough to break down our steel door. We were safely back inside our prison.

CHAPTER 27 – Home Again

I helped Blaine carry Mom up the steps to her bedroom, with Muffles trailing, and we placed her carefully on top of the covers. She still hadn't woken up.

After smoothing the pillow, I crossed her hands on her stomach so they didn't dangle over the bed. She had a big lump on the right side of her forehead. "Do you think she'll be okay?" I whispered.

Blaine didn't answer. He just shrugged.

Muffles looked at Mom and whimpered.

"Can we do anything else for her?" I asked.

"I'm not a doctor," Blaine said. "Let her rest and then maybe..." His voice drifted off.

As we stood there without speaking, I heard loud thumping noises coming from the street, following by Danny's shout: "She's tossing all the food!"

Blaine and I rushed to my window in time to see Cyndy Louise emptying the plastic bags we'd worked so hard to load and deliver here. Tin cans rolled all over the street and she went from can to can, stomping on them. Then she flung boxes of cookies and bags of chips into the street.

"Damn!" Danny yelled.

"Can we save any of the stuff?" I asked.

"Not unless we get a quick rain," Blaine said. "We were lucky to make it inside one time." He looked at me. "Besides, we know where there's lots more food."

———

Blaine, Danny, and I took showers, but the house was so warm that, for a change, the cold water felt kind of refreshing. Then we went into the kitchen for a dinner of cheese—our last canister—and crackers. Muffles was there too, lapping up his food and water from new plastic dishes because his regular bowls were still outside. That's when the screeching started.

"What's that noise?" I asked.

"Sounds like some animal," Danny said. "I'll go check." He ran to the dining room. "Cats!" he called. "A bunch of cats!"

Blaine and I joined my brother in the dining room and we took turns looking through the opening in the window. There must have been ten scrawny cats eating food from the cans Cyndy Louise had squished in the street.

"What was in those cans?" I asked.

"I don't remember everythin' we took, but I know there was some fish," Blaine said. "Tuna and maybe salmon."

"Will they leave?" I continued.

"I hope so," Blaine replied. "But there's nothin' we can do if they decide to stay here unless Cyndy Louise wants to get rid of them and right now she doesn't seem to mind sharin' the street."

As he spoke, I watched Cyndy Louise walk along the middle of the road, paying no attention to the hungry cats. When she got in their way, a couple of them hissed at her and one even bit her yellow leg. But the bite didn't bother her. After that, the cats ignored Cyndy Louise, concentrating instead on eating whatever was in the squashed cans.

———

"I'm gonna check on Mom," Danny said after dinner and he rushed out of the kitchen, followed by Muffles.

Blaine and I were alone in the rapidly darkening room. I felt kind of uncomfortable, but didn't say anything. It was almost night and that meant it was time to get ready for bed. Maybe Blaine read my thoughts, but even if he didn't, he was on my wavelength.

"Where should I sleep?" he asked, speaking very softly.

I didn't answer immediately. It was finally quiet outside. After eating all the tossed food, the cats had left so now only Cyndy Louise was on Walnut Lane and except for footsteps, she didn't make any noise.

"You can sleep on the couch down here," I said, pointing towards the living room.

"Oh."

I guess that wasn't the answer he wanted.

"My mom and brother are both upstairs," I whispered.

"Your brother will be asleep and your mother..." His voice drifted off.

"I'll find you a sheet and pillow," I said, standing. "And a towel too."

Blaine gave me a questioning look.

"What?"

"It'll be real lonely down here."

I dashed to the staircase without saying anything.

———

Before gathering the bedding stuff for Blaine, I went into Mom's room. My mother looked the same. She was still lying motionless with her arms folded and her eyes closed like some kind of fairy tale character—Snow White or maybe Sleeping Beauty. Danny was there too, sitting next to the bed in the semi-darkness, with Muffles sprawled beneath him.

"Any change?" I whispered.

He petted the dog and shook his head.

"You should go to sleep," I said softly. "You can't do anything for Mom now. If she wakes up during the night, she'll call us."

"We can stay up later if we want," Danny said. "There's no reason to get up early tomorrow with no school." He sounded a little sad.

"I know. But what are you going to do if you go to sleep late—read all night or play a video game and waste our batteries?"

"We found a lot more batteries."

"They're still in that house on Redleaf Way, in one of the bags we packed."

Danny sat quietly for a moment. Then he kissed Mom gently on her cheek and left the room.

———

I walked down the steps, my arms filled with the pillow, sheet, and towel, trying not to stumble because it was already hard to see. Our downstairs was pretty dark even in daytime since we'd covered the windows and now it was nearly night.

"Gotcha!" Blaine said, putting his arms around me as I reached the ground floor.

The bed stuff tumbled onto the floor as I held Blaine's waist while he kissed me tenderly on the lips. Then, slowly, he walked me to the couch.

"What about Danny?" I whispered, sitting closely beside Blaine.

"He's upstairs."

"But he's not sleeping."

"It's so dark down here, he won't even see us."

"He's got a flashlight."

"Shh." Blaine ran his hand gently across my mouth as if to zip it and then kissed me again, this time harder. His hand moved to my tee shirt and made little circles caressing my breasts.

"Blaine..." My eyes were closed and I spoke his name softly.

"Do you want me to stop?"

"Uh, uh."

Still kissing me, he lowered his hand to my stomach and rubbed it tenderly. Then he reached for the top of my shorts and undid the snap.

"No," I said, sitting up.

"All right."

He sounded disappointed.

"Not with my brother upstairs and then my Mom..."

"I understand."

But he didn't sound like he understood.

I stood and took a couple of small steps, groping for the things I had dropped.

"Here." Blaine switched on his flashlight. "This should help."

Without saying anything, I retrieved the bedding, tucked the sheet into the couch, added the pillow, and handed Blaine his towel. "Good night," I whispered.

"Good night," he repeated.

As I turned for the steps, hoping I could make it upstairs in the dark, Blaine grabbed my wrist. "Take this," he said, placing the flashlight in my hand. "And sleep well, Erin."

―――

But I didn't sleep well. First, I was scared about Mom. *What if she didn't wake up?* Then I thought about Blaine. *Was he mad at me and did I do the right thing? Should I've spent the night with him?*

Life was so different since the bubbles and I could die at any time. *Why'd I make him stop?*

"Erin...Danny."

I must have finally fallen asleep because my mother's whispery call jolted me. It was still totally dark so I needed the flashlight to make it into her room.

She lay as we had placed her, arms still folded on her chest, but her eyes were open and she smiled as she asked, "What happened to me?"

Reaching over, I kissed her cheek. "It's so great that you're finally awake. We think you hit your head hard on the back of Blaine's seat when a toucher threw a rock at us."

"But it's nighttime now. How long have I been lying here?" She tried to sit up. "Oww..." She frowned and moaned softly.

I moved closer and helped lower her on the bed. "Don't get up yet. You were unconscious for such a long time—and we were all so worried."

My mother smiled at me again. "I'll be okay," she whispered. "But my head feels like I just lost a ten-round boxing match...Is Danny all right?"

"He's fine. I guess he's fast asleep and didn't hear you call. Do you want me to get him?"

"No. Let him sleep."

"Should I stay with you?"

"No...What about Blaine? He was driving the car. Is he okay?"

"Yes," I said. "He's downstairs, sleeping on the couch. He carried you inside."

She closed her eyes and after I watched her for a minute and she didn't speak again, I went back to bed.

———

There was no alarm to wake me the next morning so I was surprised when I opened my eyes to daylight, checked my watch, and saw it was past eight o'clock. I threw on a pair of shorts and rushed into my mother's room.

Mom was still in bed, but she was awake, talking to Danny and petting Muffles, who was curled next to her.

"Good morning," she said, smiling at me.

"How do you feel?" I asked.

"Better, except when I try to get up."

"Then stay in bed and rest," I suggested.

Nodding, she turned her head towards my brother. "Danny's been filling me in on what happened after I conked out. All that work and we didn't save any of the food."

I shrugged.

"I wanna go back," Danny said. "We got lots more bags of stuff in that house."

Mom shook her head. "We should try someplace closer."

"But that food's already packed," I pointed out. "We just have to grab it and go."

"At least wait till it rains," she said, closing her eyes.

———

Since Mom's head hurt too much to handle the morning telephone talk, the three of us did it without her. Blaine and I stood together at my window calling to the Douglasses while Danny spoke to Mrs. Perez from his room.

Mr. Douglas tried to assure us that everyone would have enough food until supplies were delivered. "We'll manage until the next rainy day!" he shouted. "Lynne's better so I'll go with you then!"

He didn't sound real convincing to me. "What do you think?" I asked Blaine when we ended the talk. "Should we wait?"

He shook his head. "I bet the food situation's worse than what he told us—and I don't want him comin' with us. Look what happened to your mom and he's a lot older."

"Yeah. He can't move fast enough."

Danny assumed we'd be going back immediately for the food. "So what time are we leaving?" he asked as he entered my room.

"Someone should stay here to take care of Mom," I said.

"Then you stay home," Danny said. "I'm going with Blaine."

"None of us might be goin'," Blaine said, returning to my window and looking outside. "We can't take the SUV, not with the two broken windows and we don't know if Cyndy Louise's busted the tires or done somethin' else to that car." He shrugged. "I can't even see the other side."

"Can we use another car?" I asked.

"It's gotta be close," Blaine said.

"Mrs. Perez's?" Danny asked.

"Or the Douglass'?" I suggested.

"Not them," Blaine said. "Then he'll wanna go with us."

"I'm gonna call Mrs. Perez," Danny said, running back into his room.

———

Mrs. Perez didn't know if her car would start. "She said she hasn't used it since the bubbles," Danny told us. "It's still in her garage."

"Can she get in there and try it without Cyndy Louise seein' her?" Blaine asked.

Danny nodded. "That's what she's gonna do right now."

We waited quietly in Danny's room. At one point, I thought I heard the rumbling of a car's motor, but I wasn't sure if that was just my wishful imagination.

A few minutes later, Mrs. Perez opened her window and

waved at us. "I got the car to start!" she shouted. "What now?"

When Blaine told her our plan, she nodded and then asked, "Do you need me to go with you?" Although she made the offer, Mrs. Perez didn't sound anxious to take a road trip.

"No!" Blaine assured her. "We're good! Give us fifteen minutes!"

She nodded again and closed the window.

Danny and Blaine rushed into the bathroom to take another cold shower with their clothes on while I stopped into Mom's bedroom. "We're going now," I said.

"I know. I heard you talking to Norma...I wish you would wait."

"We can't. Will you be okay?"

"I'll manage," Mom whispered, raising herself higher on the pillow and then clutching my hand. "Erin, please be very careful."

"We've already done this so we know what to expect...I've got to get wet now." I gave her a quick kiss on the cheek and dashed into the bathroom, not giving her a chance to say anything else.

————

The three of us sloshed down the stairs, leaving puddles on both the carpeted stairs and the hallway floor. Then we watched through the dining room window opening, waiting until Cyndy Louise reached the other end of the block.

"Now!" Blaine ordered, rushing to the front door and opening it.

After I quickly locked the door, we ran to the right, towards Mrs. Perez's house. I hoped our neighbor had done what we asked, which would help keep Cyndy Louise away.

Mrs. Perez opened her door even before we knocked and when we were all inside, closed and locked it. "This way," she said and we followed her to the garage entrance.

"I've got a battery backup for the remote," she explained. "I hope it still works. I didn't test it."

"We'll find out," Blaine said, getting into the driver's seat of her black Camry, which was dripping wet.

"Sorry we're getting the inside all wet too," I said as I sat in the front passenger seat while Danny slipped into the back, each of us carrying two water pistols with water bottles tucked into our shorts pockets.

"No big deal," Mrs. Perez said, shrugging. "I watered the outside of the car like you wanted. You kids just get the food—and then come back home safely...Ready?"

"Yeah," Blaine said. "After we're out, shut the garage door fast."

"I will," our neighbor said. "But I've got my water gun just in case." She held up a yellow plant sprayer. "Now let's see if this works." She pressed the garage control button and the door swung up.

CHAPTER 28 – On the Road Again

It was a cloudy warm summer day so Blaine kept the air conditioning on high as he drove through the obstacle course while Danny and I watched for touchers. I gave Blaine directions to Redleaf Way, but after last time, he pretty much knew the route.

As Blaine swerved around the wrecked and abandoned cars, we passed a pack of mangy dogs that yelped at us, but didn't chase the car. They looked too weak to do anything. "Poor dogs," I whispered.

"It could be poor us," Blaine said. "Concentrate on lookin' for touchers."

I didn't see any touchers, but I did see rats—lots of them—scurrying from car to car and covering the sidewalks.

"One's coming on the left!" Danny shouted.

I stopped watching the rats just in time to see the toucher approach from the other side as my brother opened the window behind Blaine and squirted the yellow man-thing's face. "Got it!" he yelled.

The toucher stopped moving and stood in the middle of the road, rubbing its wet eyes.

As Blaine turned into a side street and zigzagged around a

smashed pick-up truck, I heard, "Help me!" It sounded like a boy's voice.

"Where is he?" I asked, turning my head.

"Running to your side, Erin," Danny said.

Blaine stopped the car and we waited for the boy to reach us. A woman toucher was three steps behind him.

While Danny and I both squirted the toucher, my brother opened the rear door to let the kid in.

"Thanks," the boy said, gasping for breath as Blaine resumed driving. "I didn't see no other people anywhere."

"It's too dangerous," I said. "What's your name?"

"Kyle Jackson."

"Glad to meet you, Kyle," I said, smiling. "I'm Erin. You're sitting next to my brother, Danny, and that's Blaine driving the car."

Kyle gave me a half smile and leaned against the seat. He was a cute little black kid with huge dark brown eyes, but he was very skinny. It was amazing he had been able to run so fast.

All that running must have used up his energy because Kyle closed his eyes and was soon fast asleep. When we reached Redleaf Way, he was still sleeping.

––––––

Blaine pulled into the driveway of the house where we'd gotten the SUV and left the bags of food. Except for the now totally-destroyed blue Honda, the street still looked empty, with no toucher in sight.

"We better move fast," Blaine said. "They must've heard our car so one of them'll be comin' soon."

"What about Kyle?" I said. "We can't leave him here."

"Wake him up now," Blaine told Danny. "Then we're goin' in."

My brother shook the boy and Kyle opened his eyes,

startled at first as if he didn't know us or why he was in the car. Then he seemed to remember and glanced nervously from face to face. "What's wrong?" he asked.

"There's no time to explain everything," I said. "We're going into this house for food. Just run inside. The front door should be open."

He nodded and we dashed from the car to the house, which was still unlocked like we had left it. When we were all inside, I locked the entrance.

Danny peeked through the front window.

"Do you see anything?" I asked.

He shook his head.

"Are them big scary yellow things here too?" Kyle asked.

"They're everywhere," I said. "We call them touchers because if they touch you, then you die."

"I know," Kyle whispered. "One of them killed my mama."

"I'm so sorry," I said, patting his shoulder.

"Guys," Blaine said as he dragged two of the loaded food bags closer to the front door. "You can talk later, but right now we've got work to do and I could really use some help."

Danny grabbed two garbage bags and Kyle and I followed.

When all the bags were piled near the entrance, Danny checked the window again. "One's coming here now," he said. "Looks like a big fat man."

"Do we have time to run to the car?" Blaine asked.

"No."

I felt Kyle's bony shoulder and realized something. "He's not wet," I said.

"Huh?" The boy stared at me.

"The touchers don't like being wet," I explained. "Water keeps them away."

"There's no time for a shower," Blaine said. "Take him to a sink and wet him good."

238

Nodding, I grabbed Kyle's hand and the two of us raced down the hallway until we reached a guest bathroom. I ran the cold water and splashed it all over his face and body. When I finished, he wasn't completely soaked, but he was pretty wet.

We returned to the front of the house where Danny and Blaine were both checking the window. "What's going on?" I asked.

"There're two of them out there now—and they don't like each other," Danny said. "We're hoping for a fight."

————

We all stood by the window, watching the touchers. There was the big man Danny had mentioned and a smaller yellow male that had once been a teenage boy. The pair circled each other silently like boxers sizing each other up, their eyes flashing with anger.

"They ain't sayin' nothin'," Kyle said as he munched on pretzels from a bag we'd opened.

"That's because they don't have mouths anymore," I pointed out. Kyle sure had a mouth. Those pretzels disappeared so fast—the kid must have been really hungry.

The teenage toucher picked up a jagged piece of glass from the street and rushed toward the yellow man, aiming at its face.

"He's goin' for the eyes," Blaine said. "Maybe that part's still human."

The man-thing ducked and the teen landed on the lawn, the glass weapon falling from its hands. The man toucher jumped on the teen and the two touchers rolled on the grass, pounding each other with their fists. But the punches didn't seem to hurt either of them.

"Which of them's winning?" Kyle asked.

Danny shrugged. "I dunno. They don't look like anything bad's happening to them. They're still yellow—no blood or scratches."

"Then why don't they stop fighting?" Kyle asked.

"I think they're like wild animals fighting over their territory," I said. "We saw this once before at our house."

"Where d'ya live?" Kyle asked.

"Walnut Lane," Danny said.

"Can I stay with you?" Kyle smiled at Danny and me, his white teeth contrasting with his dark skin.

"What about your family?" I asked him. "Do you have a dad, brother, sister, aunt—anyone?"

Kyle shook his head, not smiling any more.

"Of course you can stay with us," I said, hugging the wet little boy. *If we make it back home.* But I didn't say those words out loud.

———

The fight finally ended with the man toucher winning and the teen boy-thing running back to wherever it had come from.

"What happened?" Kyle asked.

"I guess the man-thing was stronger," I said. The two had been punching each other for nearly an hour and neither had any marks on its yellow body. We'd all been watching on and off as we gathered more food from the kitchen pantry and piled the bags by the front door. "Anyway, it's over."

"Yeah, now we've just got to worry about him," Blaine said, pointing to the man toucher that was examining our car in the driveway. The day had turned sunny and the car was no longer wet.

"I'm gonna squirt him before he messes it up like last time," Danny said, opening the window and leaning outside with his water pistol. He fired at the back of the toucher's head. "Got him!"

The man-thing grabbed its bald head and concentrated on

rubbing off the water.

"But he'll go back to checking out the car after he dries himself," I said. "We have to get him away from here because we need time to load all this stuff." I swept my hand over the bags of food and supplies.

"I'll get him to chase me," Kyle said. "I'm fast."

"No." I crouched next to the boy and looked into his eyes. "You're not faster than one of them. The touchers move much quicker than people."

"I'm all wet," Kyle said, fingering his soaked tee shirt. "You said that'll keep him away."

"He could still find a dry spot on you and touch you there."

"I'm going out the back way...I'll make lots of noise and keep him busy so you guys can take the food and then get me."

"Kyle, no!" I shouted as he dashed into the hallway and ran to the door in the kitchen. I raced after him, but the kid really was fast. By the time I reached the rear door, he was already outside.

I quickly locked the door and rushed back to Blaine and Danny.

"Couldn't...stop...him," I said, panting between each word.

Blaine shook his head. "Let's see if he can get the toucher to go after him and give us a chance to load the car—without gettin' himself killed."

———

We heard Kyle yell something to the toucher. I'm not sure exactly what he said, but it sounded like, "You can't catch me!" followed by laughter and more teasing words.

Blaine, who'd been monitoring the window, raced to the front door and opened it. "Now!" he ordered.

Danny and I each grabbed two bags and dragged them out the door, followed by Blaine, who did the same. After tossing all the bags into the trunk, we returned to the house and repeated the action. Then we all slid into Mrs. Perez's car, shoving the last two bags on the floor of the backseat.

"Is everyone okay?" Blaine asked as he drove slowly along Redleaf Way.

"Yeah," I said, breathing heavily.

Blaine honked the horn once and we checked our windows for Kyle. I didn't see him anywhere. "Where'd he go?" I asked.

"Maybe into one of the backyards?" Danny suggested.

"It's a small street," Blaine said. "I already made noise by honkin' and if we stay here much longer, more touchers'll be back for us."

"We can't leave Kyle," I whispered.

"I'm not suggestin' that, only we gotta..."

Before Blaine could finish his explanation, Kyle shot out into the middle of the road, the toucher just a few feet behind him.

Blaine swerved the car, brakes screeching, and sped directly at the man-thing, hitting it in the stomach and knocking it to the ground. "Let the kid in—quick!" he said.

Danny opened the rear door and Kyle jumped into the car as the toucher rose and lunged at him. Blaine avoided the oncoming yellow man-thing and continued driving.

Kyle leaned against the seat, his face soaked with what was probably a combination of water and sweat as he gasped for breath, too winded to talk.

Turning past the three dead bodies on the grass, Blaine zoomed out of Redleaf Way.

CHAPTER 29 – A Home for Kyle

Blaine drove without speaking as he concentrated on avoiding the wrecked cars while Danny and I clutched our water guns and stared out the windows, watching for approaching touchers.

Kyle was the only one who wanted to talk. "Told you I was faster than them yellow things," he said when he got his voice back.

"You did good," I said, smiling.

"I'm super fast." He fingered the plastic bag under his feet. "You guys got all the food?"

"Yes," I said. "Thanks to you."

"How much longer till we get to your house?"

"Just a few minutes unless another toucher comes after us," I said. "Why don't you close your eyes and rest till we get there?"

"I can't. Too wound up. Man, that was fun!"

I glanced at Kyle and as I figured, he had a huge smile on his face.

———

We had a much easier ride home this time—maybe Blaine was getting used to driving on these blocked roads—and we weren't attacked by touchers. When we reached Mrs. Perez's driveway, Blaine honked the horn.

"That'll get Cyndy Louise's attention," I said.

"Who's Cyndy Louise?" Kyle asked.

"Our toucher," Danny said. "She tries to kill everyone on our block."

"Want me to get out so she'll chase me?" Kyle asked.

"No!" Blaine and I both yelled at the same time.

Before we could say anything else, I heard a grinding noise as the garage door began opening.

"Hurry!" Danny yelled. "She's here!"

As Blaine drove into the garage, Danny opened his window and aimed his water pistol at the oncoming Cyndy Louise. He hit her in the face and she backed away.

"Good shot!" Kyle said.

"Thanks." Danny smiled at the boy.

"I hope Mrs. Perez closes this door fast," I said. Cyndy Louise had wiped away the water and was again heading to the garage.

"Give me your gun, Erin," Danny said. "Mine's out."

I handed him my pistol. As Cyndy Louise ran towards us, Danny leaned out of the car and sprayed her, this time hitting her bare yellow stomach and legs. She stopped moving and concentrated on rubbing the water off her body.

I heard the motor again and the garage door began closing—very, very slowly. Luckily, Cyndy Louise was still working on water removal when the door finally reached the ground.

———

"That was close," I said, opening the car door and stepping into Mrs. Perez's garage.

"Is this your house?" Kyle asked.

"No," I replied. "It's our next-door neighbor's. This is her car."

"How're we gonna get into your house then?" Kyle continued.

I shrugged. "We either get ourselves very wet or wait till it rains."

Kyle smiled at me. "Well, we got lots of food."

Blaine and Danny had begun unloading the bags from the trunk and piling them on the floor of the garage.

I walked up the three steps to the door to the house and turned the knob. It was locked. "Mrs. Perez!" I shouted. "Please open the door!" I heard footsteps and then the door opened.

"Sorry," our neighbor said. "When I saw Cyndy Louise coming, I closed the garage and then ran back inside the house and locked the door. I was afraid she could get in here too."

"No problem," Blaine said, waving his hand over the bags of food. "Where should we put all this?"

"Just leave everything in the garage. We can give it out from here...Hello. Who are you?"

Kyle, suddenly shy, had been standing behind me and out of Mrs. Perez's line of vision. Maybe he'd wanted to check out our neighbor first. I guess he must have approved of her because now he popped out and gave her a big smile.

"I'm Kyle and these are my new friends."

"Glad to meet you, Kyle. I'm Norma Perez. Come inside, Kyle, and all of you." She motioned us forward. "You must be tired and hungry. We'll have something to eat and you can tell me how you managed to bring back all those wonderful bags of food."

————

We gathered around Mrs. Perez's square kitchen table while she grabbed a bunch of paper plates and cups. Then she reached into a cabinet and took out a box of crackers and one can of tuna, which she opened. After placing both foods on the table, she stuck a spoon into the can of fish. "Sorry I don't have more tuna," she said. "This is the last one."

"We don't need it," I said. "We can just have the crackers."

"No," she said as she filled the cups with water from the sink. "I shouldn't have said anything. I want you to eat the fish. You kids risked your lives to get food for us and one little can of tuna isn't much of a meal for four people anyway." She smiled. "Besides, in all those bags, I bet there's more tuna."

I nodded, grabbing a fistful of Ritz crackers and scooping a small blob of the precious tuna. I hadn't realized how hungry I was.

Kyle must have still been hungry too. He didn't say anything as he shoved crackers into his mouth.

"Slow down," I told him. "You'll get sick if you eat so fast."

He turned to me and grinned, treating me to a close-up view of chewed cracker gook. Then he reached for his cup of water and guzzled that too.

"Cookies, anybody?" Mrs. Perez asked when we had finished our little meal.

"Me!" Kyle shouted, raising his hand. "What kind?"

"Chocolate chip."

"Yum!" Kyle rubbed his stomach. "I love chocolate chip!"

Mrs. Perez gave him a couple of cookies, which he gobbled up. "Anyone else?"

Danny and I nodded and Mrs. Perez gave us each two cookies. She looked at Blaine, who shook his head.

"More!" Kyle yelled.

"Sure," Mrs. Perez said as she gave him two more cookies.

I wondered when the last time was that Kyle had eaten anything—but I didn't ask.

———

After we finished our meal, I stood. "I need to get back to my house," I said. "I'm worried about Mom."

"How's she doing?" Mrs. Perez asked.

"She was a little better this morning when we left," I said. "But her head still hurt when she tried to stand."

"Should we get ourselves wet again?" Danny asked.

"I guess," I said, feeling my tee shirt and shorts. In the warm weather, my clothes were nearly dry after spending time in the car and in our neighbor's kitchen.

"Are you sure you want to do this?" Mrs. Perez asked. "You can all stay here with me until it rains."

"I want to go with Erin," Danny said, standing.

"And I'll go to make sure they both get into the house okay," Blaine added.

I gave him a dirty look. *I couldn't take care of myself?*

He shrugged and smiled.

Kyle jumped out of his seat and ran to Mrs. Perez. "I'll stay with you," he said, a huge grin on his face. "You're a real nice lady."

She bent down and smiled at him. "And you're a real nice boy," she said, giving Kyle a hug.

———

Danny, Blaine, and I again took cold showers with our clothes on. Then we scooted down Mrs. Perez's stairs, trying not to drip too much water on the steps. I wiped up some of the puddles with the towel our neighbor had given me.

"It's okay," Mrs. Perez said as she stood in the hallway watching us, her arm around Kyle. "Just get inside your house safely."

I nodded as the three of us reached her front door.

"Where's Cyndy Louise?" I asked Danny, who peeked through an opening in Mrs. Perez's neatly boarded living room window (bookshelves, I think), water dripping onto the carpet.

"She's almost at the end of the block so we should go soon."

"Just tell me when," said Blaine, who stood at the front door with his hand around the knob.

"Now!"

Blaine opened the door and the three of us rushed to my front porch.

"Hurry!" Danny yelled as I inserted the key. "She's coming!"

We all made it inside, breathing heavily as Blaine locked the door and we leaned against it, catching our breath. Cyndy Louise banged on the door a couple of times and flung her body against it before she gave up and left.

I was home again.

CHAPTER 30 – Food Delivery

"Mom!" I called from the hallway as Muffles jumped happily on my bare wet legs. "We're back!"

My mother said something, but I couldn't understand the words so I rushed up the steps. "How are you feeling?" I asked as I entered her bedroom.

"A little better." She inched up the pillow, trying to sit. "My head still hurts, but not as much as..."

Before she could finish, Danny dashed in and ran to Mom. Opening her arms wide, she hugged my wet brother. "How did it go today?" she asked, still holding Danny.

"Great!" he said. "We got all the food and saved this kid, Kyle."

Mom gave me a puzzled look.

"A little boy we took back with us," I explained. "He's staying next door with Mrs. Perez."

My mother smiled. "Good for Norma. I think she's been terribly lonely."

"Did you eat anything since we left?" I asked. We'd put a glass of water and a plate of crackers on the table near her bed, but the food looked untouched.

Mom shook her head and shrugged. "I wasn't hungry."

"I'm making you lunch," I said.

———

I opened and shut all our kitchen cabinets looking for food, but there was very little—just two boxes of crackers and half a package of sugar wafers. "Damn!" I muttered, slamming the last cabinet door.

"What's the matter?" Blaine asked as he ran into the room.

"I want to make lunch for my mother," I explained. "But we've got nothing. We should've taken some of the new food with us."

"We'll be okay till we get it."

"How can you be sure? Maybe it won't rain again for another week."

He gave me that cute smile. "If it doesn't rain, I'll fight the evil yellow dragon and run next door for you." He bowed. "What is your wish, m'lady?"

Even though I was really upset, I couldn't help chuckling at Blaine's knight imitation. "I guess we'll manage...I think we still have a little cheese spray left."

I spread a thin layer of cheese on crackers and brought them upstairs to Mom, who was sitting up and talking to Danny.

"Thank you, Erin," she said, reaching for a cheese-covered cracker and chewing it slowly.

"Don't forget to drink too." I handed her the glass of water and Mom took a sip.

"You'd make a good nurse," Mom said, smiling at me.

———

At the four o'clock telephone talk, we told the neighbors about the food stash in Mrs. Perez's garage. "Now we just need rain!" I yelled to the Douglasses.

"It's getting cloudy!" Mrs. Douglas called back.

I looked up and the sky did look much darker.

Danny, who had been talking to Kyle and Mrs. Perez from his room, reported to us afterward. "He seems real happy," my brother said. "Mrs. Perez too. They were both smiling and laughing."

It was good to hear happy stuff. But I could never forget that we were still prisoners in our own houses. Every time I looked outside, I saw Cyndy Louise, now a yellow blob, walking up and down our street and hoping to kill us all.

After dinner—more crackers with a teeny topping of cheese and sugar wafers for dessert—we prepared for bed. Blaine was again sleeping on the living room couch.

"Good night," I said to him as I turned toward the staircase.

"Wait." He grabbed my arm and pulled me into the dining room. "I can use some company," he whispered as he tenderly stroked my shoulders.

"My mother..." I murmured.

Blaine put his arms around me and began kissing the bottom of my neck. "After everyone's asleep," he said softly. "I can come into your room and nobody will know."

My body wanted to say "yes," but I didn't. "I'll know," I whispered. "I don't want to sneak around. It's wrong."

Blaine let go of me and even in the semi-darkness I could see the frown on his forehead. "Erin, we could all be dead tomorrow. Things are so different since the bubbles so we should enjoy each day. You've got to let yourself live."

I shook my head and rushed up the stairs before my body made me change my mind.

———

I didn't sleep well, tossing around a lot, still feeling bad about my conversation with Blaine. Maybe he was right. *Why didn't I let him come into my room?* Was having sex such a big deal with everything else that was going on? I sighed, covering my face with the pillow. It was still dark outside when I heard the wonderful sounds of raindrops and finally fell asleep.

Mom had set the alarm so I woke up early and immediately rushed to my window. Rain was still falling steadily. Danny, Blaine, and I hurried through breakfast—cereal with the last of our packaged milk—which I served Mom in bed.

"We should skip school today," I suggested. "We need to get the food to everyone."

Mom nodded. "That's a good idea. I don't think I'm up to teaching anyway. My head feels much better than yesterday, but it still hurts." She touched her forehead. "That must've been some bang."

I kissed my mother gently on the cheek. "If you're okay here, we're all going next door."

"I'll be fine," she said. "Muffles will keep me company."

Hearing his name, the dog, who had been lying in the corner of the room, padded next to my mother. She reached down and petted his back, which Muffles took as a signal to jump onto the bed.

"See?" Mom said.

———

We didn't even wait until the ten o'clock telephone. Before nine, we were in Mrs. Perez's garage, dividing the supplies. There were people in eight houses on Walnut Lane: us, Mrs. Perez, the Santangelos, Connie, and Blaine on our side of the block and the Douglasses, Rhonda Weiss, and the Mitchells across the street.

First we took everything out of the garbage bags and lined the stuff on top of the plastic. "How are we going to do this?" I asked. "There are different numbers of people in each house and some have kids?"

"We'll try to figure food per person and then add more for the kids," Blaine said. "Does that seem fair?"

I nodded. It sounded good to me.

"Better work fast," Danny said, staring out of the open garage. "It's not raining much right now."

My brother's weather report got us moving. We took eight bags, scribbled the name of the neighbor on a paper for each, and divided the food and other supplies as fairly as we could. When we finished, we tied up the bags. Then Danny and I each hoisted a filled bag on our shoulders and Blaine carried two.

"I feel like Santa," he chuckled. "Ho! Ho! Ho!"

"Yeah," I agreed. "This is just like Christmas, except it's summertime and the presents are all food."

Danny and I opened our umbrellas while Blaine walked unprotected and the three of us headed down the block, avoiding the smashed cans and busted boxes, courtesy of Cyndy Louise's food toss and stomp.

We started with the neighbors with kids—the Mitchells, Rhonda Weiss, Connie, and the Santangelos. While Danny continued to Bobby's house, I stopped at the Chou's and rapped on Connie's door. "Food delivery!" I announced when I heard footsteps.

"Erin!" she shrieked, opening the door and hugging me. "What a wonderful surprise!"

"It's great to see you too," I said. "But I'm not the surprise. I've got food." Stepping into the hallway, I dropped the black bag on the floor.

"Rin! Rin!" Emily slammed into my chest, almost knocking me over.

"Hi, Emmy." I caught the girl and kissed her forehead. "I brought you and Mommy something."

"Puzzle?" she asked. Emily loved doing jigsaw puzzles.

"No, I'm sorry. Just food."

"Ice cream?"

I shook my head.

"Banana?"

I reached into the bag, looking for something that might please her. "Look at this!" I announced, holding a box of cookies. "Chocolate fudge! Yum!" I rubbed my stomach and smiled.

"Eat cookies!" the girl squealed, dragging my arm towards the kitchen.

"I can't stay," I said, pulling my arm away. "I've got to give out the rest of the food." With a goodbye wave, I scooted out the door hoping Connie didn't mind her daughter having cookies after breakfast.

———

It was barely drizzling as I hurried back to Mrs. Perez's garage. We still had to get food across the street to the Douglasses. Then Blaine would take a bag back to the Fisher's and we would take one to our house. Mrs. Perez, with Kyle's help, had already carried her bag of supplies upstairs.

My brother had beaten me to the garage and was standing in front of the Douglass' door with a big plastic bag, talking to the neighbors. I started across the street to join him, but changed direction and ran to my porch instead. The rain must have stopped because Cyndy Louise was racing towards us.

"Danny!" I shouted. "Get inside! She's coming!" I opened my front door, entered the house, and immediately locked the door. Hurrying to the dining room window, I peeked through the opening. Across the street, the Douglass' door was closed and no one was outside except Cyndy Louise, who threw her yellow body against it. When the door didn't break, she gave up and headed down the street.

"Erin!" my mother yelled from upstairs. "What's going on

out there? Is Danny okay? I heard you call his name."

As I headed for the staircase, I thought about Blaine. *Where was he?* Did he make it back to the Fisher's house or was he with another neighbor? Maybe he was dead—trapped somewhere in the street where Cyndy Louise touched him.

No. I shook my head. Without an umbrella, he had to be wet. But was he wet enough?

————

I stood by my window, waiting nervously for the ten o'clock telephone. Since Mom's head still hurt, I told her to stay in bed. She didn't argue, mostly I think because she knew Danny was safe with the Douglasses. Also, she didn't love Blaine. *Did I?* I didn't know, but I wanted a chance to find out. For that, I needed him to be alive.

At last the Douglasses and Danny appeared at the upstairs windows across the street. Mr. Douglas blew his whistle and I waved as I opened my window wide. "Do you know where Blaine is?" I shouted.

All three of them shook their heads.

"I'll ask!" Mr. Douglas hollered.

I heard him relay the message to Mrs. Perez and Kyle. Then I just heard mumbling noises as I waited impatiently for the response. Finally Mr. Douglas leaned his head out the window and smiled at me. "Blaine's safe!" he shouted. "He made it into the Fisher's house!"

CHAPTER 31 – Prison Days

Once again I was trapped in my house, waiting for rain. But this time, since we'd never gotten our bag from Mrs. Perez's garage, Mom and I had very little food.

"I can get real wet and run next door," I suggested.

"No!" Mom shouted. "Too dangerous!"

So much for that idea.

My mother's head felt better, but she still got dizzy easily so I convinced her to stay in bed. I brought my sketchpad into her room and kept her company and so did Muffles, who lay on the floor watching us.

"We don't have much for dinner tonight," I said. "We ate the last of our crackers for lunch and all we have left is a tiny bit of cereal and a few sugar wafers."

"Are you sure?"

I shrugged. "I looked in all the cabinets so, unless you've got food stashed somewhere else, that's all there is."

My mother leaned against her pillow and closed her eyes. "I might have something," she whispered. "Check the bottom right of my closet."

I opened the sliding door and pushed away the hanging clothes. "There're a bunch of plastic bags," I said.

"Open them."

The first bag had two pairs of jeans, the second had some old shoes, but the third bag had two boxes of strawberry pop tarts. I carried the precious food to Mom. "Wow!" I said, excitedly. "This is some treat."

"Not the healthiest dinner, but at least it's food." She looked at Muffles, who was now sleeping. "If there was nothing in the closet, we were going to have to steal some of his food."

"Yucch!" I made a face. Then I realized that if it didn't rain soon, we might still have to eat dog food.

———

When my mother fell asleep, I returned to my room and sat by the window with my sketchpad. I'd been drawing Blaine's face again, but now I closed the book and looked outside. The view was always the same: Cyndy Louise walking up and down the block, not making noise except for her footsteps.

I realized I hadn't seen or heard any birds for a long time. The touchers didn't affect dogs or cats, but maybe they could kill birds—or maybe the birds didn't want to be around people in this screwed-up world. Maybe they flew away to high mountains or faraway places without people or touchers—or to a country like England where things could still be normal because the bubbles hadn't fallen there.

It was always quiet outside, but not in a good way. I closed my eyes and tried to remember what life had been like only a couple of months ago—the noise of streets filled with people and cars, phones ringing and buzzing. I remembered computers, TVs, lights, hot water, eating anything you wanted...

What's the use? Those days were gone. We'd have to figure out how to get rid of Cyndy Louise and the other touchers or we'd all soon be dead. People would disappear, just like the birds.

I picked up my pad and began drawing birds—mostly flying in the sky. If birds were gone forever, I wanted to make sure I remembered them.

———

I was still sitting by the window sketching birds when I heard a car's motor nearby. As the noise got louder, I put down my pencil and opened the window. Looking outside, I saw a dented black car enter Walnut Lane and stop across the street, right in front of the Douglass' house.

"Go away!" I shouted, leaning halfway out the window. "Get out of here before she comes!"

The driver must have heard me because he immediately backed up to turn into Barker Street. But Cyndy Louise had either seen or heard the car—or maybe heard me—because suddenly there she was, racing towards the moving auto, carrying a huge rock.

Before the driver could complete his turn, Cyndy Louise threw the rock at his front window. The car shook, then crashed into the sidewalk and stopped moving. Flinging open the door, Cyndy Louise reached inside and pulled out the driver.

I don't know if the man had been knocked unconscious by the crash, but I knew for sure he was dead now. Cyndy Louise dropped him on the sidewalk and then did that weird thing again—holding his arm and draining energy or something from his body to hers.

I watched, feeling totally helpless because I wasn't able to save that man. Even with my warning, he didn't have enough time to get away. As Cyndy Louise stood in the street working on his body, I studied the dead man. He had light brown hair, wore glasses, and looked like he'd been about the same age as my father. I hadn't been able to do anything to save my dad either.

———

My mother slept through the entire man-in-the-car incident. Although Cyndy Louise was a quiet killer, I had yelled and the crash had been loud, but Mom still needed lots of sleep.

The next two days were rough. Besides having to look at the dead body across the street, we were trapped in the house with nothing much to do—Mom wasn't up to teaching school and Danny wasn't here anyway—so it was hard not to think about food. We drank lots of water and tea, finished the cereal, and ate most of the pop tarts Mom had saved. Since Muffles still had plenty of dog chow, we were going to eat his stuff next.

Then, late in the morning of the third day, it rained—only a light rain—but it was steady enough to keep Cyndy Louise off the street. I didn't even grab an umbrella, just yelled, "I'm getting the food!" and rushed to Mrs. Perez's house.

I rang the bell and she opened the door, a grinning Kyle standing next to her. "Hi," I said. "Can I get our food, please?"

"Of course, Erin," Mrs. Perez said. "Come in."

I followed her and Kyle to the garage entrance and ran down the steps. There it was: the precious black plastic bag marked "Fredericks."

"Want me to help carry it?" Kyle asked. "I'm real strong." He flexed his little arms.

"Sure."

Together he and I dragged the bag out of the garage to my house. After thanking Kyle, I continued inside and called to Mom. "Come on down! It's time for a real lunch!"

———

Mom and I tried not to eat too much, but we treated ourselves to a feast of tuna on crackers, followed by canned peaches in heavy syrup. It was great to taste fruit again—even if it wasn't fresh. We had almost finished lunch when Danny came home.

"Do you want some peaches?" I offered. "These are delicious—really sweet."

He shook his head. "That's okay. I just ate."

Mom still tired easily and was struggling to keep her eyes open. "Go back upstairs and rest," I suggested. "Danny and I can go out by ourselves." The rain was now coming down heavily, pounding hard against the windows. It was a wonderful sound.

"Please be careful, both of you," Mom said, glancing from me to Danny. "If the rain looks like it's letting up, come right home. I don't want you getting stuck in another house again—or worse."

"I'll take Muffles out," Danny said, getting the dog's leash. "He can run with me to Bobby's house." My brother took an umbrella, put a leash on Muffles, and dashed out of the house.

Mom turned to me and smiled. "So where are you going, Erin?"

I gave her the answer she already knew. "I thought I'd check on Blaine."

My mother nodded. "Just remember what I said about coming home," she said. "I want you back here safely."

———

I checked the mirror and didn't like what I saw. With a sigh, I tied my hair into a neater ponytail since there was nothing much else I could do with it. Then I got into my raincoat, grabbed an umbrella, locked the front door, and stepped into the pouring rain.

I was glad the dead man was gone. His dented black car was now parked in front of the Kaplan's house. And the street was clean again—no more busted cans, bags, and boxes.

I passed Mrs. Perez, sitting on her front porch with Kyle and the Douglasses, and waved to all of them.

"Had a good lunch?" Mrs. Perez called.

I nodded and smiled at her.

The Santangelos were opening the door of Mr. Ortega's house, wheeling their baby in a covered stroller. I waved to them too and continued walking.

Connie and Emily weren't out yet, but I didn't stop and knock on their door. Instead I continued to the Fisher's, stepped on the porch, and rang the doorbell.

No one answered.

I moved away and scanned the rest of the block, but I didn't see Blaine outside. Across the street, Danny and Bobby were running along the sidewalk with Muffles, playing some kind of goofy tag.

Where was he? I turned and started walking back to my house, not sure where else to look.

"Hey, Erin!"

I lifted my head at the sound of the familiar drawly voice—and there he was, standing at the Chou's front door with Connie and Emily, a huge grin on his face.

————

I forced myself not run straight into Blaine's arms. But I did walk very fast.

"Rin!" Emily shouted when I reached Connie's house, grabbing my ankles from her seat in the stroller.

"Hello, Emmy!" I bent down to give the little girl a kiss.

Connie smiled at me and then at Blaine. "We're going across the street to see Rhonda and Jake," she said. "You two have fun." Without another word, she opened her umbrella and wheeled Emily into the road.

Blaine and I stood facing each other. "I really missed you," he whispered, spreading his arms wide.

"I missed you too," I said, snuggling against his chest. "I was so worried."

"I'm too smart to let her catch me. Did you make it home with the food bag?"

I shook my head. "If it didn't rain today, our next meal would've been dog food."

"Woof," Blaine whispered.

"How about you?" I asked. "Did you have enough to eat?"

"I did okay...That's enough talking." He tilted my head up and kissed me tenderly on the lips. "I wish we could be together," he said afterwards.

"Me too."

"We've got some time now. How about we go to my place?"

I looked at the sky. It was raining, but not as hard as before. I remembered my mother's warning—and she still wasn't okay. "No," I said. "Let's just be together out here for a while."

———

Holding hands, Blaine and I walked along Walnut Lane, letting the warm rain trickle down on us. My hair was getting soaked, but I didn't care. "You never told me how you escaped from school during the bubbles," I said.

Blaine sighed. "I was in my room, studyin' for the history final, when I heard someone screamin' to stay away from Rob Stewart. I opened the door carefully, stepped into the hall, and found bodies of kids everywhere. Then Zach—the guy who'd screamed—saw me and explained what was goin' on outside with the bubbles. We made it from the dorm to my car and drove away. So Zach saved my life."

Poor Zach. "I wish he'd jumped into the Fisher's pool," I said, shaking my head. "What'd you and Zach do next?"

"We headed south because his folks lived in Delaware and that's on the way to Atlanta. But everythin' we saw on the road was scary..."

His voice trailed off and I remembered that first awful day.

"We were lucky the car had a full tank of gas," Blaine continued. "When it got dark and the bubbles stopped, I drove into a rest area. But that place was bad."

"What happened?"

"Touchers, many of them, were walkin' around outside with dead people lyin' all over the parkin' lot and entrance. We were starvin', but couldn't get out of the car."

"How'd you manage to eat?"

"In the lot, we saw a dead man next to a bag of food so Zach opened his door and snatched the bag."

After that, Blaine and I just walked quietly in the rain, thinking our own sad thoughts.

All the neighbors were outside. Danny and Bobby continued to play with Muffles. Now they were doing Monkey in the Middle, with Muffles jumping up and trying to snatch the ball away. Connie and Emily were across the street with Rhonda Weiss and Jake, the two moms talking to each other under umbrellas while the kids played in their covered strollers. The Douglasses still sat on Mrs. Perez's porch and they had been joined by the Santangelo family and Bobbie's mom. My mother was the only one inside.

"I want to check on my mom," I said as we reached my house. "Do you want to come with me?"

"Sure."

I unlocked the door and we stepped into the hallway. "I'll just be a second," I said, dashing up the steps.

The bedroom door was open and I walked in. Mom lay on top of the sheet with her eyes closed. She looked pale, but her chest moved steadily up and down so she was breathing okay.

I tiptoed out of the room and darted down the stairs.

"She's sleeping," I whispered to Blaine.

He grabbed my waist, twirled me around and kissed me hard on the lips. "Why don't we just stay here?" he asked softly, speaking into my ear as he nuzzled my neck. "This way you'll be near your mother."

I didn't say anything as Blaine guided us backwards into the living room and we landed together on the couch. We sat there, getting the couch pretty wet, but I didn't complain. Somehow that didn't seem to matter.

We kissed each other until, a minute or so later, we heard footsteps on the porch followed by a key turning the lock. By the time Danny walked in, Blaine and I had smoothed out our damp clothes and were sitting innocently on the couch.

"What's up?" I asked.

"The rain's almost stopped," my brother said. "Everyone went home."

"Then I better be goin' too." Blaine stood and smiled at me. "See you soon."

CHAPTER 32 – Hope and Fear

Very early the next morning, even before Mom's alarm went off—school was back in session—I heard a rumbling noise in the street, louder than a car's engine. Jumping out of bed, I banged on Danny's door. "Get up! Something's happening outside!"

My brother could sleep through an earthquake. "One second," he muttered. Then he opened his door, still rubbing his eyes. "What's so important?"

"Just listen."

The rumbling sound was even louder.

"Trucks?" Danny asked.

"Maybe."

"Should we wake Mom?"

"No. Her head still hurts. We can watch the street from my window and if it's something important, we'll tell her."

Danny and I stood together in front of my open window in the early dawn, listening and waiting. The rumbling noises seemed louder, but we couldn't see anything except a shadowy Cyndy Louise pacing up and down the block.

"Whatever it is, it's not coming into Walnut Lane," Danny said. "It's just staying on Barker."

"Wait...I think there's some kind of announcement. Listen."

Both of us leaned our heads out the window trying to figure out the message—if there was any. I could only understand two words, "army" and "help." Nothing else sounded clear. Finally I pulled my head back inside the room. "Did you get any of the words?" I asked.

"Just 'help' and 'wet.'"

"I heard 'army' too."

"So what do you think this is about?" Danny asked.

"I hope it's the army saying they're going to help us," I said.

"And the 'wet' could mean you have to be wet so the touchers can't hurt you, like we already know," Danny added. "You think there's still an army?"

I shrugged. If there was an army, it couldn't have many soldiers anymore—and did they know how to kill the touchers?

———

When Mom's alarm went off a few minutes later, Danny and I told her what we'd heard. "It's a good sign," she said. "There must still be people in charge, working to fix this." She smiled at us. "But until they do, after breakfast, we've got classes."

At our break for the ten o'clock telephone talk, we asked the Douglasses what they'd heard.

"Just a few words!" Mr. Douglas shouted. "'Army,' 'help,' and 'weapon!'"

"I thought I heard 'wet!'" Danny yelled from next door. "But maybe it was 'weapon!'"

"I hope they're right about 'weapon,'" I said to Mom, who sat on my bed.

"It makes sense since both you and the Douglasses heard 'army,'" she said.

"Maybe the others understood more words!" Mr. Douglas

hollered. "I'll ask!"

We waited while the message was relayed down the street. A few minutes later, Mr. Douglas called back. "Jennifer and Bobby think they heard the word 'soon!'"

When we returned to Mom's bedroom to continue our classes, I had trouble concentrating. I kept stringing together all the words shouted from the truck or whatever had rumbled down the streets in the early morning. *Army, help, weapon, soon.* Was it just wishful thinking on our part—or were we going to be released from prison? And what time did they mean by "soon"?

———

Danny, Mom, and I eased back into our boring routine. The only difference was we now had enough food.

Since it was summer and the weather was hot, we were okay taking icy cold showers. But what would happen when it became fall and then winter? We didn't even have a fireplace to heat the house.

In the afternoons, I sat in front of my bedroom window with a pad and colored pencils on my lap. While I still drew pictures of Blaine, I mostly sketched scenes of Army tanks riding along our street with huge guns that blasted Cyndy Louise with something that killed her. In all my drawings, she was lying dead in Walnut Lane.

I had no idea what weapon would be powerful enough to kill Cyndy Louise and the other touchers. But thinking the army was coming gave me hope there was a way out of this prison. Life would never be like it was before the bubbles, but maybe we'd be free to go outside again—all the time—not just when it rained.

And it didn't rain often enough. In fact, it hadn't rained for a week. I missed Blaine, I missed walking outside, I missed my friends. Most of all, I missed having a normal life. I was a teenager and I was supposed to be having fun. Then I thought about my dad, who I knew I'd never see again. I missed him too.

––––––

The next afternoon, I was back in front of my window, mostly drawing, but occasionally peeking at Cyndy Louise. I lowered the pad and concentrated on her. Something was different, but I wasn't sure what it was.

Mom was resting since she still got tired easily so I didn't want to disturb her. That left Danny. I stuck my head into my brother's room. "Can you please look at something?" I politely asked.

"What?" He was lying on top of his bed, reading a magazine, and didn't even bother to glance up.

"I have to show you. Please!"

He tossed the magazine on the floor and rolled his eyes at me. "What's the big deal? Nothing's happening outside unless it rains or some dumb person gets near Cyndy Louise." He walked slowly into my room like I had interrupted something important.

I pushed Danny towards the window and stood behind him. "Shut up and look."

My brother didn't say anything as he watched Cyndy Louise. But then he must have noticed something because he went from being real pissed off to being real serious. "Erin..." he whispered.

"What is it?" I moved next to him.

"Look at her back," he said.

Cyndy Louise was walking away from us, heading down the block, and I tried to zero in on her naked yellow back. It didn't seem completely smooth anymore. "Is something growing there?"

"Yeah," Danny said.

"What do you think it is?"

My brother didn't answer right away. "Wings," he finally said. "I think she's growing wings."

————

We stepped away from the window and sat on my bed together.

"She's going to fly?" I asked.

"That's what things and animals that have wings do," Danny said. "Airplanes, bees, butterflies, birds..."

"I haven't seen a bird in weeks. Have you?"

Danny shrugged. "I dunno. I hadn't thought about it."

"If the touchers fly, how are we going to stop them?" I continued. "We can't even stop them now when they're just on the ground."

"And then they can get into those places where the bubbles didn't fall because of the rain—like England." My brother stared at me. "They'll kill everybody."

"Do you think the army knows?"

Danny shrugged again.

"There's got to be some way we can tell them—get a message to them to hurry."

"How?"

"I don't know yet, but I'm working on it." I closed my eyes and tried to concentrate, hoping my brain would cooperate. But all I pictured was a winged Cyndy Louise and other flying touchers dive-bombing at people, who all lay dead on the ground.

————

When Mom got up a few minutes before the afternoon telephone talk, we took her to my window to see Cyndy Louise.

"You could be wrong," she said to Danny. "Those little nubs on her back may turn out to be nothing. We don't know for sure they're the start of wings."

"They're wings," Danny insisted. "I'm sure."

"What else could they be?" I asked. "And why would something be growing on her back like that in two places?"

"I don't know," Mom admitted.

"She's gonna fly," Danny continued. "All of them are gonna fly and then we'll never be able to kill them."

"But you both heard an announcement that the army's coming with some kind of weapon," Mom pointed out.

"We think that's what we heard—or maybe we just hope we heard it. I didn't hear the word 'weapon' and Danny thought he heard 'wet.'"

My brother returned to the window and stared outside. "We gotta do something before she grows those wings."

A thought popped into my mind. "Danny, that megaphone you used to play with," I said. "It was part of the carnival game you loved and I always told you was too loud. Do you still have it?"

"I'm not sure."

"Go look for it before Mr. Douglas blows the whistle," I said.

For a change, Danny didn't argue. Instead, he nodded and dashed into his room.

My mother smiled at me. "You think you can warn the army with a toy megaphone?"

I shrugged. "I don't know, but it's worth a try."

———

The telephone talk started before Danny found the megaphone. My brother told Mrs. Perez about the growths on Cyndy Louise's back and she relayed the message to Connie and the others down the block.

"They might not be wings!" Mr. Douglas called, echoing Mom's thoughts.

"Danny's sure they are!" I hollered back. "We've got to stop her before she can fly!"

"If they're wings, the army must already know!" Mrs. Douglas yelled.

"But what if they don't know?" I shouted. "We have to tell them!"

"How?" Mr. Douglas called.

"Do what they did!" I hollered. "Spread the word in the streets!" Of course that was only if Danny found the megaphone. But my brother was a packrat. He saved everything and he used to love that dumb carnival game so it had to be somewhere in his room.

The message relayed to us from the other end of the street was that although no one else had noticed the growths on Cyndy Louise's back, they all saw them now. And Connie and Blaine agreed with Danny and me that they were the early stages of wings.

"What can we do?" Mr. Douglas asked.

I told him about the megaphone. And when the telephone talk ended, I ran into Danny's room to help him find it.

———

It was nearly dark when we found the megaphone, on the bottom of Danny's closet behind piles of old games and wrinkled, yellowing comic books.

"Why do you save all this crap?" I asked, waving one of the crumbling comics in his face. "You're never going to read this stuff."

"Maybe I will, especially since there's no more book stores or libraries."

I shook my head and picked up the dusty megaphone. "Get some batteries and let's see if this thing still works."

While Danny went to find four C batteries, I stepped into the bathroom and used a tissue to clean the megaphone. Muffles, curious about what I was doing, followed me inside.

"This thing makes a loud noise," I told him, pointing to the black cylinder. "You might not like it."

The dog backed away. He wasn't crazy about loud sounds.

My brother returned with the batteries. "Mom said to give them back if it doesn't work. We don't have many C's left."

After inserting the batteries, I switched the megaphone on. "Testing! Testing!" I said. I thought I felt vibrations and heard an echo. "Did it work?" I asked Danny just to make sure.

"Yeah and it sounded loud."

I turned off the machine, not wanting to waste any of the precious batteries, and smiled at my brother. "Then we're ready for a road trip."

CHAPTER 33 – Spreading the News

I didn't want to wait until the next rain to get the word out about Cyndy Louise's wings. We didn't know how fast those stubs were growing and maybe she'd be able to fly in just a couple of days.

I made my pitch the next morning during breakfast. "Mom," I began. "Now that the megaphone works, we should go for a ride and make an announcement about the wings."

"It's not raining today."

"I know, but we should still do it. We have to make sure everyone knows before she and all the others start flying."

My mother shook her head. "It's much too dangerous."

"If we get ourselves soaking wet and are in a car, we'll be okay. It's worked before."

"They attack cars. Look what happened to that man here and to me when they threw rocks." She massaged the spot where she'd hit her head. "The headaches have finally stopped."

"You shouldn't go out again," I continued. "Let me do this with Blaine."

Danny had been listening quietly, but now he spoke. "I want to go too. I can be a lookout for touchers and warn Blaine and Erin."

"No."

"Mom, please!" I pleaded.

"Neither of you is going anywhere unless it's raining."

———

We made arrangements during the telephone talk. Mrs. Perez said we could use her car again and Blaine agreed to drive.

Two mornings later, it finally rained—not a heavy downpour, just a steady drizzle—but that was enough to keep Cyndy Louise off the street.

As I showered with my clothes on to get ready for the ride, Mom admitted she still wasn't a hundred percent well. "My head doesn't hurt, but I get a little dizzy at times—and the sound of the megaphone blasting..." She shook her head. "I'm not sure I can take the loud noise."

Although she'd agreed to let me go with Blaine, Mom refused to let Danny ride shotgun with us.

"Why not?" my brother asked angrily. "I'll take the water guns in case it stops raining and you know I'm the best shooter."

"It's not necessary for you to go," my mother said. "Erin and Blaine are only going out for a half hour and if the rain stops, they're coming back here immediately, not staying on the street to fight touchers." She turned to me. "Right?"

I nodded.

"So it's settled." Mom smiled and tried to grab Danny's shoulders, but he frowned and moved away. "You'll have a chance to get together with Bobby again and have fun, play ball..."

My brother turned and ran up the stairs. Then we heard the loud slamming of a door.

"I'm just trying to keep him safe," Mom whispered, more to herself than to me.

"Nobody's safe anymore," I said, taking one of the filled water pistols Danny had left on the table and tucking it into my jeans pocket. "Not until we get rid of them all."

———

The rain was warm and gentle and I was already wet so I didn't mind getting wetter during the short walk to Mrs. Perez's garage. When I got there, the overhead door was open and our neighbor and Kyle stood next to the car, talking to Blaine.

"Hi!" Kyle said, rushing to me and grabbing my legs. "I wanna go with you guys, but Miz Norma ain't gonna let me."

"Don't feel so bad," I said, smiling at him. "My mom won't let Danny go with us either. Anyway, we're only going to be out for a little while."

Kyle pointed to the megaphone in my hand. "Can I yell into that thing?"

I turned the machine on and handed it to him. "One time only. It's very loud."

Putting his mouth inside the cylinder, he shouted, "All you bad yellow touching things—go away!"

Kyle's words boomed. Blaine took the instrument from the kid's hands, turned it off, and gave it to me. "That's exactly the way you should talk into this," he said, rubbing the boy's head and grinning at me. "I hope you do as good a job."

———

"So how've you been?" Blaine asked as he drove out of Walnut Lane, entered Barker Street, and turned left. "I really missed you." He reached for my left hand and squeezed it tightly.

"I missed you too," I said softly. I would have said more, but we had a job to do so I picked up the megaphone. "Go slow and I'll start making announcements."

Opening the window, I stuck the megaphone outside. It

smelled awful, thanks to the rotting bodies on the street. As Blaine drove, the rats hurried away from the corpses, but the bugs were still everywhere. I swatted the ones in the air and tried not to breathe through my nose as I placed my mouth in front of the opening of the megaphone. "The yellow touchers are growing wings!" I shouted. "Soon they'll be flying! Pass along this message!"

I lowered the megaphone and turned to Blaine. "Did that sound okay?"

He nodded. "It sure was loud enough. Should you say somethin' about the army comin'?"

I thought about his suggestion. "Yeah, maybe, although I'm not even sure that's what I heard."

"Then just say, 'this is to the army or whoever said they were goin' to help.'"

I picked up the megaphone and stuck it out the window again. "This is for the army or whoever made the announcement about helping us!" I said. "You should know the touchers are growing wings! They're going to fly soon! You need to kill them now!"

With Blaine weaving around smashed cars and dead bodies, I repeated, "the wings are growing!" warning along the main street. At one point, I saw a gold car at the intersection ahead so I pulled down my window, signaling the driver to stop.

"Hi," I said, lowering the megaphone since the woman driver was close enough to hear me. "We're warning people that the yellow toucher monsters are growing wings. Did you know that?"

A girl about my age in the rear seat opened the window. "I told my mom I saw something on the back of one of them, but she didn't think it was anything."

"It's wings," I said, nodding. "And they're all going to fly."

"Oh, God!" The driver shook her head and stared at the sky. "What next?"

———

We looped around to Thornwood Street, the two-lane road that ran parallel to Barker, so I could continue to spread the word as we headed home.

"Close the window—fast!" Blaine ordered as I finished my announcement.

"Why?" I stuck my head back inside the car and pushed up the window.

"The rain's stopped." He pointed to the front window, which was dry, the wipers now off. "They'll be comin' out soon. They always seem to know right away when there's no more rain."

He had just finished speaking when we saw the first toucher, a tall man-thing that rushed at us with a large tree branch. "Watch out!" I yelled.

Blaine swerved the car and the toucher fell against a storefront, the stick shattering into many pieces.

"I'm gettin' off this main road," Blaine said as he turned into a side street. "I hope you can direct me back."

"Don't worry about that. We're close enough so I know all these roads...How're you doing on gas?"

"We still have more than a half tank."

I looked out the back window and saw a woman toucher running our way. "There's another one behind us," I told him.

Blaine checked his rearview mirror. "I can't go much faster here," he said. The small street was full of wrecked cars and broken glass.

The yellow woman-thing stopped to pick up a jagged piece of glass. "She's going to throw glass at us!" I shouted.

Blaine navigated his way past a smashed gray truck and

sped up a little.

"Duck!" I yelled, crouching and covering my head with my hands. I heard the loud shattering sound of broken glass, but didn't feel any impact. When I raised my head and looked outside, I saw more pieces of glass next to the truck.

"What happened?" Blaine asked.

"She must've hit the truck," I explained. "Our car's okay. Let's get out of here."

———

"I'm opening my window just enough so I can stick the megaphone out," I said to Blaine as we cut across Needham Road to head back to Barker Street. "Otherwise all this time riding in the car going home is a waste."

"You're gonna draw them to us."

"Maybe. But they see and hear the car anyway." I pushed the megaphone through the window and made my, "The wings are coming!" announcement. Then I quickly closed the window.

"There're two touchers behind us," I said.

"There's one up ahead too," Blaine reported. "I'm gonna turn into another side street—and no more megaphone. Bad idea."

I didn't say anything because he was right. I'd become more like the Pied Piper than Paul Revere.

"Keep your head down," Blaine said. "They're throwin' stuff at us again."

I ducked and heard a series of thumps and booms followed by the shattering of the rear window. When I turned around, I saw two touchers on top of the trunk pounding the smashed back window—so hard that it broke—pieces of glass flying into the car.

"Drive fast!" I yelled as I grabbed my gun and, still crouching, squirted the opening until both touchers jumped off the car. "Got them!" I shouted. "They almost got in. Are we nearly home?"

"Yeah. Keep down and I'm gonna make a left into Barker Street. We're only a block from Walnut Lane."

I listened to Blaine, keeping my head down until the car stopped. When I looked up again, we were parked in Mrs. Perez's driveway.

Blaine honked the horn. "We need her to open the garage door," he said. "Cyndy Louise is already runnin' here and with the back window busted...You got your water gun ready?"

"Yeah." I didn't say anything else, but I had very little water left and couldn't keep her away from us for long. Thankfully, I heard the garage door open.

Cyndy Louise reached us just before Blaine drove the car into the garage and I squirted her with the last of my water. I wasn't as good a shooter as Danny, but I must have hit her enough because she backed away as the garage door closed. Then we were inside and Cyndy Louise was still outside, hitting the house in anger.

———

"Are you two okay?" Mrs. Perez asked as she rushed to us.

"We're good," I said, stepping out of the Camry. "Sorry about your car's back window though."

"I don't care about that—but what's wrong with him?" She pointed to the front seat where Blaine still sat, head down and slumped forward.

I ran to the driver's side and opened Blaine's door. The edge of his gray seat was now dark red.

"I'll be okay," he said, looking up and smiling at me. "Just a little scratch."

That's when I saw the piece of glass embedded in his left side. "You drove like this?" I whispered.

He didn't answer as Mrs. Perez and I helped him out of the car. Then, with Blaine leaning on both of us, we walked slowly into the house.

"Let's get him to the bathroom," Mrs. Perez said as she opened the door. Kyle was standing there.

"Is he gonna die?" the boy asked.

"No," I said. "He's going to be fine once we get the glass out." I sounded more confident than I felt. It was a big jagged chunk and Blaine was losing lots of blood.

I sat him on the toilet seat while Mrs. Perez washed her hands and gave me a clean white towel. "When I take out the glass, I need you to press the towel tight against his side. Okay?"

I nodded, hoping I wouldn't faint first.

Kyle stood in the hallway, watching us.

"Get another towel from the closet, Kyle," Mrs. Perez said. "We might need it."

The boy ran to the linen closet and returned with a blue towel, which he gave to Mrs. Perez. Then he quickly left the bathroom.

"Ready?" Mrs. Perez asked Blaine.

He nodded, closing his eyes.

With one quick move, she yanked the glass out of his side and the blood, which had just been dripping, gushed out.

"Now, Erin!"

Pressing as hard as I could, I shoved the towel against the wound. In seconds, the white cloth turned bright red.

Mrs. Perez handed me the second towel and I placed it over the soaked one. A little blood seeped through the light blue fabric, but the bleeding slowed. I let out a deep breath. "I think it's stopping," I said.

"Good," Mrs. Perez said. "But keep applying pressure. If you get tired, let me do it."

"No, I'm fine."

As Mrs. Perez and I talked, Blaine didn't say a word and his face was very pale. But he was awake and breathing normally.

"How are you doing?" I whispered.

"I'm okay." His voice was very faint.

"You sure are," I agreed, smiling. "I can't believe you drove back with that huge chunk of glass in you."

"He's tough," Kyle said, entering the bathroom again. "Like one of them superheroes."

Blaine didn't say anything, but he did smile.

———

After Mrs. Perez put two gauze pads over the wound, she and I carefully guided Blaine to the living room couch and sat him down. He still looked very pale.

"Does it hurt a lot?" I asked.

He shook his head. "I'm just real tired," he said, closing his eyes and leaning against the couch. "I'll be okay after I rest a little."

"Sure." I kissed his forehead gently and backed away.

Mrs. Perez signaled me from the kitchen. When I entered, she whispered, "He can't go anywhere for a while. He's too weak."

"I know," I said. "It's not even raining anymore and Cyndy Louise is out again. Even if he gets all wet..."

"He couldn't get to his house even if she wasn't outside. He lost too much blood." She grasped my hand. "But he'll be fine here with us. We'll take good care of Blaine, won't we, Kyle?"

The little boy, who'd been sitting at the table and listening to us, smiled. "Yeah. Don't you worry 'bout your boyfriend. Me and Miss Norma'll get him all better."

"Thanks," I said to Kyle before turning to Mrs. Perez. "I should go home now. I'm sure my Mom's worried so can I use your shower?"

"Of course."

I took another quick cold shower with my clothes on, not drying myself at all. Then, placing the towel Mrs. Perez had given me under my feet to catch some of the dripping water, I waddled down the steps, into the hallway, and back to the garage.

"Sorry I got everything so wet," I said as my neighbor pressed the button to raise the garage door.

"It's not a problem, Erin. Everything will dry. Just get home safely."

I nodded as I raced outside. Cyndy Louise ran towards me, but immediately backed off when she saw the water dripping from my body and clothes. "Get away!" I said, sticking my tongue out and waving the water pistol in my wet arm, for a change feeling all-powerful as I unlocked my front door.

CHAPTER 34 – Water Fight

As Blaine recuperated in Mrs. Perez's house, I kind of spent time with him. He'd open the upstairs bedroom window that faced my house and I'd open Danny's window. This way, we were able to see each other and talk, sometimes for hours.

My brother wasn't thrilled with our arrangement. "I wanna use my room," he complained.

"Just give me another couple minutes. Blaine's hurt and he's really bored over there."

"I'm bored too," Danny whined, "and it's my room!"

In the beginning, Blaine was too weak to yell to me from next door. But then I remembered something. "I left the megaphone in the car!" I shouted. "Ask Kyle to get it for you!"

For that first day, Blaine used the megaphone. Of course he couldn't say anything romantic or personal as his words boomed so loud that the Douglasses and maybe even Connie could hear them. And I was yelling too so Mom and Danny could definitely hear what I said. But at least we could talk to each other. He told me his dreams and I told him mine.

"I want to find my mother and sister in Atlanta when we get rid of the touchers!" he shouted through the megaphone. "Will you come with me?"

"Yeah!" I yelled. "I've been stuck here for so long—I really want to travel!"

"What do you want to do?" he asked.

"What do you mean?"

"When all this is over!"

"Oh." *The future.* I hadn't thought much about it. "I was planning to go to college and study art—be an artist somewhere!"

"Maybe you can still do that!"

"You think there'll still be colleges?"

"I hope...I want to finish school!"

"You said you wanted to major in sports management! Doing what?"

"Helpin' pro athletes with their careers—if there's still any pro sports!"

We talked like this, back and forth, for three days. Then everything changed.

———

Danny, Mom, and I were finishing lunch when we heard a strange noise.

"What's that?" I asked.

"It sounds like water being squirted from a hose," Mom said.

"The hydrant?" I jumped out of my chair and ran upstairs to my room, followed by Mom and Danny.

"Do you see anything?" I asked. I still heard the noise, but nothing outside looked different. Cyndy Louise was heading down the other end of the block, her yellow back now sporting mini-wings. The hydrant across the street wasn't running and I didn't see a hose pouring water.

I dashed into Danny's room and opened the window. "Blaine!" I shouted. "Did you hear that?"

A minute later, Mrs. Perez's window opened and Blaine waved to me. "What's up?" he hollered.

"Listen!" I called.

We were both quiet and again I heard a noise like something being poured.

"Sounds like a concrete mixer!" Blaine yelled. "You know, those trucks that spin when they move!" He twirled his hands.

"It's coming closer!" I shouted and ran back to my window for a better view of the street. Mom and Danny were still there, staring outside.

"What is it?" I asked as a strange-looking black jeep with a large gray container tied to the roof turned into our street.

"It must be some kind of special truck for killing touchers," Danny said. "Look—it's got hoses for spraying them." He pointed to green rubber tubing tied to the outside.

The truck continued slowly down Walnut Lane. Cyndy Louise had turned and was marching towards it.

"She looks like she's gonna do something," Danny said.

There were two people in the truck. The man in the passenger seat opened the window and fired his water pistol at Cyndy Louise. But she darted to the left and he missed. Before he could shoot again, she hurried towards him, touching his exposed arm. The man immediately went limp and collapsed in the truck.

The driver must have turned on a switch because water began flowing onto the street from the hoses attached to the truck. Cyndy Louise quickly stepped onto the sidewalk before any of the liquid reached her. She stood in front of Mrs. Perez's house and didn't move.

———

Without saying a word, I rushed into Danny's room again, opened the window, and yelled Blaine's name.

"You see that?" Blaine shouted when he opened the window opposite me.

"Yes! She's right in front of the house! I need you to spray water on her!"

"Why?"

"I'm going out there before she kills the other guy!"

"No!"

"Yes!"

I didn't waste time arguing. Slamming the window shut, I jumped into the shower. It was freezing, but I didn't care.

"What do you think you're doing?" my mother asked as I stepped onto the bathroom floor. Danny stood next to her.

"I'm going outside."

"Erin!" My mother reached for my wet arm.

"You can't stop me!" I shouted, wrenching my arm free.

"I'm going too," Danny said, turning the water back on and getting into the shower.

Before Mom reached me, I squished down the staircase, grabbed a water gun, and opened the front door.

—————

The truck was still outside, parked in front of Mrs. Perez's house, its water turned off. I didn't see Cyndy Louise, but there was a big puddle on the sidewalk where she'd been.

"Toucher thing ran away!"

I glanced up at the open upstairs window of my next-door neighbor's house and a smiling Kyle waved at me. "Me and Blaine squirted her good!" he shouted.

"Where's Blaine?" I called.

"Right here."

I turned and there he was, dripping wet and standing next to me. "But you're hurt—your side."

"I'm a quick healer."

"Kids, watch out!"

Blaine and I stopped talking when the man in the truck yelled to us. Cyndy Louise, moving so quietly that we didn't hear her coming, was just a few feet away.

"Grab a hose!" the man continued. "And keep it aimed on her!"

Blaine and I each grabbed a green hose attached to the truck. I felt the hose expand as the liquid burst through, heading for Cyndy Louise. She backed away and then tried to get up on the sidewalk, but I yanked out more of the hose and kept blasting water at her.

She crossed the street, running to the other side. But Blaine was there with the other attached hose and he squirted her. Then she switched direction again, trying to race down the block.

The truck followed her, the driver moving slowly at first so Blaine and I were able to keep pace. "I've got to go faster!" the man yelled to us. "Try to keep up with me!"

Blaine and I ran alongside the truck in pursuit of Cyndy Louise. I held on to the hose at first, but the water was shut off so I dropped it. When I didn't see Blaine, I looked behind me. He had stopped and was holding his side. Blood was seeping through his jeans.

"Stay there!" I hollered as I raced down the block after the truck.

Cyndy Louise was already at the end of the street in front of the woods. The truck was there too, its water again turned on. The driver, wearing military camouflage, had picked up one of the hoses from the ground and was squirting Cyndy Louise. I took the other hose and sprayed water on her too.

"Keep the hose aimed at its head!" the man yelled.

I tried to follow his instructions, although Cyndy Louise made it hard because she kept moving to keep from getting wet. But she wasn't succeeding because every time she changed direction, one of us squirted her. She seemed weaker, not strong enough to run away and soon she was completely soaked. Then, for the first time since the bubbles, Cyndy Louise stopped moving and her naked yellow body crashed heavily to the ground.

The man stepped forward, continuing to squirt her as he did. He stood over the fallen toucher and sprayed her again and again until finally, the water ran out. He dropped the hose, walked up to me, and smiled. "It's dead," he said.

———

I heard footsteps behind me and Blaine was there. He tried to put his arm around my shoulders, but winced and gave up. His face was very pale again and his left side was bleeding heavily. "Sit down and don't move," I said, lowering him to the ground. He didn't protest.

The man from the truck came over to me, holding out his hand. "Thanks for your help," he said. "It takes at least two of us to kill one of them and when the girl-thing touched Captain Hitchcock..." He nodded sadly at the passenger seat of his van.

"What's in that water?" I asked.

"It's a chemical formula that our scientists have been working on. They keep making it stronger and it's finally doing the job although it still takes too much water and too much effort to kill them." He pointed the empty hose at Cyndy Louise. "But this one won't be bothering you any more."

"And all the other touchers out there?" Blaine asked.

"We'll get them...The scientists just have to improve the formula—make it stronger without hurting us."

"Is she dead?"

I heard Danny's voice behind me and when I turned, saw my brother followed by Mom, Mrs. Perez, Kyle, and the

Douglasses.

"Yes," the man said, answering Danny's question. "She's dead."

"Who are you?" my brother continued as the front door on the left opened and Bobby Mitchell and his mother raced towards us.

"I'm Major James Figueroa of the United States Army and we're starting to take back our country from these yellow things."

"I didn't know we still had an army," I said softly.

"We do—much smaller, of course—but it's still there."

"What happens now?" my mother asked, putting her arm around me and Danny. "Are we going to be safe?"

Major Figueroa shrugged. "Not yet. We've got to kill all of them first. But we will. This is just the beginning."

And it was.